Final Sky

ELIAS WITHEROW

**THOUGHT
CATALOG**
Books

THOUGHTCATALOG.COM
NEW YORK·LOS ANGELES

THOUGHT
CATALOG
Books

Copyright © 2020 Elias Witherow. All rights reserved.

Published by Thought Catalog Books, an imprint of the digital magazine Thought Catalog, which is owned and operated by The Thought & Expression Company LLC, an independent media organization based in Brooklyn, New York and Los Angeles, California.

This book was produced by Thought Catalog Books. Cover by Ira Rebeca.
Visit us on the web at thoughtcatalog.com and shopcatalog.com.

Made in the USA.

ISBN 978-1-949759-21-1

This book is for the fantastic friends in my life:
Kyle, Matt, Kozy, Zach, Dave.
You guys are the best.
Here's to many more trips and years of friendship.
And Kozy? Sorry for saying you play the bass.
You're a phenomenal guitarist, dude.

One last thing:
This book is not for the faint of heart.

Chapter 1

L iam pulled his hood up, protecting his face from the relentless wind. It was bitterly cold, a silent current flowing across the near-dark sky, slicing through camp like a blade. The campfire flickered beneath the assault, threatening to extinguish but never quite losing the will to endure. Inky clouds funneled across the sky overhead, passengers to this endless gloom.

"Should we get more wood?" Dekker asked from across the clearing. Liam stared at the Transistor, his form enveloped by a thick wool blanket, the firelight casting shadows across his weathered face.

"Let it be," Avalice stated quietly from Liam's side. We don't want to draw too much attention to ourselves."

Liam grunted his agreement and pulled his wife deeper into him, feeding off her warmth.

Dekker shrugged, a roll of his blanket, his pale blue eyes staring intently into the fire. "I feel like I'll never be warm again. How long have we been at this? A week? Two?"

Liam barely heard him as he stared off into the distance, into the trees, knowing The Chain was out there somewhere, dozens of miles in the distance, unaffected by the weather. He envied it, its massive iron links chilling, but never freezing. In that moment, he felt like the furthest thing in the world from iron. He felt like water, solidifying and cracking at the bone.

"We've almost made it to Maltor," Avalice said between the wind. "We'll find a place to stay and warm up for a day or two before we head back out."

"Head back out?" Dekker asked. "Head back where?"

"We'll get another job," Liam said flatly, breaking the seal between his lips. "Just like we always do."

"How many Tablets do we have left?" Dekker asked, fighting against the chatter of his teeth. The dark forest around them shuddered, the canopy coming alive in the rising storm.

Avalice reached into her pack and fished around for a moment before pulling out half a dozen iron sheets. They were rectangular in shape, about the size of a small plate, and stamped with an intricate engraving—a fist holding an ear of corn.

"Six," Avalice said, turning the paper-thin ironworks over in her hands before stuffing them back into her pack.

Dekker looked at her, the lines in his face tracing the years of his life. "That's it? Yikes. This old boy is going to get mighty hungry if we don't earn some more soon."

"We'll get another job," Liam said without really listening. "We always do. We always...we always do…"

He thought he heard something in the darkness, past the wall of trees that squeezed them to the campfire. The rustle of leaves overhead overwhelmed any other sound and whatever it was had been lost beneath it.

Avalice squeezed his arm gently. "You OK? What is it?"

Liam let his eyes pull apart every shadow before he answered. "I don't know. Thought I heard something."

Dekker snorted and smiled. "I don't know about you, but I'm hearing a lot of things right now." He cocked his head to the side. "Ah, yes...there it is again. The bitter sound of our impending end."

The end. Liam let the words roll into the back of his mind, down his throat, and then into his guts. Was there an actual end to all this? His mind's eye went back to The Chain, its massive presence absorbing the skyline, soaring forever up into the heavens and beyond the ceiling of cloud. How long had it been since he had traveled to its base and stared up at its mysterious construction? Five years? Ten? He brushed the thought aside and turned his head toward the silent fourth member of their group.

"What about you, Isaac? Do you think the end is near?"

The young man shifted his tall form and kept his eyes closed as if he hadn't heard the question. He sat against his massive sword, the wide blade piercing the ground, acting as a prop.

Dekker smiled gently at the youth's casual indifference. "Who cares, right, kid? Just so long as you got that titanic slab of steel at your side, nothing else matters, am I right?"

Isaac opened one green eye and stared across the fire at the Transistor, his dark hair blowing across his stony face.

Dekker chuckled. "You know, I've said it a thousand times and I'll say it again—I have no idea how you wield that thing. It's almost as big as you and half as wide. What do you eat to get so strong? It certainly isn't anything out of the Factories, I'll tell you that much."

"Leave him alone," Avalice said. "We're just lucky we all found each other. Isn't that right, Liam?"

Liam nodded out of duty, "Sure...yeah, of course." Something distracted him again, that sound between the trees.

Dekker sighed heavily and watched the flicker of the flame before him. "Yeah, don't listen to me, kid. I'm just running my mouth to keep warm."

Slowly, Liam stood and stared out at the wall of black forest across from him at Dekker's back. There it was again. A noise. A snapping of wood. Out of the corner of his eye, he saw Isaac watching him.

Avalice looked up at her husband, concerned. "What is it?"

Liam held a finger to his lips, silencing her. She stood quickly and reached for her bow, the iron weapon reflecting the dim light as she brought it to her side.

Dekker stayed huddled where he was, casting a look over his shoulder. "You hear something creeping up on me or something?"

Liam winced against another blast of wind, almost positive this time that another sound floated through the air with it. He bent his knees and picked up his axe, twirling it in his hands as he rotated the shaft.

"Something's out there," he said quietly, eyes trained on a patch of darkness just past the treeline.

Dekker quickly scrambled to his feet, the blanket falling away to reveal his bandaged forearms. He scuttled over behind Liam and Avalice, peeking between their shoulders.

"It gives me the heebie-jeebies when you say stuff like that," he said nervously, now wrapping his healing arms around his shivering form. He jumped when Isaac plopped a blanket down over his shoulders, a squeak escaping his lips.

He pulled the warmth over him and cleared his throat, embarrassed. "Much obliged, kid, but maybe make some noise next time so I don't piss myself. I swear you move like a shadow some—"

"Quiet!" Liam hissed, squinting. Something was moving between the trees, a slow sway of dense darkness. Isaac had pulled his colossal sword out of the ground and stood at Avalice's side, the massive thing resting on his shoulder, the tip of the weapon extending a good six feet from the hilt. The trio of small rocket thrusters lining the blunt side remained cold, but Liam knew Isaac could bring them to life with a twist of the hilt, bringing the blade roaring down at whatever was out there. It made him feel slightly better.

"There, to the left," Avalice whispered, pointing with her free hand.

Liam saw it. It moved without grace, jerking and sputtering forward through the trees and out into the small clearing.

"Creator above," Dekker whispered, his face paling.

It was a man, dressed well but filthy. His eyes were completely black, save for tiny pinpricks of orange at the centers. He was caked in dirt and his hair hung in greasy clumps around his eerie eyes. His mouth was agape and moving as if he were searching for his next breath. When he spoke, his voice was ragged and distant.

"Where...where's my son? Where did he go...?"

Liam swallowed hard and gripped the polished handle of his battle axe. The man stayed where he was, staring at the small group, his brow furrowed in anguish, his orange-pierced eyes roaming around wildly.

"Rockflesh," Avalice said sharply, bringing her bow up and notching a steel-tipped arrow.

Dekker quickly raised a hand and pushed the weapon away. "What are you doing?!"

Avalice shot him a dagger of a look. "Don't you see he has the disease? He's *dangerous.*"

Dekker shook his head stubbornly, his blanket falling away. "He's in the early stages still. The fever has him." He pushed between Avalice and Liam. "And look at his face, his arms, do you see any threatening mutations yet?"

"There is no cure for his affliction, Dekker," Liam said evenly, keeping his eyes locked on the intruder. "Avalice is right. He's dangerous. What if he brings others?"

Dekker took another tentative step toward the man, his voice soft. "He's in pain, Liam. What if it were you? Wouldn't you want someone to show some compassion?"

"I would want a quick death," Liam stated thinly. "Anything is better than what comes next for him."

Avalice reached for Dekker. "Don't get near him. He could blow at any moment."

Dekker shook her off. "Nonsense. Do you see any Rockflesh jutting from his body? Where is the mass of pulsing crystals? Do you see any? No? Then let me help the poor soul."

He stepped around the campfire and held his hands out to the swaying man. "Easy, pal, it's going to be OK."

The man rolled his eyes around his head to meet Dekker's, taking a step back as he did so.

"Where...where is everyone...? What happened to the Factory?"

"Nothing happened to the Factory," Dekker said slowly, still approaching. "You're not in Maltor, I'm afraid. I'm not going to hurt you. I'm a Transistor. I can help you, if you'd like. Would you like that?"

The man's mouth twisted in sorrow, his voice a plea. "I just want to...see my son...I don't know...what...what happened to him...? Do you know what happened to him?"

Dekker reached for the man and gently took him by the arm. "Hush now, lost one. Turn your head for me, would you?"

The man just stared into Dekker's eyes as if he were a wandering child. He obeyed, and Dekker scaled his fingers across the back of the man's scalp.

"There it is," Dekker said gently, parting the man's hair to reveal a cluster of small, glowing abnormalities embedded in the man's head. It looked like a handful of neon orange gravel had been planted beneath the man's skin, bursting through the flesh to pulse with life of its own.

"Dekker, your arms—you shouldn't exert yourself," Liam warned, stepping toward the pair.

The Transistor waved his bandaged appendages casually. "This will take very little effort. I can handle it."

"It's poison," Avalice hissed. "It will only come back. You can't heal him."

Dekker smiled kindly into the man's blackened eyes. "No, but I can ease his suffering, if only for a little while."

Liam looked at Avalice, and then at Isaac, as if waiting for another argument. When none came, he released an exasperated hiss and lowered his axe.

"Just be quick about it. We need to get to the city."

Dekker nodded and closed his eyes, holding the lost man in place with one hand while the other wrapped around the back of his head where the orange rocks were. The only evidence that anything was happening came from a sharp intake of breath as Dekker worked, his eyes remaining shut. He remained perfectly still, the wind blowing an icy gale through the clearing.

The lost man suddenly gasped, an explosive exhale that brought with it all the relief in the world. His body shuddered once, twice, and then he was slumping over in Dekker's arms. The Transistor slowly lowered him to the ground, watching his face intently, a sweat breaking out across his forehead. The man's eyes cleared some as Dekker laid him down, the black turning gray.

"Rest now," Dekker said, a sudden weariness in his voice. "It might be the last chance you get."

The man blinked as if he was lost in a haze, his cloudy eyes meeting Dekker's. "What is...happening to me?" he wheezed, and then he was gone, lost to fatigue.

As Dekker slowly stood back up, Liam heard a crunch of leather and turned to see Isaac had been gripping his sword tightly. The young man caught Liam's look and cast it away, curling his wrapped hands into fists and then releasing them.

"He'll sleep for a while," Dekker said heavily, his face pale, "probably for the last time."

"You shouldn't have done that," Avalice said. "You can only channel so much."

Dekker wiped his brow and smiled without humor. "The Creator once chose to save us all from the disease. As his follower, it's my duty to do the same. Compassion is a weapon we should all brandish before anything else is considered. Wouldn't you say?"

"Not for someone who has Rockflesh," Avalice muttered, turning away.

Liam went to Dekker's side, keeping an eye on the sleeping man at their feet. "Are you OK? I know what your religion teaches, but you need to think about yourself once in a while." He looked at the bandages around Dekker's arms, "Avalice is right, you can only channel so much."

Dekker searched Liam's face for a moment before sighing, the aged man's wrinkles showing themselves. "You've known me for some time now, Liam. You know what's important to me." He spread his hands. "The world is dying. We all know it. I just don't want it to fade without kindness."

Liam put a hand on the Transistor's shoulder, nodding. "I know, Dek. I know. Now why don't you get rid of that poison, OK?"

Dekker nodded and slowly raised his hand, palm out. He aimed it at the woods and closed his eyes, taking a breath as he did so.

After a moment, a sickly yellow glow surrounded his arm.

"Easy now," Liam warned, keeping his hand on the man's shoulder.

Still aglow, Dekker flexed his fingers once and then a thin stream of viscous liquid materialized out of his hand and sprayed out onto the dirt. It was blackish-orange in color, and Liam could feel a dangerous heat coming off the growing puddle. The air stank of it and after a moment, the flow ceased and Dekker snapped his eyes open.

"Void below, but that stings something fierce," Dekker hissed between his teeth, his eyes watering. He gripped his bandaged arms protectively and gingerly massaged them.

"You OK?" Liam asked cautiously. He could feel Isaac watching them, an unmoving pillar wrapped in firelight.

Dekker nodded slowly and his arms fell away. "I'm fine. It was a minor thing. There wasn't much in him yet. I'm still just a little sore from our last encounter with the Profanes." He snorted. "May the Creator have mercy on their godless souls. Buncha wild heretics..." he trailed off, muttering to himself and Liam left him to it. He went back to his wife, Avalice, who was breaking camp.

"You've got the right idea," he said, joining her. "No telling if there's more Rockflesh coming this way or not."

"We're close to Maltor," she said with her back to him, "a couple hours walk I'd say. We need to rest and regroup out of the cold, Liam."

"We will," he said, stuffing blankets and gear into their packs. "What I wouldn't do for some damn horses…"

"Or one of those automated machines the Factory Caps use."

"Eh, I don't trust anything those militarized freaks use."

They continued to ready themselves for travel, the conversation dying. Isaac came and helped, sliding his coffin-sized sword into a slot in the back of his leather armor. Dekker seated himself next to the sleeping man and seemed content to let the others do the work. When they were finished, they shouldered their bags and took one last look at the sleeping man, his features peaceful beneath the dying fire.

"Good luck to you," Dekker whispered, and then they were away.

They passed through the dense trees with as much speed as they could muster, making their way through the final stretch of forest. Liam was glad to leave it behind, the swaying canopy almost as dark as the sky above. They had been traveling for days now, maybe weeks, passing between two of the last cities this side of the Red Ravine. They had come up empty when they had gone searching for work, most of the jobs being Factory related and unfit for a group of wandering mercenaries. Frustrated, they left Titan and began making the long journey to Maltor, with hopes that something lie in wait for them there.

As much as Liam hated the cities, he would be glad to be back in one. The wilderness was growing more and more dangerous, each year bringing with it new horrors that crawled from the Red Ravine. The disease, Rockflesh, seemed to be seeping from the Void at a greater rate these days, with more and more infected showing themselves with alarming frequency. They were a curse on the land, a constant threat that weighed heavily on the surviving population.

Silently, he wished the diseased would just wander over to the edge of the world and throw themselves down into the Void, back into the hell from which they had been spawned. What kind of existence did they hope to gain by staying alive? He shook his head, his worn leather boots crunching over dead twigs. He knew it wasn't their fault. Once you were infected, the fever stage came and went quickly, leaving madness and mutation in its wake.

What had the Creator really accomplished in saving them from the plague? Why had he cast The Chain down from above and hauled up this chunk of the world? So everyone could live another couple hundred years in agony and misery before the gases slowly reached them all?He remembered reading something once, a history book, about how in the early days, back when technology wasn't so rare, a group of people had tried to plug the Red Ravine. Once they went down into it, confident in their fire and explosions and metal, they would succeed.

No one ever saw them again.

His mind wandered back to when he had made his own journey through that hellscape,onto the other side of Tectonic, across to where The Chain held the world like a piece of meat on a string, just out of reach from the nightmare below.

"We're through," Avalice said quietly, breaking him out of his trance. He looked up and saw they were passing through the treeline and out into the open plains. As the four passed across the threshold, the darkness of the forest remained at their backs. Liam craned his head back and took a long breath of open air, the oil-thick clouds rolling overhead.

"What I wouldn't do for a sun splash," Dekker said, earning a glance from Isaac. "Just one, just for a couple seconds. I can't remember the last time the Creator gifted us with one."

"Enough talk about the Creator," Avalice said as they began to cross the long, open terrain. "It's depressing."

Dekker offered her a small smile in the gloom. "Even so, He is with us in the darkness as well, Avalice. Have faith."

"Just don't see the point," she muttered as the wind scoured the hard packed earth and blew grit into everyone's face. Liam winced and held his hand up to protect his eyes, turning around to view the fading woods.

Rising out of the far horizon, soaring high above the trees and into the heavens, was The Chain. It was a needle-thin pillar of darkness, tethering Tectonic to whatever was holding the other end, above the endless clouds.

"Don't drop us just yet," Liam muttered, turning his attention back to land before him. "Not quite yet."

Chapter 2

The small party trudged through the gloomy world in silence. Their trek took them over rising foothills and across dried creek beds, the dead grass and hard-packed earth crunching underfoot. The sky remained a swath of gray-black smog, the sun an almost distant memory. Now and again they would hear the call or chirp of an animal, the noise sounding eerily alien. A flock of crows cawed somewhere in the distance and Liam shivered. The wildlife was not immune to Rockflesh, and the disease had a tendency to warp an animal's vocal cords, creating an unnerving sound that pierced the skull when heard.

Liam cursed the wind as it continued to billow across the dark world. He rubbed warmth into his arms as he walked, clamping his teeth together so they wouldn't chatter wildly. Avalice had her hood up and Dekker was encased in his familiar blanket. Isaac was the only one who seemed unaffected, his tall figure clothed in nothing but his black pants and leather armor, a crisscross of belts and loops clinking gently as he strode ahead.

Despite outward appearances, the trek was getting to them. The road was long and the constant threat of danger had a tendency to drain the muscles. Liam rolled his shoulders, releasing some of the tension in his neck. He prayed they would make it to Maltor without another run-in with the religious heretics, a group that called themselves the Profanes. Liam wasn't an especially religious man himself; he barely believed in the Creator at all, but he had grown to loathe the ignorant violence of the Profanes. Their hatred for Dekker's kind, Transistors, had grown to become a real danger. Liam thought they were just envious. Envious that some were not only immune to the world-ending disease, but that they could also drain and use that same power that killed so many. Snorting to himself, he shook his head. It turned his stomach knowing that such moronic people still existed and survived even now. Even though no one really knew why people like Dekker could do what they did, Liam didn't see them as something to fear. He considered them a blessing. A means to survive just a little longer. A few of the remaining scientists mused that the immunity might have something to do with a Transistor's blood type, but the technology no longer existed to test such theories.

"How we've regressed," Liam mumbled to himself, his breath pluming out before him.

"You say something?"

Liam turned to his wife, Avalice. "It's nothing. Just getting lost in my own head again."

"Dangerous place to get lost," Dekker chided from their backs.

Avalice pointed ahead of them as the group crested a rocky foothill. "We're getting close. See the light on the horizon?"

Liam nodded, pausing for a moment to catch his breath, the landscape fanning out around them like an empty crater. "I see it. I can smell the Factory from here as well."

"At least it's still running," Dekker said, hiking his pack up higher on his shoulders. "When we were in Titan, I heard talk that the Caps were having some problems with the one there."

"They better figure it out, then," Avalice said, tugging at her hood. "Once they go, we won't be far behind."

"We could always eat each other," Dekker mused.

"Now that's a lovely thought," Liam said, the wind teasing metallic smoke.

Dekker tilted his chin toward Isaac. "We could probably get a week's worth of meals out of this one, don't you think? You wouldn't mind that, would you, son? If worse came to worst?"

Isaac didn't dignify the older man with a reply.

"Come on," Liam said, walking down the slope before them, "let's get going. I'd like to make it to Maltor before we all turn to ice."

The wind filled the sky as the four continued toward the distant city. Liam could make out the bones of the past resting on the horizon, a scattering of highrises from the Old World, along with the makeshift, cruder structures that had been built after The Chain had come. Resting in the center of his vision, between the towering buildings, was the Factory. The massive dome couldn't be missed, its windowless, metal shape sprouting dozens of smoke-stacks that churned out thick smog. It was one of the last places in the world that produced a food source, and Liam knew that his wife was right. Once the Factories went, everything else would follow. Despite his cynicism, he had to give it to humanity. The Factories were the only reason survival had been possible for this long, nearly three hundred years now. After Tectonic had been ripped away from the Void, the technology that had come with it had been used to construct a place that could sustain the population.

The Captains, or Caps as they were called, had been formed and it birthed some kind of order out of the chaos. It had given people purpose, something Liam found himself longing for during the deep hours of the night. He had thought about joining them at one point, enlisting in their ranks, but found that he simply couldn't. They were a self-sustaining people with no regard for anything or anyone else but their militarized system. Protect the Factory, produce Tablets as a form of currency and control, and murder anyone who crossed them or stepped outside the boundaries of their regulations.

As they walked toward the looming city, Liam thought back to when they had been in Titan. During the first night there, they had all witnessed some-one getting caught with fake Tablets. It was a common occurrence, a risk the desperate took to eat. Liam felt the cold creep up his neck as he reminisced, the memory still fresh. The Caps had come, confronted the man in the street, and then proceeded to beat him to death once his deception was unmasked.

Don't mess with the Factories, leave the Caps alone, and don't try to steal or fool the system. It was a rule Liam held the group to. Let them be and they won't mess with you.

It was a cruel system, but sometimes Liam wondered if there was some logic to it all. Everyone was living on the edge of a knife and it wouldn't take much for humanity's survival to end. There were no laws, no government, no police. There were only the Factories and their guardians. Mess with either and you were killed without trial. There simply wasn't time for anything else.

Liam sighed quietly and shut his mind off.

An hour passed. And then another. As the third one approached, the small party reached the outskirts of Maltor with a collective sigh. Small houses began littering the flattened landscape, most made of stone and wood. Ragged eyes met them as they passed, families and children standing like statues to make sure the travelers wouldn't hurt them. A road formed from the dirt and twisted them deeper and deeper inward, taking them toward the heart of the city. The houses were joined by small shops now, each selling simple things to make life a little more comfortable. Clothes, tools, weapons, armor, shops with signs boasting cures to Rockflesh. Nothing was regulated and there was no one to check the validity of anything. Goods and services were traded for Tablets, each exchange a gamble, a faith placed that everyone could survive until the next time the Caps distributed more of them to the population. In Titan, that had happened every five days, the great Factory doors opening to roll out more Tablets to distribute. Once they were, the shopkeepers and vendors who were licensed to sell the Factory-made food would turn in ninety percent of their earnings to the Caps. They were allowed only to keep ten percent of their earnings for their own pleasure.

It was a hard system to live by, but Liam didn't feel like anyone had a choice. If it was discovered that you were hoarding more Tablets, you were confronted and murdered without mercy. It didn't matter who you were or how well your shop was doing. Steal from the Captains and you were dead. Liam didn't like it, but he had to acknowledge the balance of it all. Too many Tablets on the street meant an imbalance in the food distribution. It made it too easy for someone to gain power and try to monopolize control over the less fortunate.

Liam reminded himself of his rule. Don't mess with the Caps.

He was shaken from his thoughts as a little girl ran across the street in front of him, laughing as a young boy chased her between the shoddy houses. He glanced at Avalice and saw her eyes soften and her mouth tighten. She saw him looking at her, and she offered him a rare smile, small as it was.

He felt his heart harden and then soften almost immediately. It was a constant source of strain between him and his wife. He watched the children disappear into the streets, ducking between vendors and the wandering population. He just couldn't live with himself if he mindfully chose to bring a child into this terrible world. He simply couldn't.

They continued deeper into the city, the streets growing denser as they went. The houses turned more industrial the closer they got to the Factory, which sat at the center of Maltor. Signs of the Old World began to show themselves, the last remains of a distant memory. Torches flickered high up on metal poles, casting an ever-moving shadow across the shuffling masses. Carriages cluttered across the broken asphalt and cobblestone streets. A dull murmur seemed to float above everyone's head, mutterings of business being dealt, of conversations being whispered.

The Factory loomed ahead like a monument, its bubble-like surface catching the light and absorbing it against its dull gray frame. Blinking lights dotted the exterior, the last remains of an electric world. Smokestacks cut high into the air, exhaling great, stinking wafts of black into the dark clouds.

Liam led the group down the streets, bumping past the moving populace, keeping one hand on his axe. He didn't trust city people. They all reeked of desperation, trusting only in the Factory like it was some kind of god.

They passed storefronts and stables, houses and hostels, the dull rumble of life all around them. Ahead of them, at an intersection, a trio of Caps rolled past in their mechanical contraptions, the drivers hidden behind blackened glass and heavy doors. The great wheels of the machines bounced and skidded along the potholed road, trusting the population to get out of the way.

Liam turned down a side alley, the rest of the group following without question. The alley dumped them into another street that Liam quickly crossed, heading for a lit-up building two stories high. As he mounted the wooden steps, he could hear loud conversation from inside, a milling of voices and the clink of drinks being dispersed down thirsty throats.

He reached the double doors and turned around, addressing the others. "We'll rest here at the Inn for the night and try to find some work in the morning. I know we could all use a little bit of a break, so make sure to get some sleep tonight." He met their eyes. "We have six Tablets left. That should be more than enough for some hot food and maybe two rooms. Anyone have a problem with that?"

"A bed sounds wonderful right about now," Avalice said.

Dekker stepped out of the way as a pair of women mounted the stairs and pushed past him, disappearing into the Inn. He turned to Liam, his voice low. "I think I'm going to head over to the Church and see if I can offer any assistance for a couple hours." He looked at Isaac, "Save me a couple crusts of bread, would you, son? Just tuck 'em under my pillow or something. I'd appreciate it."

Isaac nodded.

"You sure that's a good idea?" Liam asked. "There's got to be a lot of Profanes wandering the street. I don't want you running into trouble."

Dekker smiled. "I'll be fine. Besides, I'm sure my brothers at the Church could use some help. It would feel good to do something...useful."

"Just be careful," Liam warned. "Please."

Dekker winked at him. "Who would want to hurt a face like this?"

Avalice snorted. "Plenty, trust me."

"Try not to miss me," Dekker said, turning away and waving a hand over his shoulder, "Oh, and Isaac, there better be some food waiting for me when I get back or my sobs of grief will wake the dead."

Isaac snorted and pushed his way into the Inn, leaving just Liam and Avalice standing there.

Avalice was about to go inside when Liam reached out and took her hand. She turned and looked curiously into her husband's eyes.

"What is it?" she asked.

Liam squeezed her hand gently, his voice quiet. "Hey, uh...I just..." he took a step closer. "I want you to know that I still love you."

Avalice's face softened slightly, her dark brown hair falling down across her bright blue eyes. "I know you do. I love you too, Liam. Is that all you wanted to say?"

Liam nodded and let go of her hand. She gave him a smile and then went inside. Liam followed her, shoving the doors aside and stepping into the bustle of the Inn.

A well-lit room met them, warm and wafting with smoke. Tables were littered around a large hearth, men and women talking loudly before the dancing flame. Food was brought from a kitchen in the back, and a long bar ran the length of the establishment. Liam took a moment and breathed it all in, the burst of life a refreshing contrast to the hush and gloom outside.

Avalice pushed ahead and found Isaac in the far corner, sitting at a wooden table, his massive sword propped against the corner. Liam noted more than a few eyes staring at it, hungrily examining the rocket thrusters lining the blunt side of the blade. Technology like that could earn someone quite a few Tablets if turned into the Caps, and everyone seemed to know that. One look at Isaac though dispersed most schemes and Liam felt no danger as he followed his wife over to the young man and took a seat.

"Hell, but does it feel good to sit down," Avalice groaned, plopping herself down in the chair next to Isaac.

Liam took his place next to her, sliding his pack from his shoulders with a relieved sigh. His neck felt like one large knot, a dull throb up the base of his skull. Wearily, he ran his hands down his face and realized just how loudly his stomach was rumbling.

A young woman made her way over to them, a horribly dutiful smile plastered across her pretty face.

"Welcome, I hope you've found the warmth and relief you're looking for!" she greeted, her voice almost nauseatingly flat.

"We're going to need some food as quickly as you can manage, dear," Avalice said, taking off her gloves and pulling her hood down.

The young woman bobbed her head and Liam hoped the thing wouldn't pop off her shoulders.

"Of course! I'm going to have to see your Tablets first, though." She flashed an apologetic smile, her eyes lingering on Isaac's muscled frame. He ignored her and stared into the fire, his face unreadable.

"Right, right," Avalice groaned. As she dug in her pack for the iron-stamped sheets, Liam looked up at their server, keeping his voice low.

"Is Henry here tonight?"

The young woman bobbed her head again. "Yep, sure is! He's in the back. Do you want to speak with him?"

"That would be great, thank you."

"And who should I say is asking for him?"

"Liam."

"Well, OK, Mr. Liam, I'll go fetch him right away then!"

Avalice held out four Tablets to the girl. "Here, come back with some food, would you please?"

"It would be my delight!"

As she scampered off, Avalice watched her go, shaking her head as she did so. "Don't know where she finds the energy to be so...bubbly."

"She's doing her best," Liam said, pulling his cloak off and hanging it on his chair. He considered removing his leather breastplate but decided against it. The thing stank enough where it was.

As they waited for their food, Liam allowed warmth back into his body. The heat from the hearth filled the air and made his head swim in a pleasant kind of way. He could feel his muscles relaxing, the tension fading. He closed his eyes and allowed himself a couple moments of peace. They didn't come often these days.

It wasn't long before the server returned, carrying with her a tray of food along with a trio of mugs. She plopped them down on the table and Liam surveyed the offering. Two lumps of gray matter rested on a plate, looking like some kind of half-dried mud. Sitting alongside it was a small loaf of bread that looked a couple days past edible. Isaac immediately leaned forward and snatched the bread up, pulling a mug of ale along with it. Wordlessly, he buried his face in the warm brew and drank with vigor.

"Let me know if you need anything else!" the young woman chirped, her smile looking more like a fatal wound.

"This is fine, thank you," Liam said, breaking off a piece of the gray matter and shoving it into his mouth. He didn't know why he expected anything different. This was the standard ration the Factory produced, nothing more than flavorless fuel for the human body. There were a couple other items in their production, like the bread, but the majority of it was this. A slightly chewy glop of protein and nutrients. Liam swallowed it down, trying not to wince. It never seemed to get easier.

As Avalice broke off a piece for herself, a man bustled toward them through the crowd, mopping sweat off his bald head. He was skinny and appeared to be in his late thirties, only a couple years older than Liam himself.

He nodded to the table and sat himself down, letting out a dramatic sigh as he did so.

"Liam! Avalice! How wonderful to see your cheery faces again!" he said, his voice loud and fatigued. He mopped more sweat off his clean-shaven cheeks and wiped them on his pants. Avalice grimaced.

"Hello, Henry," Liam said, daring another bite of food. "Wasn't sure if you'd still be running the place. It's been a while."

Henry scratched his chin, musing. "Couple months, I'd say. Where'd you all go this time?"

"Titan."

"Ah, of course. Where else is there to go?" Henry said, casting a look at Isaac. "I see you're still hanging around these bums, huh?"

Isaac drained his mug.

"Still as annoyingly chatty as ever, too," Henry rumbled, turning back to Liam and Avalice. "I gotta say, the pair of you look a little worse for wear these days. Was Titan not the dream you hoped it to be?"

Avalice took a gulp from one of the mugs before answering. "If you held a mirror up to Maltor, you wouldn't know if the reflection was Titan or this stinking pit."

Henry waggled his finger at her. "Now now, don't go talking poorly about my city. I won't have it. This wonderful place is the heartbeat of Tectonic!"

"Yeah, well, it must have heart disease, then," Avalice mumbled, tipping her mug back once again.

Henry scoffed at her and waved a hand. "Oh, enough of your cynicism. I heard you asked after me. Do you need something? I mean, besides this wonderful feast I have provided and the beds you'll sleep in tonight."

Liam nodded. "Yeah, actually. We're looking for work. I was hoping you'd know of some. Any chatter recently?"

Henry tapped his chin with a finger. "Hmmm. As a matter of fact, there might be. There's this fella that's been coming in here quite a bit recently. He's been asking for you specifically. Meant to tell you that next time I saw ya."

Liam cocked an eyebrow. "Asking for me? What about?"

Henry shrugged, "I dunno. He's been pretty insistent, though. I would bet the whole Inn that he has work for you."

"What's he like?" Avalice asked.

"Ahhh, let's see. Older fella, I suppose. Very serious look about him. Bald, graying beard. Probably the same age as that other guy that's always with you. The Transistor." Henry looked around the table suddenly. "Say, where is he? He hasn't kicked the bucket, has he?"

"He's at the Church," Liam said. "He'll be by later."

"What a martyr he is," Henry said sarcastically. "Speaking of the Church, there's been a real influx of Profanes in town. Don't really know why. They're always coming in here, stirring up trouble, talking too loud, shittin' on everything to do with the Creator, The Chain, the whole thing."

"Why are there so many these days?" Avalice asked.

Henry shrugged, "Who knows? I think the Rockflesh is getting worse out there in the wild, driving more people to the cities. Seems to be popping up everywhere lately, just sprouting out of the ground in those great lumpy knots of stone. It's getting bad, ya know?"

"We've seen," Liam said darkly, his mind going back to the lost man they had encountered at camp. "And it's infecting more of us."

"Creator help us," Henry said miserably. He looked around the table glumly. "See? Now you've gone and ruined my mood. And I was having such a good night, too."

"We'll let you get back to it," Liam said, leaning back in his chair. "I didn't mean to bring you down."

"Ach, we're all dead anyway," Henry said dramatically as he stood.

"It was good to see you," Liam said.

"You stay safe out there," Henry said, patting Liam's shoulder, "and keep this pretty bird safe," he continued, throwing a wink at Avalice.

"This bird has a very sharp beak," Avalice threatened.

Henry walked away, clutching his chest, his voice carrying back to them. "Oh, and how I dream of it!"

"He's such an ass," Avalice muttered, but Liam saw she was smiling around her mug.

The three of them finished their meal and departed for their rooms, climbing the stairs to the second level. Isaac went down the hall to a room he'd share with Dekker while Avalice and Liam took another.

The furnishings were as bare as could be—a single wide bed with a nightstand that held a bowl of water for washing, along with a single candlestick. Liam went to it as Avalice closed the door behind them. Once the room was lit, Liam and Avalice stripped themselves of their leathers and clothing, stepping out of their boots and collapsing into the bed.

"Oh, but does that feel nice," Liam murmured, pulling his wife close to him. She rested her head on his chest and closed her eyes, her voice soft.

"I've missed this."

Liam kissed the top of her head, feeling the worries of the world fade away for a few precious seconds.

"We could do this in camp, you know."

Avalice snorted and looked up at him, her blues meeting his browns. "With Dekker watching? Please. I don't think I could take his commentary." She lowered her voice. "No, this is just for you and me to share."

"I suppose it is," Liam said, closing his eyes and allowing himself to breathe.

"We should probably hunt down that man asking for you, huh?"

"We will," Liam said, his eyes remaining closed. "Let me just enjoy this bed with you for a minute, though."

Avalice grinned. "Always the sweet talker."

A few moments passed in silence, the bustle of the Inn muted by the safety of the room. He brushed his fingers along his wife's bare back, his mind wandering back to their arrival.

"I saw you looking at those kids earlier," he said quietly.

He could feel Avalice bristle slightly. "And?"

Liam continued to rub her back, her cheek warm against his chest. "I just don't want you to be upset with me."

Avalice let out a long sigh. "We've been over this a thousand times, Liam. I understand your stance. I just so happen to have a different one."

"So...where does that leave us?"

"The same place we always end up." She suddenly propped herself up on her elbow and looked down at him. "What's this all about?"

Liam shrugged and brushed a strand of hair from her eyes. "I don't know. It's like we were telling Henry. Things are getting worse out there. I'm just worried about losing the few things I still care about."

Avalice placed a hand on Liam's cheek. "I'm not going to leave you, if that's what you're scared of."

Liam nodded, enjoying the feeling of her fingers against his stubbled jaw. "OK. I just..." he trailed off.

"I love you, Liam. However that may be for us."

"I love you, too, Av."

She leaned down and kissed him. He kissed her back, and then the two of them were tangled in one another, hands groping, breath hot and frantic. They made love and fell into a fatigued slumber, lost in one another's arms.

It wasn't long before they were jolted from sleep, a sudden pounding on the door blasting through the room like Rockflesh exploding.

Liam leapt to his feet, panicked and dazed. He grabbed his pants from the floor and went to the door, opening it cautiously.

Henry stood panting before him, sweating and out of breath.

"What is it!?" Liam barked, his heart racing.

Henry jerked a thumb over his shoulder, "There's trouble outside and you're going to want to get down there."

Liam clenched his teeth. "What now?"

Chapter 3

L iam rushed down the stairs of the Inn, Avalice at his heels. The previ-ously packed main hall was now mostly drained of patrons, the dull roar of a crowd emanating from outside. Liam, still pulling his clothes on, felt his heart begin to race as he followed Henry past the hearth. The three of them burst through the front doors and almost ran into a gathering crowd, all pushing and shoving for a spot.

"What the hell is going on here!?" Liam yelled over the din. He avoid-ed a stray elbow as dozens of men and women pushed forward, down the stairs, and into the street. He tried to understand what everyone was shout-ing about. The eerie way everyone was riled up set the hairs on his arms at attention.

"Look!" Henry yelled, grabbing Liam and shoving people aside so they could get a good look at what the commotion was all about.

Liam pushed a woman away and stepped forward, breaching a circle of people who seemed to be focused on something at the center of the ring.

"Oh, hell," Avalice hissed at Liam's side, one hand reaching out and grip-ping his shoulder.

Liam felt his stomach turn sour, a cold hand caressing the back of his neck.

Dekker was on his knees, his face beaten and bloody, one eye swollen shut. Blood trickled from a split lip and it seemed to take all his energy to just stay on his knees and not collapse in the street.

The men and women surrounding him wore black tunics with the image of a white broken chain inked into the fabric. They jeered at Dekker, spat on him, and slapped the old man whenever he tried to clear his face.

"Profanes," Liam growled, his pulse thrumming.

Avalice gripped Liam's shoulder even harder, her voice urgent. "We have to stop this. They're going to kill him."

A woman stepped in front of Dekker and his weary eyes rose to meet hers. He was rewarded by a kick to the groin, finally bringing him to the ground in a gasp. The dozen odd Profanes cheered, and the crowd seemed content to watch the show, a couple stray cries joining the Profanes.

Liam looked desperately at Avalice. He grabbed at his belt loop, cursing himself, "I left my axe upstairs!"

Another Profane stepped toward Dekker and kicked him hard in the ribs, bringing forth a pained wheeze from the old man.

"Why hasn't the Creator come and saved him!?" The Profane yelled to the crowd. "If he exists, where is he!? Surely he wouldn't let one of his believers go through something like this!" Another Profane delivered another kick.

"Why don't you pray some more!?" Another yelled, leaning down into Dekker's dazed face. "Pray and maybe your precious god will come and stop this!"

"To hell with this," Liam snarled, bracing himself.

But Avalice wouldn't let him go, her voice frantic. "Liam, there's a dozen of them! They'll kill you!"

Liam tried to shake her away, his lips curling. "We have to do *something!*"

Suddenly the crowd was swept with an unexpected and abrupt silence, all eyes turning toward a figure that had pushed his way through the crowd and now stood opposite from Liam.

"What is going on here?" Isaac asked quietly, his colossal sword planted between his feet. The wind rustled through his dark hair, his voice rising with the breeze.

The apparent leader of the Profanes faced Isaac, Dekker sprawled at his feet.

"This has got nothing to do with you, kid," the man spat, his followers gathering at his back. "So why don't you piss off and mind your own business?"

Isaac didn't move, his voice flat and even. "Let him go."

The Profanes snickered, kicking Dekker over onto his back. The old man coughed and blinked blood away, his chest rising and falling weakly.

"Do you know what this man is?" The leader asked loudly, making sure the crowd could hear him.

Isaac didn't even look at Dekker, his green eyes boring into the leader's pale grays.

"He's a Transistor!" The Profane yelled, earning a cry of affirmation from his followers. "He's a freak! A monster! A wielder of the poison that is killing this world!"

Isaac remained a statue, his face carved from stone. "Walk. Away."

The Profane stepped toward the young man, staring up into his face without fear. "This isn't a fight you wanna pick, kid."

Without warning, Isaac shifted, his shoulders lowering, his sword swinging back, eyes going dark.

"Oh shit," Liam hissed, grabbing Avalice and Henry and yanking them away.

CLICK.

The roar of Isaac's sword as he activated the rocket thrusters was loud enough to rattle Liam's teeth. A burst of light followed and Isaac stepped forward, the wide, razor-sharp slab of iron screeching through the air in a wide horizontal arc.

The group of Profanes didn't even have time to scream as Isaac delivered death upon them, a half-dozen exploding at the waist in halos of blood. The blade passed through them with ease, severing them in half, raining gore across the faces of the other six that had been spared the blow.

The leader of the Profanes just stared at Isaac in horrified shock, and then the life drained from his eyes and his body fell in two across the cobblestones, followed in suit by the others who had been caught in the projection of the blade.

Isaac let the thrusters die as red sprayed across the ground, his stance wide, his sword warmed by the impact. He looked up at the remaining Profanes, their faces horrified as their companions collapsed in pieces.

"Walk. Away."

In a great scramble, they obeyed, scattering and dispersing through the equally shocked crowd. Isaac pulled himself up to his full height and slid his massive sword into the slot in the back of his armor. Then, kneeling, he helped Dekker gingerly get to his feet.

"Are you OK, Dek?" he asked the old man, his voice calm and soft.

Dekker winced around the bruises, his voice weak, but still his own. "Oh I've been worse." He coughed and wiped his face. "You know, for a second there, I wasn't sure if I'd make it out of that."

Liam and Avalice rushed to their friend's side, helping Isaac carrying the weight.

"Sorry we didn't make it sooner," Liam babbled apologetically. "They really did a number on you, huh?"

Somehow Dekker found the strength to bark a laugh. "Oh, relax, I'm tougher than I look." But even as he said it, Liam saw pain fill his eyes.

"You should have eviscerated them," Avalice said fiercely, ripping off a piece of her sleeve and dabbing at the Transistor's face as Isaac and Liam helped him up the stairs of the Inn. Somewhere behind them, Liam heard Henry angrily scold the dispersing crowd.

Dekker looked at Avalice through puffy eyes. "And what would that have accomplished? What would that have shown everyone watching? That I really am the monster they accuse me of being? No. I won't give them that."

They took him inside, Henry bustling at their backs, instructing them to bring Dekker into the kitchen. Limping past the stoves, they finally lowered the Transistor into a chair. Liam wasn't sure what groaned louder—the wooden backing or Dekker.

"All right, everyone back it up," the old man moaned, shooing them. "I just need a breather, that's all."

A pair of bewildered servers stood across from them, wringing their hands. Henry barked loudly for them to get back to work, and they went scurrying from the kitchen to attend to the Inn's patrons. Avalice grabbed a cloth from the counters and wet it, passing it to Dekker who took it gratefully.

"How did they get to you?" Liam asked.

Dekker dabbed at his bloody lip. "Caught me as I came out of the Church. It's like they were waiting for me. Probably saw me go in and decided to hang around." He grunted. "Lucky me."

"They infuriate me," Avalice growled, bunching her hands into fists. "Bunch of brain-dead morons going around making life harder for good people. Hell, you didn't even do anything to them."

Dekker wiped his chin of blood. "Yes, but I exist and that's enough for them. While I don't appreciate their violent nature, I still hope that one day the Profanes will put their faith in the Creator."

"Wouldn't hold my breath on that," Liam said, helping the old man as he struggled to remove something from his pocket.

"What is this?" Liam asked, taking the small brown purse. It was heavy and sealed shut by a pair of drawstrings.

"Might want to put that on the counter and leave it alone," Dekker said.

Liam pried the purse open and felt his heart sputter when he realized what the contents were.

"Oh, hell, take it back!" Liam said, tossing the bag back to Dekker.

Dekker closed the purse and set it on his lap. "Told you."

Avalice cocked an eyebrow. "What is it?"

Liam looked around the kitchen, first at Avalice, then Isaac, then Henry. "It's Rockflesh, glowing like wildfire."

Henry took a step back, his voice suddenly nervous, "Hey now, I'm all for helping out a couple friends, but I am not OK with—"

Dekker help up his hands passively. "Take it easy. It's OK. It's just a couple of stones still in the early phases of growth. There's absolutely no risk of detonation."

"There better not be!" Henry yelled, unconvinced. "The last thing I need tonight is a bomb going off in my kitchen, not to mention all the gases that would be released and then I'd be responsible for starting a city-wide pandemic—"

Without warning, Dekker tossed the bag at the Innkeeper. Henry shrieked as he fumbled to catch the purse, cursing loudly.

"See?" Dekker said, smiling around his bruises. "Perfectly harmless. The Church harvests them solely to channel. They're very careful and make sure the stones they gather are still in the early phases. Just enough to be useful, but not so powerful they could be dangerous."

"Yeah, unless one of em breaks open and all that gas—"

Liam plucked the bag from Henry's shaking hands and gave it back to Dekker, who made it disappear before addressing the startled man.

"I don't think anyone here has any intention of doing something so stupid," he said, "so why don't you go back to attending your Inn, OK? I thank you for your hospitality and I'd very much like to get some sleep now, if that's all right."

Henry nodded nervously. "Yeah, OK. Sure. Just, uh, make yourself at home."

Muttering to himself, he left the kitchen, mopping his brow as he went.

Dekker looked up at Isaac, appraising the young man. "You didn't happen to stash away some food for me, did ya? Despite the beating, I'm absolutely starved right now."

"Of course," Isaac said quietly. He turned away and exited the kitchen, almost bumping into someone as he passed through the doors.

"Oh, pardon me," the new arrival said, bowing his bald head to Isaac, "I didn't mean to get in your way." Isaac ignored him and disappeared into the main hall.

Avalice looked at the man who now approached them, wringing his hands together as he did so.

"Who're you? We're kind of in the middle of something here."

The man smiled, though it was a fragile thing. His eyes were ringed with hard lines and a short beard peppered his face with grays.

"I don't mean to intrude," he said, taking a tentative step closer, casting a glance at Dekker, "but I couldn't help but observe the spectacle outside. Are you OK?"

Dekker snorted, then winced. "I'm just fine, especially now that I know Maltor is occupied with such concerned citizens. What's your name, friend?"

The man smiled, encouraged. "I'm Rezin. I really don't mean to barge in like this. I hope I'm not interrupting anything?"

Liam crossed his arms, quietly sizing up the newcomer. He cleared his throat and shot a glance at Avalice before speaking.

"You wouldn't happen to be that guy Henry told us about, would you? The one asking about me?"

"Oh, heavens," the man bumbled, wringing his hands even more vigorously, "I'm sorry about that. I promise you I mean you no ill will; I was simply told you visit this establishment from time to time and so I inquired about your presence often."

Dekker chuckled in his chair. "Creator above, pal, relax, would you? You're making *me* uncomfortable."

The man, Rezin, offered another weak smile and his shoulders drooped a little. "Of course, I'm sorry. It's just, I've been looking for you for so long that I'm a little nervous now that you're here in front of me."

Avalice stood next to Liam and shrugged. "Well, here we are. Spit it out, would you? Henry mentioned you had a job or something."

Rezin nodded and ran a hand over his bald head. "Straight to business, of course, of course, very good." He exhaled heavily and let out a broken laugh. "Work. Yes, I have a job for you if you'd be so kind as to take it."

"Well, that all depends on the work and what you're willing to pay," Liam said flatly.

"Oh, I can most assuredly pay!"

"That's a good start then," Avalice said, then paused. "But Henry mentioned that you were specifically asking for my husband, Liam. Why?"

Rezin chewed on his lip. "Ah, yes, Henry is correct, I was."

"That's been established. Why?"

"Because Liam here has crossed the Red Ravine."

Avalice looked at Liam, and Dekker groaned from their backs.

Rezin examined their faces, suddenly concerned. "Was I mistaken?"

Liam slowly shook his head. "No, you're right. I have. But that was over ten years ago. It was back when the gases were much more...subdued. It's been getting worse lately, as you may have noticed."

Rezin's eyes came alive with curiosity. "But you have crossed it, correct?"

"More like went around it. But yeah, I've been to the other side."

Rezin stepped forward now, his voice low. "And The Chain. You've been to it?"

Liam's memory soared back a decade, taking him to another time. Carefully, he nodded. "I've been to it."

Rezin, now face to face with Liam, reached out and gripped his arm, his voice full of energy. "I would like to hire you, all of you, to take me to it."

Avalice pulled the man's hands off her husband, shaking her head violently. "Now hold on—"

She was cut off as Isaac reentered the kitchen. Clutched in one hand was the bread from dinner. He brushed past Rezin without so much as a look and knelt by the Transistor and handed him the food.

Dekker took it with gratitude, his eyes meeting Isaac's. "Oh, bless you, son. You've saved me from the Profanes *and* starvation today."

Isaac stood and faced Liam and Avalice, raising his brows at Rezin.

"He wants us to take him across the Red Ravine," Avalice said, shaking her head, waiting for Isaac to object.

The young man said nothing.

"Why I expect an opinion from you is beyond me," Avalice muttered, turning back to her husband. "You're not actually thinking about doing this, right?"

Liam found it hard to meet her eyes. "Av..."

"It's way too dangerous!" Avalice said, throwing her hands up. "Why would we take on a job like that?"

"She's right, Liam," Dekker said around a mouthful of bread. "I don't care how much this nice man here is willing to pay us."

Rezin's face sagged. "It's not much, but I could pay you at least two hundred tablets..."

Liam's jaw dropped.

"Well, I suppose there's no harm in discussing it," Dekker said quickly, swallowing hard.

"Where the hell did you get that kinda iron?" Avalice whispered incredulously. "And how have you managed to keep that kinda wealth hidden from the Caps?"

Rezin flashed her a nervous smile. "I'd rather not discuss my practices. No offense, of course."

"None taken," Liam said carefully. He could feel his heart racing. Two hundred tablets? They could live off of that for months, take some serious time off the road, actually live a life. It almost seemed too good to be true. He paused at that, exhaling through his nose. He was getting blinded by the payout and forgetting what it was going to take to earn that kind of iron. Cross the Red Ravine...he felt a worm of unease wriggle in his gut. What kind of hell awaited them on that road? What kind of nightmares lay down that path?

And yet...

"Two hundred..." Avalice muttered, taking Liam out of his thoughts. "You're a man of surprises, aren't you, Rezin?"

"I hope not!" he half-laughed, wringing his hands together.

Avalice turned to her husband. "What are you thinking? I know the pay is"—she looked at Rezin—"very good, but you have to think of the insane risk we'd be taking. We don't have to do this. There will be other jobs in the city we can find."

Liam turned it all over in his head, fighting with himself. "I know. There's just...I mean...damn it, though, that's a lot of currency."

"Sure is," Dekker said from his chair.

Avalice touched Liam's shoulder, eyes meeting his. "Remember what's important."

Liam nodded. "I know, I know. Damn it all." He let out a frustrated sigh, running a hand through his hair.

Isaac's gentle voice cut through the air.

"We'll take the job."

Everyone turned to stare at him, the kitchen filled with silence.

"We need this," Isaac said quietly. "We all know it."

Liam looked at Avalice, who let out a hiss before nodding slowly. "Fine. To hell with it."

"Guess that's that," Dekker muttered.

Chapter 4

After getting a couple hours of sleep, everyone met outside the Inn. The sky was still a swath of rolling gloom, heavy clouds mixing with trails of smoke that wafted from the Factory. The people of Maltor bustled past the small party, a muted conglomerate of hooded faces leading horses down the broken streets, children chasing dogs between the organized chaos, and the steady rumble of the Factory in the background.

Liam watched as Dekker slowly unwrapped the bandages from his arms, the old man looking much better after some much-needed rest. His face was still bruised, but much of the swelling had gone down and it looked like he had washed his face and hair.

"You sure you should be doing that?" Avalice asked, casting a glance at him as she secured her bow across her back.

Dekker continued to peel away the dirty cloth. "I don't think they're necessary anymore. Despite the rest of me, I believe my arms have completely healed." He finished with the task and held out his arms for the group to see. Contrary to what he suspected, Liam saw that Dekker was right. The skin was scarred slightly, but beyond that he looked good as new.

"What'd I tell you?" Dekker beamed, his scabbed lips stretching up his face. "Don't ever count me down and out unless I stop breathing, you got that?" He swung his eyes over to Isaac who stood watching the street, arms crossed over his breastplate.

"You hear me, son? Anytime you wanna spar, you just let me know."

"Maybe wait until your face loses all that black and blue," Avalice said, checking her arrows now.

Liam turned around and faced the Inn, gnawing on his lip. "What the hell is taking Rezin so long? I thought he wanted to get going."

A couple of Caps rumbled by in one of their machines, leaving a trail of grumbling complaints in their wake as the citizens jumped out of the way, pulling their horses and carts with them so as not to get run over.

Dekker watched them go, returning his attention back to Liam a moment later. "I saw him earlier. He's paying Henry for road supplies. Food, water, all the things you didn't think about."

Liam rolled his eyes.

"Are we really doing this?" Avalice asked after a couple seconds, her eyes meeting the others. "I know the money is good, but I meant what I said earlier. This is going to be a high-risk job."

Liam looked at her. "We can do it. We just have to be extremely careful. I want everyone to keep their guard up and their eyes open. This is going to be a long haul, but once it's done, we'll get to lay low for a while. We'll actually get to live like human beings for a couple weeks." He paused. "To me, that's worth it."

Before anyone else could voice their opinion, Rezin came bustling out of the Inn. The bald man had a massive pack strapped to his back and he seemed to be struggling beneath the weight of it. He walked down the steps to meet them, casting a bashful smile to the group.

"Sorry to keep you waiting. I just had to finalize some business with Henry. He, uh, drives a hard bargain, that one does. Not sure who came out on top, honestly..." he trailed off, muttering to himself, wincing beneath the weight of his pack.

Liam raised an eyebrow. "I know this is your show and everything, but how the hell do you plan to march across Tectonic carrying that load? You're going to be dead two miles outside the city."

Rezin smiled, but it was closer to a wince, a trickle of sweat running down the side of his face. "Don't worry about me. I'm stronger than I look. Lots of endurance. I won't fall behind."

Without saying a word, Isaac stepped forward and plucked the pack from Rezin's back and slung it over his shoulder next to his own.

Rezin sputtered, unsure of what just happened. Avalice chuckled and slapped him on the shoulder.

"I think the words you're looking for are 'thank you.'"

"Right, of course, much appreciated," Rezin mumbled, turning red.

Liam checked to make sure his axe was in his belt loop before sizing Rezin up, a question bubbling to the surface.

"You know, we agreed to take on this job, but there's something we all need to know."

Rezin nodded. "Sure, anything."

"Why do you want to go see The Chain?"

Rezin licked his lips and his eyes fluttered toward the ground. "Well, yes. A perfectly natural question. One I expected." He exhaled and looked at the four. "Have you heard any of the rumors lately? The ones about the man in the west?"

Liam looked at Avalice, who shrugged. Dekker was the one who answered. "You're talking about Desmond."

Rezin released a relieved smile. "Yes, Desmond. Are the rest of you familiar with his existence?"

Liam shook his head, shooting a glance at Dekker. "I haven't heard of him."

"The brothers at the Church spoke of him," the Transistor said. "They said he's recruitingProfanes and anyone afflicted with Rockflesh."

Avalice frowned. "Why? What's he want with them?"

"I don't know, but there are some theories. Nasty ones."

Liam turned his attention back to Rezin. "Well?"

Rezin shuffled his feet. "It's my belief that he wants to destroy The Chain."

"Hell," Avalice hissed, "Why would he want to do that?"

"I'm sure he has his reasons," Rezin said. "But I would like to prevent this from happening, as you can imagine."

"If he actually manages to destroy it, Tectonic would plummet back down into the Void. It would be a free fall. It'd kill us all," Liam said slowly, his brow furrowed. He shook his head. "Is he insane?"

"I'm not unfamiliar with the man, but I don't think he's insane. Like I said, he has his reasons," Rezin said.

"Wait, you know him?" Liam asked.

"That's putting it too strongly, but he used to be an associate of mine, yes," Rezin said, avoiding everyone's eyes.

"What pushed him over the edge?" Liam pressed. "What did you two do together?"

"I'd rather not talk about the details right now," Rezin said.

"You have to give me something," Liam insisted.

Rezin licked his lips nervously. "All you need to know is that he's bad news for all of us. We worked together outside the city some time ago. We had a job to do, and it went south. Now he poses a threat to Tectonic. If further details are required, then I'll provide them as the need demands. Is that satisfactory?"

Liam looked around at the group. "What do you think?"

"What do we do if all this turns out to be true?" Avalice asked.

Rezin looked at the ground. "I'm not sure. Alert the Captains? I know they're mostly concerned with their Factories, but if this man actually wants to send us all plummeting to our deaths, then I would think they might intervene."

"This is crazy," Avalice said, shaking her head.

Rezin just rolled his shoulders. "Unfortunately, it's what I seek."

"But why you? Why do you want to go?"

Rezin offered a weak smile. "I have my reasons. Like I stated, I used to work with this man some time ago. I feel responsible for his fractured state of mind. I want to ensure he doesn't harm anyone."

"The Creator would never allow someone to break The Chain," Dekker said suddenly. "He saved us once, He would do it again."

"You sure about that?" Rezin asked. "I don't mean to question your faith, but when's the last time you saw any proof that He's even still up there?"

"The Chain remains," Dekker answered firmly, "And he holds the end, keeps us suspended, keeps us alive."

Rezin shrugged. "Perhaps. As you can see, there are far too many questions and far too few answers. This journey, this job that I've asked you to take on—I'm just looking for some clarity." The bald man set his jaw. "So enough of this. Let's be off, shall we? I would like to lay eyes on The Chain, up close, and if we happen to meet Desmond, then I would very much like to speak with him."

"Hold up," Liam said. "There is the matter of payment."

Rezin nodded. "I'm a man of my word. I brought the tablets with me and I trust you won't just take them and leave."

"Where are they?"

Rezin pointed to the pack Isaac was holding. "I believe your friend just collected them."

Isaac jostled the pack and was rewarded with the sound of clinking metal. Liam looked at Isaac, then at Avalice and Dekker. "Right...I guess that about covers it, then. Unless either of you have anything else you'd like to add?"

They both shook their heads. Liam looked up at Isaac. "You?"

"I'm ready to be out of this city," he answered, surprising everyone.

Liam turned back to Rezin. "Then I guess we should be off."

Together, the five of them departed from the front of the Inn, a sense of weight settling over Liam's mind. As they walked down the streets, pushing past the crowds, his thoughts went to what Rezin had said. He was surprised he hadn't heard of this Desmond person and he hoped that it was because the rumors were false. He couldn't imagine anyone wanting to separate Tectonic from The Chain, not unless they had gone completely mad. And if he really was mad, how did he expect to complete the task? The Chain was enormous, the base of it almost as big as one of the Factories.

He walked on, pushing the questions away. Maybe madness was the answer, as simple as it was.

When they reached the outskirts of Maltor, the crowds thinning, the buildings spreading out, a distant shout stopped everyone in their tracks. Liam turned around and looked back down the street from which they had just come, a rising shriek piercing the gray skies, followed by others. After a moment, he realized that they weren't cries of pain, but of fear.

"What now?" Avalice said, turning to stand with her husband, one hand reaching for her bow.

"Trouble already?" Dekker groaned, the five of them standing in the middle of the street, searching for the source.

It didn't take long to spot.

"Void take us," Avalice whispered as the cause walked into view, stumbling toward them from around the bend in the street.

It was a woman, horribly bent over, mounds of glowing Rockflesh sprouting out of her shoulders and neck. Her eyes were wild and lost, drool and spittle leaking down her chin. The clusters of disease pulsed brightly in the dim light, threatening to detonate at any moment. Men and women scrambled to get away from her, screaming in terror, ushering children away with cries of fear, wagons and horses hurriedly yanked down opposite roads.

But the woman remained, hobbling miserably down the center of the street, straight toward Liam and his companions.

"How the hell did she get this far into the city?" Avalice rasped, pulling her bow out and notching a steel-tipped arrow.

Dekker sprang forward, blocking her aim. "No! Don't! If you shoot her, she'll erupt and everyone will be exposed to the gases!"

Liam held his arms out and backed up, pushing everyone with him. "Everyone just stay calm. She's clearly in the late stages and I'd rather not work her up into a frenzy."

"I can help her," Dekker urged. "I can pull the poison from her."

"Have you lost your mind?" Rezin almost yelled, his eyes wide. "She's done for, look at her!"

Dekker grit his teeth. "I have to do something. Everyone here is at risk."

The woman continued up the street, twenty yards away now, her mouth opening and closing, releasing a guttural moan of pain. The protruding orange rocks blazed with raw energy, sprouting from her skin like hardened boils.

"I have to do this," Dekker said.

He stepped forward but was stopped as a large hand pulled him back. Sputtering, Dekker struggled to release himself, turning to glare at his captor.

"You're still weak, Dek," Isaac said softly, his calm green eyes staring down at the old man. "Let someone else deal with this."

"She's in pain," Dekker almost pleaded, some of the fire leaving his eyes. "*Please.*"

But before anyone could react, a sudden mechanical rumble filled the air. Liam turned away from Isaac and Dekker and saw Caps roaring toward the diseased woman in one of their strange vehicles. They passed her on the side of the road, the wheels of the machine screeching and then coming to a sliding halt in front of the woman.

A pair of metal doors opened along the sides, and four Caps exited the machine, dressed from head to toe in metal armor, complete with helmets and reflective glass faceplates. Without a word, they approached the woman, pulling out deadly-looking batons as they went.

"Stop this," Dekker begged, pulling at Isaac. "She's in enough pain, look at her!"

The Caps formed a circle around the woman and then struck out at her legs, the clubs thudding into the back of her thighs.

Liam winced as she went down, heart leaping up his throat as the Rockflesh hit the asphalt. Mercifully, it didn't detonate.

"Leave her alone!" Dekker yelled, tugging to get to her. Isaac's grip remained tight around the old man, keeping him in place.

The woman wriggled on her stomach, reaching out toward the Caps, horrible, gasping chokes sputtering from her lips. One of the Captains stomped down on her hand, bringing forth a scream that sounded more animal than human. The other three went to the back of the vehicle and pulled out a handful of thick metal sheets. As if rehearsed, they began slotting pieces into place, forming a small box about waist high.

"Creator help us," Dekker cried as they all watched the woman get roughly shoved into the contraption.

She screamed once more before the top slid into place, sealing her inside, her howls now muted.

One of the Caps activated something along the side of the metal coffin and then they all stepped back, sliding their batons back into their belts.

Horrified, Liam watched as the box began to compress in on itself, a slow, grating sound filling the air. He closed his eyes and turned away once the woman's bones began to break.

"What is this…?" Dekker whispered, his eyes wide, the air ringing with agony.

Without warning, a muffled explosion shuddered from the box, bringing an abrupt end to the woman's suffering. As soon as it happened, the Caps stepped forward and hoisted the contraption up and into the back of their transport.

Slowly, Liam turned to his companions. They looked at him with varying degrees of horror, all except Isaac, whose face remained impassive. Rezin licked his cracked lips.

"Had to be done, didn't it? I mean, she would have poisoned everyone..." he trailed off, dry-washing his hands in distress.

"Let's get moving," Liam said quietly, ushering them away from the scene. "What's done is done."

Dekker let out a pained grunt and jerked himself away from Isaac, eyes boring into the young man's. "Let go, you brute. Next time you lay hands on me, I won't be so complacent." His words were harsh, but his heart wasn't behind them. He dropped his eyes to the ground and fell into a sickly silence.

"Let's just get away from here," Avalice said, forming up next to Liam.

As one, they all turned away and continued down the street, a grim silence filling the air between them. Liam felt sympathy for the woman, but he agreed with Rezin. It had to be done. He snuck a look at Dekker and saw the man's face was pale, his jaw clenched shut. He knew the old man just wanted to help, but there was a line between hope and hopelessness, and that woman had crossed it long ago.

The rumble of the Caps' vehicle sputtered across the broken asphalt, a departing sigh from Maltor as the small group passed further into the outskirts. The road stretched out ahead of them like a long black tongue, buildings and houses fading to be replaced by rolling hills of rock and patchy clusters of dead forest. In the far distance, beyond the gloom-dipped horizon, stood The Chain. It was a barely visible line of darkness that stretched between the gray earth and the billowing smog that filled the heavens.

Liam shivered as a cold wind swept in from the west, casting itself over his face like a splash of freezing water. He hadn't missed that. It was one of the few things he liked about the cities. The Factory had a way of heating everything around it, blocking the worst of the cold out. But now that they had returned to the open road, he found that the miserable temperature had waited for them.

Liam was tugged from the thoughts as Avalice touched his arm, her voice concerned.

"I think they're following us."

Confused, Liam turned around and looked back at Maltor. It didn't take long for him to understand what his wife was talking about. Racing toward them were the Caps, bouncing along the fragmented road in their vehicle.

"Everyone slow down," Liam instructed, stepping off the road. "I don't know if they're coming for us or not, but we're about to get run over."

"Maybe they're going to Titan," Dekker said quietly, the sound of the engine drawing nearer. Together, they clustered around Liam and Avalice, content to let the metal transport pass. Liam noticed his wife was holding her bow, one arrow casually notched, but not drawn. He looked at her and their eyes met. He nodded, but held up a finger.

Just wait.

Liam's heart sank when the Caps came to a screeching halt, the transport jerking to a stop as the brakes were engaged. Without pause, the doors snapped open and the four Captains from earlier poured out. They faced Liam and the others, a wall of featureless armor.

"Can we help you with something?" Liam asked, his voice combating the wind. He noticed Rezin hovering behind Isaac.

The Caps pointed to the bald man, who was now peeking out from behind Isaac's large frame. One of them addressed the group, his voice buzzing behind his faceplate, like he was speaking through some kind of mechanical filter.

"He has stolen from us."

Isaac didn't move to expose Rezin, but Liam swung his head around to stare at the bald man, feeling his throat tighten. Steal? From the Caps? How? Why?

The Cap who had spoken pointed to the rest of them, his voice retaining that same strange resonance.

"You have all stolen from us."

"Now wait just a second," Dekker said, stepping forward. "We just met this man last night and have no idea what you're talking about. We're just working a job here, OK?"

"You have stolen from us."

"I don't like this," Avalice whispered urgently.

"What's been stolen?" Liam asked, trying to keep his voice neutral.

The Cap spoke again, his companions unmoving statues of armor. "Tablets."

Liam felt his stomach sink and he swallowed hard, directing his attention back to Rezin. "What the hell are they talking about?"

Rezin stayed where he was behind Isaac, his brow mopped with sweat now. He said nothing.

"Please tell me you didn't do something so *stupid*," Liam said from between his teeth, fighting against a sudden panic.

As if to answer, the Caps pulled their batons from their belts. A moment later, as a unit, they bent down and pulled long, thin blades from their boots. Standing back up, they stepped forward and took on a combative stance, knees bent, arms loose and ready.

"You have stolen from us," the leader said again. "We will not tolerate it." The Caps began to approach, spreading out in a semicircle before Liam and the others.

"Wait wait wait!" Dekker cried, backing up. "We can talk about this! There's been a misunderstanding!"

Isaac reached out and pulled the Transistor behind him. Without a word, he drew his colossal sword, holding it in one hand while the other pushed Rezin and Dekker away, shielding them from the coming violence.

Liam hefted his weighty axe in his hands, cursing their luck. He shot Rezin a venomous look, then returned his attention to the pressing Caps. Their stances looked trained and deadly, their weapons held with an unnerving confidence.

"Isaac?" Liam hissed.

"With you," the young man said, his eyes dark.

The Caps sprang into action, collapsing their formation in a rush of speed, each one flowing in tandem with the others. Avalice let an arrow fly as she fell back, the steel tip whistling for one of the Caps' exposed throats. The kill shot missed its mark as the armored man ducked and then rolled, coming up in front of her, his baton crunching into her knee.

Avalice screamed and went down, trying to roll away as the Cap raised his long knife to stab at her stomach. Liam's axe caught the blade with a crash, driving the deadly thing down into the hard dirt. Using his momentum, Liam stepped into the blow and brought his knee up into the Cap's stomach, doubling him over. Before he could follow up the attack, the Cap's fist was plowing into his jaw, leather-clad knuckles dazing him.

He tasted blood on his tongue as he fought against an explosion of stars, the cries of the others filling the sky at his back. The Cap that struck him spun under Liam's reach and brought his baton back around and delivered a vicious strike, the heavy club smashing into Liam's breastplate, knocking the wind from his lungs.

Gasping, he clutched his chest, the speed of his attacker surprising him. He hoisted his axe and managed to deflect the Cap's knife, a slice aimed for his throat. A split-second later and the baton was back, whistling through the air straight for his face. With one hand, he reached out and grabbed the Cap's wrist, stopping the blow a second before his nose was obliterated.

Sweating now, he fought against a very real panic, knowing the knife was coming. The Cap's shielded face was hidden, inches from his own, and he could see the strike being prepared, everything happening way too fast.

He squeezed his eyes shut, gasping, as a sudden splash of blood sprayed across his face, blinding him. He stepped away, releasing his attacker, blinking frantically. When his vision cleared he saw the Cap fall to his knees, an arrow protruding from his throat. He wiped his face clean as Avalice rushed the dying Cap, another arrow held tightly in her grip. She stabbed the gurgling man again in the throat, bringing forth another eruption of blood across the ground.

"LIAM!"

Rezin's cry brought Liam spinning around to face the others. Isaac was holding back two of the Caps on his own, his huge sword acting as a shield against a flurry of lightning-quick attacks. Sweat ran down the young man's face and it was clear that he was losing ground, his body taking stray batons, his efforts focused on the knives.

The last Cap had Dekker by the throat, knife raised directly over the old man's face. Liam's heart exploded up his throat, knowing he wasn't going to make it over to them in time as he watched the Transistor fumble with something in his pocket.

A split-second before the killing blow was delivered, Liam saw Dekker shove his hand over the Cap's face plate, his other hand suddenly glowing a fierce orange.

In an explosion of light, a stream of red-hot energy burst from Dekker's hand, engulfing the entirety of the Cap's face.

There was no scream, no slow realization of death. The Cap's head simply ceased to exist, disintegrating in a moment to leave nothing but empty space above his shoulders. Dekker fell to the ground gasping as the Cap's grip fell away, followed by the thud of his headless body.

"Liam! We have to help Isaac!" Avalice was yelling, scrambling to draw another arrow.

Seeing that Dekker was still alive, Liam turned his attention to Isaac as the young man caught another blow to the ribs. The two Caps were pressing him hard, the speed of their attacks wearing out the young man at an alarming rate.

Bursting into motion, Liam sprinted for them, axe in hand. At full speed, he bull-rushed one of the two with his shoulder lowered, the impact crunching across his body but sending the Cap flying onto his back. Avalice's arrow found the stunned Cap a second later, puncturing his throat with a sick pop and spray of flesh and blood.

With only one attacker left, Isaac managed to block the next two swings of the knife, quickly ducking under the baton as it came next. As he stood back up, he dropped his sword to the ground and reached up for the Captain's head, clamping it firmly between his gloved hands.

Gritting his teeth, he headbutted the remaining attacker, shattering the man's face plate, sending shards of glass into the Cap's eyes. Screaming, the wounded man dropped his weapons and clawed at his shredded sockets.

Isaac quickly adjusted his grip on the man's head, stepped behind him, and then confidently snapped his neck so viciously that the skin tore, spraying blood out of the lacerations.

Taking a slow breath, Isaac dropped the corpse and stepped away from the violence.

A cold wind swept across the road, bringing a deadly silence with it. Liam felt the sweat on his face chill and then freeze, along with the splatters of blood streaking down his cheeks. He looked first to Avalice to make sure she was all right.

She was sitting on the ground, bow at her side, massaging her knee. Her eyes reached his.

"I'll be fine," she said, reading his face. "Bastard had quite the swing, though."

"You sure? Is it broken?"

"No. Check the others."

Liam gave her a curt nod and then turned to Dekker, who was slowly getting to his feet, rubbing his throat as he did so.

"That was a close one," the old man muttered.

Liam looked at Dekker's arms and winced. "You OK? I saw you channel. Not a second too soon, I might add."

Dekker looked down at his exposed forearms, examining the skin, now bright red and inflamed.

"Didn't have much of a choice, did I?"

"I'm sorry," Liam offered, going to him. "I had my hands full with that one." He pointed to the dead Cap, Avalice's arrows still sticking from his throat.

Dekker grimaced. "What a mess this is, huh?"

"You sure you're OK?"

"I'll be fine. Give me an hour and it'll be like I didn't channel at all. For once the wind feels good." Dekker looked at his hands and realized he was still clutching something. He opened his fist and a black rock fell to the ground, drained of power.

"Maybe it was a good thing you went to the Church earlier," Liam said. "Seems it saved your life."

Dekker nodded, his face twisted in a scowl as he surveyed the dead bodies. Avalice was up and attending to Isaac who didn't seem to want the attention. Instead, he retrieved his sword and slid it into the slot on his back.

"Thank you, Isaac," Liam said, going to his side. "Didn't mean for you to have to take on two of them. Are you hurt?"

Isaac met his eyes. "We just killed Caps, Liam. Four of them."

Liam ran his hand over his head, nodding. "I know." He frowned. "I know. Damn it."

And then he found Rezin. He was standing off to the side of the road, arms wrapped around himself, eyes wide, face pale. Liam felt anger seep into his head, burning away everything else. He strode over to the bald man and grabbed him by the shirt collar, hoisting him up so that they were nose-to-nose.

"You mind telling me what the *fuck* that was all about!?"

Rezin sputtered around Liam's grip, gasping for air. "I'm sorry! P-please let me go! I'll explain everything!" He coughed and his eyes began to water. Liam set him down with a disgusted thud.

Avalice came to Liam's side, her face as dark as her husband's. "Were you planning on telling us you're a wanted man!?" she yelled, a vein pulsing in her temple.

"I didn't know they would be coming like this," Rezin said meekly, massaging his throat. "We were supposed to be gone before they found me."

Liam stepped forward, jabbing a finger into Rezin's face. "Am I to understand that you paid us in *stolen* tablets? Do you have ANY idea what kind of price that puts on our heads?! Do you!?"

Rezin flinched. "I—I'm sorry! I don't know what else to say! I was desperate!"

"How the hell did you even manage to steal that kind of currency anyway?!" Avalice yelled, not backing down.

"Does it even matter? It seems we're all in this together now," Rezin said sheepishly.

Dekker stepped between them, raising his hands. "Enough. What's done is done and yelling at each other isn't going to solve our problems."

"He just made us the most wanted people in all of Tectonic!" Liam cried, his face red.

"I know. Which is why we need to get out of here and fast."

Liam stared at Rezin over Dekker's shoulder. "I swear—"

Dekker stepped in front of him. "Stop. Focus, Liam. We need you calm. We're in trouble and we need to act. There will be time for finger-pointing later."

Liam stepped into Dekker, his voice a hiss. "Get the fuck out of my face, Dek. Do *not* lecture me right now."

Avalice pulled her husband away, her voice cooling. "Hey, come on. We don't have much time before more Caps come. Once they realize we killed the others, it's going to get nasty. We need to figure out what we're going to do."

"Shit," Liam snarled, letting himself be pulled away. He shut his eyes and let the wind wash over him, chilling the fire in his chest. He forced himself to take a deep breath and then opened his eyes.

Isaac was over by the Caps' vehicle, scrounging around inside. Liam watched as he pulled a jug of something out from between the seats, taking his sword in hand as he did so.

"What's he doing?" Liam asked quietly.

Dekker glanced at the young man who was now unscrewing the top of his sword's hilt. "Looks like he found some fuel for those rocket thrusters. Could have used that a couple minutes ago."

Liam glanced at the Transistor, pressing his anger away. "I'm sorry for losing my cool. You didn't deserve that."

Dekker clapped him on the shoulder, his face grim. "No harm done, old friend."

Liam continued to watch Isaac, his eyes drifting over the vehicle, an idea blooming. He shot Dekker another look. "You think you can figure out how to drive that thing?"

The old man let out a surprised huff. "Me? Huh. Don't see why not. Though it's powered by the old technology, not the power I channel. Different beasts."

"Are you saying you can't do it?"

"I'm saying be patient with me when I try."

Liam looked behind him at Rezin and then at Avalice. "Well, let's get the hell out of here then before anything else happens. Or before I break someone's nose."

As they walked to join Isaac at the vehicle, the dark clouds above parted for a split-second, exposing a brief ray of sunshine. It winked down at the dying world, a golden pillar of light that momentarily swept away the chill in Liam's bones. They all looked up at it, eyes going wide, everything else suddenly unimportant.

"Will you look at that?" Dekker said in awe.

"It's a sun splash," Avalice whispered, her eyes igniting in the light, practically glowing.

Dekker brought his hands together, his voice reverent. "Thank the Creator. He's still up there looking out for us."

The words died on his lips as the sun was engulfed in rolling darkness, robbing the world of its light once again.

Liam felt the cold return. "I wouldn't bet on that."

Chapter 5

The inside of the transport was cramped and smelled of dirty leather. Dekker sat in the operator's seat, hands on the wheel, confidently guiding them down the road. It had taken him only a couple minutes to figure out how to work the levers and pedals, and once he had, the group was on their way again.

Isaac sat in the front with the Transistor, his eyes scanning the dim road ahead as it zipped past. His sword had been too large to fit inside, and so he had tied it to the roof. Liam sat in the back next to Avalice, who had wisely taken the middle seat. Rezin's head rested on his shoulder, his eyes closed, his breathing soft.

"Don't know how he has the audacity to sleep right now," Liam muttered, casting an annoyed look across his wife.

Avalice put a hand on his leg. "Let it go. What's done is done."

Liam exhaled, feeling irritable. Everything had happened so fast and now returning to the city seemed like a distant dream, at least for the time being. He had always kept them on the right side of the Caps, never straying too far into their circle of interest. But now they were sought after, hunted even. How had things gone so wrong? He ran a hand over his eyes, feeling tired from the fight. Tired and responsible.

"Maybe this is a stupid question," Dekker said from the driver's seat, "but what are we doing? You know, besides fleeing for our lives."

Liam stared out the window and watched the dark landscape roll by. "Well, we can't go back to Maltor, that's for sure."

"That much is obvious."

The transport bounced across a hole in the road, rocking Liam in his seat. He gritted his teeth before continuing. "I don't really see any choice but to continue with the plan. There's nothing to be done about the stolen tablets now; we might as well keep them. Creator knows I'd like to take back this whole mess, but there only seems to be one way through this and that's forward."

Avalice looked at him, her face pulled down into a frown. "You mean we're not dumping this moron?"

Liam glanced again at Rezin, who seemed to still be asleep. "As much as I'd love to, we can't. That's just not how we do things. We've always seen a job through and I intend to see this one to completion as well. It's my fault for not asking more questions. I should have asked how he had acquired such a large sum of currency. That one's on me and I apologize for not doing my job."

Dekker waved a hand back at him. "You don't have to be so dramatic. Any one of us could have been more thorough, but let's face it—we were kind of desperate. I mean we had what, two Tablets left? I don't think we've ever gotten that low before. Plus we had been on the road for a while and we were tired. Nothing clouds judgement worse than being on the wrong side of your eyelids."

"We could just give him the tablets back," Avalice said quietly. "That way we could maintain our reputation and put an end to this. I know it's just a job, but I don't like this guy. There's something about him that just sets my teeth on edge. I think he's hiding something from us. Something important."

"Hey, go easy," Dekker said.

"He's asleep," Liam muttered. He took Avalice's hand in his own, his voice gentle. "Listen. I hear what you're saying and a part of me wants to do just that. But if we give him back all that currency, then we're screwed. We can't go back to Maltor to look for more work and we just left Titan. Where else is there to go?"

Avalice looked out the window. "There are camps. Pockets of people out here who could probably use our help."

"So what, we just wander around with our fingers crossed until we freeze to death or starve?" Liam asked.

Avalice looked at him sharply. "It was just an idea."

He sighed. "I know. I'm sorry." He looked out the window again, the dark hills spilling into patches of forest now. "I'm just pissed off. The last thing I wanted was for us to be on the Cap's kill list."

"And yet here we are!" Dekker said, slapping the wheel. "And you know what? We're all still breathing, so let's stuff the sour mood and focus on what the next step is, OK? Can we all do that?" He nudged Isaac next to him, grinning. "What do you say, kid, show me a smile, will you?"

Isaac just stared out the windshield, face slack.

"I could always sing us a song," Dekker offered.

"Don't you dare," Avalice threatened.

"All right, all right," Liam said. "I get your point, Dek. The bottom line is that nothing has changed. We're still going to take this lunatic to The Chain so he can poke around and find this Desmond guy or whatever it is he wants to do. Once we do that, we're out. So in order to do that, we're going to have to go around the Red Ravine."

"Won't that be fun?" Avalice muttered.

"It's been a long time since I've been over that way," Liam continued, "and I don't feel comfortable relying on the old route I took. The Ravine has changed, grown, since then. For us to get around it while avoiding the gas, we're going to need some kind of map or chart." He looked at Avalice. "Or find someone who knows the area extremely well."

Avalice grunted, her lips twisting in a smile. "We're going to see Kell, aren't we?"

"That's right."

"Who's Kell?" Dekker asked, swerving the wheel to avoid another massive hole in the road.

Liam touched his wife's leg. "She was the one who married us almost eight years ago."

Dekker turned around, surprise written across his face. "No kidding? Is she a minister AND a cartographer then?"

"Something like that," Liam answered. "She lives in a house out in the woods, not too far from the outskirts of the Ravine. If we have any chance of making it past the Ravine, she'd be the one to talk to."

"Consider our course charted then, sir," Dekker mocked. After a moment then, "Um...where *exactly* does she live, though? In case you haven't noticed, I'm kind of just blindly driving this hunk of machinery without a clue in the world as to where we're going."

"Stay on this road," Liam instructed. "Once we get deep into the woods, we're going to hit a river. Shortly after, if memory serves, there's an intersection there that we'll take."

"And how long is that going to take?"

Liam scratched the stubble on his chin. "In this thing? I'm not sure. On foot it's about a three-day march. So I don't know. Eight, nine hours?"

Dekker groaned. "Better get comfy back there, then."

"At some point we'll break for camp and rest," Liam said, formulating the journey in his head. "I don't want you falling asleep while you're driving this thing."

"It hasn't been that long since we left the Inn," Dekker said. "I'm fine right now."

"I know, but you channeled," Liam said carefully. "I know how much that takes out of you. I just want to be careful and do this right. I've gotten us into enough trouble as it is. Last thing I need is to push us to the brink of exhaustion and end up in a ditch somewhere."

Dekker smiled. "Your concern is noted and appreciated."

Liam turned to the window once again, letting his eyes travel across the land and then up the sky. The eternal mass of dark clouds spilled over one another, muted grays mixing with the inky expanse, casting just enough light across the road for Dekker to see where he was going.

As he examined the sky, his eyes found a flock of crows high above, soaring away from them. They all glowed in the gloom, dots of orange marking their progress across the heavens.

"Everything is dying," he muttered to himself, turning away from the infected birds.

They were all silent for a long while, the hum of the engine holding a conversation of its own with the rest of the machine. The patches of forest around them grew dense, finally swallowing the road down its throat, filling the interior of the vehicle with darkness. Dekker slowed down and began fumbling with the knobs next to the wheel. After a moment, he let out a victorious cry as a splash of light expanded out in front of the transport.

An hour passed, then two. Rezin remained asleep and Avalice gently reached into a pack behind them and distributed food throughout the car. When they were finished, a canteen was passed around, the cold water near its freezing point.

The dark trees pressed tight to the road, the outside world a blanket of tar between the foliage. After the third hour had passed, Dekker suddenly cursed and slowed down quickly, the lights on the transport picking up movement ahead of them on the road.

"What is it?" Liam asked, leaning forward.

"Travelers, it seems," Dekker said, squinting. "They're on horses, just ahead. You seen them?"

"Yeah. What the hell am I looking at, though?"

Avalice peered out the windshield, brow furrowed. "Hell below, is that infected with them?"

As the transport approached the large group from behind, Liam saw that his wife was right. There were about twenty mounted riders making their way down the road, their heads turning as the light illuminated them. Tied to the horses and trailing their captors were over two dozen infected, the Rockflesh lining their bodies glowing a deep orange. Their hands were bound and they stumbled along, a miserable march that made no sense to Liam.

"Careful, go around them," Avalice warned as Dekker guided their vehicle to the edge of the road, passing the first of the infected prisoners.

"What are they doing with them?" Dekker muttered, careful to keep distance between the two groups.

Liam's gaze swept across the mounted riders as they passed them and felt a boulder plummet into his guts.

"Profanes," he whispered.

The riders were all armed, various swords, clubs, and spears strapped across their telltale clothes, the broken-chain insignia glaringly apparent on their chests.

"Where do you think they're going?" Avalice asked as they finally got around the large group.

"Nowhere I want to be," Dekker said, throwing a look over his shoulder at the fading travelers.

"Are they stupid?" Avalice asked. "Don't they know how dangerous it is to be around infected?"

"The Rockflesh didn't look that advanced," Liam said. "Unless they're forcibly detonated, I don't think they're going to blow anytime soon."

"Those poor people," Dekker whispered, gripping the wheel. "Why can't they just leave them alone to die in peace?"

No one seemed to have an answer, and so the group fell into silence once more. At one point he felt Avalice's head on his shoulder and he looked down at her. Her face was impassive, eyes staring forward out the windshield. But after a second, she quietly took Liam's hand in her own and held it gently.

"You need a bath," she whispered after a moment.

Liam allowed himself a small smile and squeezed her hand.

The hours continued to roll out before them, the journey feeling more laborious than it should from inside the transport. Liam found himself resenting this mode of travel the longer they went. As much as he hated the cold, he realized how much he missed the open air, the mark of time each footstep ticked away, the alerts his body gave him when it needed to rest. He found it hard to keep his awareness about him, the false sense of security causing his mind to wander. Every time he realized he wasn't paying attention to the road, he cursed himself and tried to shut down his thoughts. It wasn't easy, though, the rumble of the road lulling him into complacency.

Finally, after what seemed like an eternity, they reached the river. Dekker carefully drove them across a small bridge, everyone holding their breath, praying it wouldn't collapse beneath their weight. Once they were over, it was only a few minutes until they hit an intersection, the road splitting into four different directions. Liam instructed Dekker to go left, and once they had gone a mile or so down the abandoned stretch, they decided to call it a day.

"I swear, I'm going to lose my mind if I have to sit in this transport a second longer," Liam said as Dekker pulled off to the side of the road and switched the engine off.

"I don't know, I kind of like it," Dekker said, stretching dramatically.

Isaac was the first one out, his large frame stooping out his door and into the open air. Liam and Avalice were next after rousing Rezin from slumber. The bald man blinked furiously after Avalice shook him, looking around with curiosity.

"Where the heavens are we?" he asked as he scurried out of the transport, following Liam and Avalice.

"The woods," Liam said. "Look around and you'll figure it out."

"Right, right, of course," Rezin mumbled, scrubbing at his eyes, "but where exactly?"

"A lot closer to The Chain than before," Avalice answered, grabbing their packs from the back of the vehicle.

"We should head into the woods a little and make a fire," Liam said, the cold wind rustling the trees above. It sounded like running water, the rustle overhead filling the sky.

"I don't know about you all," Dekker said, "but I'm not sleeping out here in this chill. I'll join you by the fire for a bit if you'd like, but this old man needs to keep his bones thawed, thank you very much."

"Does anyone else want to sleep in the transport?" Liam asked, sweeping his eyes across everyone's faces.

"I feel very refreshed," Rezin said, raising his hand, "and if you'd like, I'd be more than happy to keep watch while you get some shut-eye."

"First useful thing you've said this whole time," Avalice said, "and I for one would like to sleep in front of a fire, as far away from that stinking machine as possible."

Liam looked to Isaac, who was now untying his sword from the roof. "What about you?"

"I'm sleeping outside," he said quietly.

It didn't take long for them to gather wood and start a fire, a meager pile that crackled loudly and pushed some of the shadows away. Avalice had taken their packs out of the transport and piled them next to her, the one with the tablets closest to where she lay. Liam joined her, spreading his own blanket down alongside his wife. He set his axe aside and lowered himself, already feeling the cold trying to make its way past the fire's heat. Isaac propped himself up against a tree opposite them, throwing a thick cloak around his shoulders. Liam watched as he closed his eyes, his massive sword resting across his legs.

Rezin sat cross-legged with his back to the fire, staring out at the road. Liam wasn't sure how much he trusted their employer to keep watch, but he realized he really didn't have a choice.

Dekker confessed he was more tired than he thought and resigned himself to the back seat of the vehicle, closing the door as he crawled inside. Liam worried that each time the old man channeled, he was losing something he could never get back.

Sighing, he laid down on his side, facing his wife. She pulled a large blanket over both of them and stared at him, the firelight dancing across her eyes.

"Here we are again," Liam said quietly, allowing his body to relax against the hard ground.

"Seems like we spend most nights like this now," Avalice responded just as gently. "Freezing, uncomfortable, and praying we'll make it through the night without something creeping up on us."

"Things will get better once we finish this job," Liam assured her, not really believing what he was saying. "We'll be able to rest for a while. Live normally."

Avalice snorted. "I don't think I even know what normal is anymore."

Liam scooted closer, keeping his voice low. "You remember where I took you after we got married?"

Avalice's face softened slightly. "Of course I do. You took me to those falls. Told me it was the last place like it on Tectonic."

"When all this is over, I want to take you there again. Camp out, even, if you want. Spend some time alone, just you and me." Liam reached out and ran a finger across his wife's cheek. "I miss that. Being alone with you."

"We get plenty of time alone," Avalice said.

"I don't mean like this, while we're working a job. I mean time where we just get to enjoy each other. Remember what that was like?"

Avalice smiled slightly in the soft light. "Barely."

Suddenly her face twisted and she was biting her lip, curling into herself. Liam propped himself up, concern written across his face. "What's wrong?"

Avalice closed her eyes, breathed, and then relaxed. "It's nothing."

"Av…"

She looked at him. "I think I'm just sick. All this running around, the cold, the fighting. It just upsets my stomach sometimes."

But Liam didn't back down. "You sure? Because you felt like that back in Titan, too."

"It'll pass. It always does."

"Av, if it's Rockf—"

"It's not," Avalice said firmly. "You know I check myself for that. It's not. I'm just tired, Liam. Tired of all this. I'm ready for a break."

"We'll get one," Liam said confidently. "As soon as this is over."

"Do you promise?"

"If we don't take a break after this, I give you permission to cut my manhood off with Isaac's sword. How's that?"

Avalice cracked a smile. "You got yourself a deal."

"Good, now shut up, I'm trying to sleep, lady," Liam said, closing his eyes, grinning.

He felt a fist thump into his arm and he chuckled, opening his eyes again to find his wife preparing another blow. He grabbed her wrist and pulled her close, his voice so quiet it was barely audible.

"I love ya, Av. Always will. You know that, right?"

Avalice kissed the tip of his nose. "OK, softie, get some sleep before you turn into a melon." She turned away, but before she did, she squeezed Liam's hand, her voice as quiet as the wind. "I love you, too."

The pop and sizzle of the fire echoed through the camp, pulling eyes closed. The wind let up a little and the cold lost some of its bite. The air smelled of woodsmoke and dirt, the road remaining an empty stretch of darkness across from them. Liam felt himself slip into a light doze, his thoughts tumbling into one another before taking a life of their own and sprinting into a tangle of dreams.

He wasn't sure how long he had been asleep when a firm hand shook him awake. His eyes snapped open in an instant, a hand reaching for his axe. Heart hammering, he looked up and saw Rezin's worried face hovering over his own.

"What is it!?" Liam hissed quietly.

Rezin put a finger to his lips and motioned for Liam to follow him. Careful not to wake Avalice, Liam did as he was told, pulling himself from his wife's warmth and out into the open cold. He shivered and forced his heart to stop thundering in his chest. Taking his axe, he crept to the edge of the small clearing where Rezin had stopped, staring motionless out into the wall of wooded darkness.

"What's going on?" Liam asked, feeling uneasy.

Rezin put a finger to his lips again. "Shh. Listen."

The knot in his stomach expanded as Liam silenced the drumming of his pulse, focusing his attention on where Rezin was staring, wide-eyed, into a patch of black between the trees.

And then it came. A sound so slight he almost missed it.

Liam's blood turned to ice.

"What the hell is that?" he whispered, the words dying on his lips.

"I have no idea," Rezin answered in a hush.

The wailing came again, a distant cry that sounded more animal than human. It sounded like something was dying out there, a low howl that rose into a rolling screech. It bounced off the thick darkness and echoed from the crowded forest like a call for help.

"I think it's getting closer," Rezin gulped.

A full minute ticked by before the ungodly sound came again.

This time, there was no mistaking it. Whatever it was, was coming their way.

"I need to wake the others," Liam said, a shiver running down his spine. He turned back toward the dying fire and almost ran into Isaac.

"Fucking void *below!*" Liam almost screamed, slamming a hand over his heart. "You trying to give me a heart attack?"

Isaac cocked his head as the low wail came again, rising into a screech.

"You ever heard anything like that before?" Liam asked, his pulse racing. Isaac shook his head.

Suddenly, Rezin grabbed Liam's arm and pointed out into the woods to their left, his voice almost a shriek. "Liam! Look! Look!"

Liam squinted in the low light and when he saw what Rezin did, his throat tightened with fear.

"You see the orange glow?!" Rezin pleaded, tugging Liam's sleeve. "Do you see it?!"

"Isaac, go wake the others," Liam said, taking a step back. "Hurry."

As Isaac did as he was told, Liam hoisted his axe and watched the moving light flicker between the trees. After a moment, he realized there was more than one, the orange glow expanding into a dozen swaying orbs that moved within the masses of shadow, fanning out to fill his sight.

"Get back to the transport," Liam instructed, pushing Rezin away. "Get inside and don't come out." It didn't take much convincing to get the bald man running.

Liam kept his eyes trained on the shapes, each one now echoing the cry they had heard earlier. Dead twigs crunched from the wall of night as the eerie lights walked closer.

Avalice and Dekker appeared at Liam's side, out of breath and wide-eyed. Isaac brought up the rear, his sword held at the ready. Liam eyed it and shook his head.

"Whatever they are, they're infected. Melee weapons are just going to get us all killed in an explosion." He looked at Avalice and Dekker. "If they get too close, I'm counting on you two, but Dekker, don't channel unless absolutely necessary."

The Transistor nodded, but Liam could see he already wielded a handful of power-filled stones, the disease flickering dangerously from inside.

"If we're rushed, I want everyone to pile into the transport. Dekker, you're our driver so you'll go first. Understood?"

The screeching wail came again, a shrill, piercing thing. Liam could now make out shapes, strange, large shadows that continued to walk closer, the Rockflesh pulsing like infected fireflies.

A couple breaths later and the shapes emerged from the trees, entering the clearing at a slow stride.

"Oh, hell," Avalice gasped, taking a step back. Liam's eyes went wide and he involuntarily took a step back as well, his stomach turning sour.

It was a pack of wild horses, their features and flesh mutated and twisted beneath an onslaught of Rockflesh. Their fur peeled away in strips, exposing patches of bone and muscle. Their eyes were bloated, some almost as large as rotting apples, the disease changing the color to a sickly orange. Their mouths were pulled open in a constant gasp, their lips pulled back, almost like they were smiling. Strands of drool dripped from broken, blackened teeth, their tongues bloated and dangling, most of them crawling with bugs.

Mounds of Rockflesh covered their bodies like massive boils, the largest of them the size of a human head.

The trio of the mad horses approached from the left, stumbling forward. They were coughing and shaking their heads, their engorged eyes rolling with fever. One of them arched its head back and let out a shrieking wail, a sound so alien to its source that Liam felt the hairs on his arms stand up. Six more emerged from the woods, closer to the road this time.

"Everyone get to the transport," Liam whispered, "right now."

Without argument, everyone slowly backed up, keeping their eyes trained on the approaching monstrosities. One of the horses arched its back and screamed, the sound a haunting cry.

And then they charged.

"Look out!" Liam screamed, diving out of the way as the ground rumbled beneath the stampede. Avalice released an arrow, her aim true, the steel tip thudding deep into the lead horse's head, bringing it crashing to the ground.

Isaac grabbed Dekker and dove in the opposite direction of Liam, rolling hard as the pack thundered past them, heads lowered, teeth bared. Four of the horses turned around, shaking their unkempt manes, spinning and preparing for another charge.

The other five didn't slow, their target marked. When Liam saw what was happening, he cursed and sprang to his feet, axe in hand.

The horses slammed into the transport at full speed, rocking it over onto its side, metal screeching, windows shattering in an eruption of glass. Liam could hear Rezin cry out from inside as the vehicle tilted and then crunched over again, upside down now.

Two of the horses dropped to the ground, their skulls crushed, the orange disease lining their backs and glowing dangerously. It was a miracle they hadn't detonated on impact.

"Isaac, grab our packs!" Liam yelled, squaring up as the four horses before him stamped their hooves and crouched, readying to attack.

Avalice drew another arrow from her knees, letting it fly a second later. A horse went down screaming, its throat gurgling in a spray of blood.

"They're going to charge!" Dekker yelled, scrambling in his pocket. "Get out of the way, Liam!"

The horses came for him, all thunder and hooves. Heart in his throat, Liam dove away once more but felt something thud hard into his side, lifting him up and throwing him through the air. He came down with a thud by the transport, stars exploding in his head.

He winced and squeezed his eyes shut, the sound of Rezin's screams ringing close. Pulling himself up, he opened his eyes and saw the horses by the vehicle were now reaching in through the broken windows, their large teeth snapping and biting.

Liam threw a look over his shoulder a second before the darkness ignited.

A stream of raw power coursed through Dekker's open hand as he channeled, the white-hot beam eviscerating two of the horses by the transport.

Avalice let another arrow fly, this one burying itself into one of the horse's ribs. The horse stumbled but didn't go down until two more arrows pierced its skull.

Liam rushed the transport and slid across the road, opposite the horses. He reached inside the broken frame, calling out for Rezin. A shaking hand gripped his own and then he was pulling as hard as he could. Rezin let himself be dragged from the wreckage, his bald head scarred with shallow cuts that dripped blood across his shell-shocked face.

"Th-thank you," he sputtered, his whole body trembling.

Liam looked over the flipped transport and saw the three remaining horses were now charging Isaac who now had their packs slung over his shoulder. Teeth gritted, Dekker unleashed another current of blinding power, the air sizzling as the beam struck two of the horses, evaporating their flesh in an instant.

The last horse didn't stray from its course as the others died, its wild eyes set on Isaac.

Isaac saw it coming and braced himself, one hand on the packs, the other gripping his sword. At the last instant he twirled, spinning his cloak so that it covered his mouth, his sword turning to a blur as he swung at his attacker.

The sharp steel cleaved the horse in two, the massive weapon separating the animal front to back.

In the same instant, the Rockflesh lining its body exploded. The blast caught Isaac in its radius, throwing him hard to the ground, his mouth and nose shielded from the wave of gas that erupted outward.

"Get away!" Liam screamed, jerking Rezin further out onto the road. "Run! RUN!"

Avalice grabbed Dekker and pulled him backwards, half-dragging him toward Liam, the old man in visible pain.

Head pounding in a panic, Liam watched as Isaac dragged himself across the ground and then stood with a groan. He kept his cloak planted over his mouth as he hurriedly limped over to the others, dragging his sword and the packs in his wake.

Liam ran to him and took some of his weight, the tall warrior slouching across Liam's shoulders.

"Are you OK?!" Liam cried, pulling them both away from where the gas had been dispersed.

Isaac nodded, but his eyes were hazy.

"Everyone, down the road, let's move!" Avalice instructed, hustling the group away from the bloody battlefield. "We need to get away from the gas! Go!" She looked at Dekker, who she was still helping. The Transistor's arms were bloody, the skin splitting and inflamed, the damage horribly obvious.

"Damn it," Avalice hissed, hoisting Dekker's weight. "We'll get that bandaged up as soon as we're clear, OK? You with us still?"

Dekker just nodded, mouth open, his eyes streaked with pain as his wounds trailed blood down his body.

"Goddamn it," Liam growled as they fled down the road, deeper into the forest.

They didn't slow for a long time.

Chapter 6

A handful of miserable hours had passed since their encounter with the diseased horses. Isaac was coughing, but he seemed OK, his cloak mercifully protecting him from the dangerous gases. Rezin was shaken up but had only suffered mild scrapes, the blood drying on his head as the wind roared across the forest road.

Dekker had suffered the worst of it. Avalice had helped him wrap his arms, stemming the bleeding as best she could. Liam had given the old man his cloak, but the Transistor still shivered as they trudged along. His eyes seemed distant and his face was pale. Without him, they would have suffered a worse fate, but the encounter had taken its pound of flesh.

"We're almost to Kell's place," Liam said from Dekker's side. "We'll be out of this cold soon, I promise." Dekker didn't respond, his eyes dropping to the road, concentrating on putting one foot in front of the other. Liam exchanged a worried look with Avalice, noting how pink Dekker's bandages were becoming.

Isaac coughed again and Rezin shot him a concerned glance. Isaac ignored it, lugging their packs over his shoulder, his sword slotted across his back.

"He's fine," Liam said sharply, eyeing Rezin. "Save your eyes for the woods in case more wild animals come for us."

"I didn't mean—" Rezin started, but Avalice cut him off.

"No one wants to hear it right now."

They fell into silence once more as the winding road cut deeper into the thick forest, the dark sky howling with the ever-present wind. Liam fought against it as best he could, his eyes drying beneath the gale, forcing him to blink.

"How much...longer...?" Dekker whispered, his voice thick.

"Shouldn't be much furth—" Liam started, but Avalice silenced him as she raised her hand and pointed down the road.

"Light. I see light."

"Thank the Creator," Dekker mumbled, bunching his cloak around him.

"Is that your friend's house?" Rezin asked, the trees swaying overhead.

"It has to be," Liam said, "if memory serves."

"Is she going to be up for guests? There's quite a lot of us," Rezin said nervously.

"Just keep your mouth shut and everything will be fine," Avalice said.

Exhausted, the five marched wearily toward the light. As they rounded a bend, a small cabin came into view. It wasn't much to speak of, a single-story construct with a proud chimney that puffed woodsmoke into the open air. A pair of windows lined the front, the glass panes glowing with firelight from inside.

The party trudged the rest of the way to it, an air of silent relief sweeping through them. As they approached the front door, the trees giving way to a tiny yard of packed dirt, Liam held up a hand, stopping them.

"Let Avalice and I go ahead first. I don't want to alarm her."

After receiving no complaint, Avalice and Liam walked to the front door. Before he could even knock on the sturdy wood, a dog announced their arrival from inside. Liam knocked anyway, a quick rap of the knuckles.

The door opened after a moment, a cautious sliver of warmth slithering through the crack as a face peeked out at them.

"Kell?" Avalice asked, offering a weak smile.

The woman peering at them didn't move, her wrinkled face squinting beneath a tumble of gray hair.

"Kell, it's Liam. Don't you remember us? It's Liam and Avalice. You married us a couple years ago?"

The old woman's face finally broke, recognition flooding her tired eyes. Her lips parted in a smile.

"Well, I'll be. Liam? Avalice? Is that really you?" she asked, her voice warm and grandmotherly. "I'm not still dreaming, am I?"

Avalice smiled in relief. "It's really us, Kell. We didn't mean to wake you." The old woman pulled the door open, waving a hand at them. "Oh, think nothing of it. Loo was the one who woke me up, always barking her beak off whenever the wind blows." From inside, the dog barked again. Kell turned around, voice stern.

"Oh, hush! Don't you recognize these nice people? It's our friends Liam and Avalice, you silly mutt."

"We've had quite a journey," Avalice said, huddling close to her husband as the wind came again. "And we don't mean to put you out, but we really could use a place to warm up for a couple hours, if that's all right."

"Of course it's all right!" Kell said merrily, pulling the door all the way open. "Heavens, it's so rare I get company! Welcome company, that is!"

Liam looked over his shoulder. "We didn't come alone, Kell. We brought some friends with us. Some of them are a little worse for wear. You got room for five?"

Kell looked over Liam's shoulder, spotting Dekker, Isaac, and Rezin. She snorted and nodded. "If they're friends of yours, they're friends of mine. Just so long as they don't mind Loo slobbering all over them, then they're welcome to come in."

"Thank you," Avalice said, reaching out and taking the old woman's hands in her own. "We can't tell you how grateful we are."

Kell smiled. "Anything for you, dear. Now get in here and get out of the cold. It's particularly nasty tonight."

"That we can agree on."

Liam waved the others to follow them into the house, and soon they were all seated before a roaring hearth, warming their hands and feet as the flames burned away the chill clinging to their bones. Kell stood in front of them with her arms crossed, examining the newcomers. Loo, a small mixed breed with golden fur, was conducting an examination of her own, slowly going to each of them to sniff their clothes. She stopped in front of Rezin and just stared at him. The bald man reached out to pet her, but she scurried away and cuddled up next to Isaac, who gently scratched her ears, his eyes trained on the fire.

"It seems you all have been through a lot," Kell said, focusing her attention on each one of them. "Creator only knows the trouble you've gotten into. Honestly, I don't even want to know about it. But rest assured, you're safe here." She looked over Rezin, Isaac, and Dekker, her eyes lingering on Dekker's arms. "Liam and Avalice are old friends of mine and they vouched for you. Don't go and embarrass them by doing something silly, you got that?"

"We wouldn't dream of it," Rezin said from the floor, hands outstretched toward the fire. "We're just grateful for your hospitality. Kindness is such a rare thing these days."

Kell gave a curt nod. "It is indeed, so don't go spoiling it or you'll catch the wrong end of my knives."

Isaac grunted.

"Still got some fire in your bones, eh, Kell?" Liam said, hiding a smile.

The old woman returned the smile. "Just got to make sure these ruffians know who's running the house." Her eyes fell on Dekker, her voice softening. "I have some salves for your wounds, if you'd like. It wouldn't be any trouble at all."

"Thank you," Dekker whispered, his voice weak.

Kell looked up at Liam. "You didn't tell me you had a Transistor with you."

"He's a good man," Liam said. "You won't get any trouble out of him, I promise."

Kell went to the kitchen, her voice trailing back to them. "Oh, it's not him I'm worried about."

As she gathered her salves from the cupboards, Loo the dog wandered away from Isaac, resting her head on Dekker's lap. The old man petted her gently, wincing, but her presence seemed to calm him some. Kell returned, kneeling in front of Dekker to uncork a small bottle she now held. "I'm going to have to take those bandages off, if that's OK," she said gently. Dekker nodded.

While she worked, Liam wandered over to the window, trailed by Avalice. He crossed his arms wearily and stared out into the night. After a moment, he felt his wife's hand on his arm.

"We did good, Liam."

He looked at her, feeling slightly lost. "Yeah, I guess so. At least we'll be OK for a while. Everything just feels so..." he rubbed his face, exhaling. "I'm tired."

"I am, too. We'll rest here for a while. There's no rush." She looked over her shoulder at Dekker. "I think some of us need a break. We have the Tablets. There's no need to charge ahead recklessly."

Liam nodded, keeping his voice low. "I know. I just want to be finished with this, though. Back there at camp...that was too close. I don't want us walking the line like that. I don't know how much more Dek can take. If he has to channel again..."

"We'll be careful," Avalice assured. "You know I don't like this job, but I've been thinking."

"Yeah?"

She stood close to him, sharing his warmth. "Yeah. About what you said. About being able to live like human beings again. We'll be able to do that once this is over. We'll be able to get away from all the noise, if we want, just the two of us." She looked up at him, their eyes meeting in the firelight. "I think I want that. I think I really, really want that. Being on the road for so long like we have, I think I've forgotten what it's like to be alive, and that scares me. I don't want to just survive. I want to live. With you. Together. So let's get this thing done and do that, OK?"

Liam smiled, his face softening. "You got it."

They turned back to the group just as Kell was finishing up, her hands carefully wrapping Dekker's arms once more.

"Remember," she instructed, "no more channeling for at least a couple days. If you do, then the salve won't work properly."

"Thank you," Dekker said, his face appreciative. "Sorry you had to waste that on me."

Kell stood. "It's not a waste if it makes you feel better." She corked the bottle and brushed a strand of gray from her face. "Now, I want you to march into the back bedroom over there and get some sleep."

"Oh, I don't need—"

"Don't you argue with me," Kell scolded, helping the old man to his feet. "Just do as I say or I'll sic Loo on you."

The dog raised its head from where it lay.

Dekker chuckled weakly. "Yes, ma'am. And thanks again. I'm sorry to put you out like this."

Kell shooed him into the bedroom, and Liam approached the hearth with Avalice, sitting down and crossing his legs next to Isaac.

He looked at the young man, carefully examining his face. "Hey. You OK?"

Isaac glanced at him, then back at the fire. "I'll be fine."

"I know, I just—"

"I'll be fine, Liam," Isaac pressed. Then, quietly, "I didn't breathe any of it in. I'm sure of it."

Liam nodded. "OK, then. Why don't you get some shut-eye? I feel like we could all use it."

In response, Isaac leaned back and stretched out on the floor next to his sword, hands behind his head. The firewood popped and sparked from the hearth, filling the cabin with a sense of welcome calm.

"Think I'll catch a few winks as well," Rezin said from where he sat. Without gaining a response, he laid back and turned over on his side, content to lie on the floor in front of the fire.

Kell returned from the back bedroom, shutting the door behind her. Liam and Avalice joined her at the kitchen table, the walls rattling beneath the wind.

"Mercy, it *is* good to see you two. How long has it been?" Kell asked quietly, taking a seat.

"Eight years, I think," Avalice said, sliding into a chair next to her husband. "I honestly wasn't sure if you'd even remember us."

Kell made a dismissive gesture. "When you get as old as me, you'll realize time moves at an alarming rate. It only feels like a couple weeks ago you two were standing right over there, lost in each other's eyes as I wed you." Kell smiled affectionately. "That was a good day, wasn't it?"

"One of the best," Liam agreed.

Kell folded her hands and leaned forward. "You know, I didn't want to ask before, but just what are you two doing all the way out here?"

"We're working a job," Liam explained, pointing to Rezin who lay curled up by the fire. "For him. Us being here is no accident. I need your help with something."

Kell sighed and looked at Avalice. "I was hoping you two wouldn't still be on that path. It's such a dangerous way to live."

"We don't have much of a choice right now," Avalice said. "But I can promise you we're on our way out."

Kell nodded and looked at Liam. "She deserves better than this, you know. You got yourself a good one here."

"I know," Liam said, holding up a hand as Avalice began to object. "I know I do. I'm working on it. That's why we're here."

"Oh?"

Liam leaned on the table, keeping his voice low. "We have to get around the Red Ravine. This Rezin guy, he wants to go see The Chain. That's where we're headed, but a lot has changed since I crossed over the first time. Do you still map the area?"

Kell closed her eyes. "Oh, Liam, do you have any idea how risky that is?"

"I do, but it's gotta get done. Can you help us?"

Kell sighed and stood. "I can, but it's been over a year since I went over that way. I'm getting too old to be running around charting maps."

"We can pay you," Avalice offered.

"Nonsense," Kell said, going to a cabinet. "All I ask is that you two return safely. And when you do, promise me you'll stop by so I know you're OK."

"Only if you make us dinner, just like you did that night we got married," Liam said, grinning.

"It's a deal," Kell said, pulling out a piece of rolled-up parchment. She returned to the table and pressed it into Liam's hands. "Here. This is the most up-to-date one I have."

"Thank you."

"Just be careful," Kell begged. "You two are such a rare find these days, and I'd hate for the world to be without you."

"We'll be careful," Liam assured. "You have my word."

Kell nodded. "It's settled, then. I think this calls for a drink, yes? I have a bottle of something special under the house, if you'd like."

Avalice smiled. "Best idea I've heard in a long while."

Kell stood and went over to the corner of the kitchen where she bent and pulled at an iron loop attached to a small door in the floor. Cold air immediately filled the room as Kell positioned herself down the small ladder that led to a crawl space. When she returned, slamming the trapdoor behind her, she carried a large black bottle.

"A cold drink is always better than a warm one, no matter what the weather's like," she said, winking.

But before she could pour it, a noise came from outside. It was a clattering on the front porch loud enough to raise an eyebrow.

"Expecting someone else?" Liam whispered. Kell shook her head and slowly put the bottle back down.

Everyone jumped as a sudden knock came at the door. Three loud raps and then a pause.

Isaac immediately sat up.

"Stay where you are, I'll get it," Kell said quietly. "Probably some damn fool who got himself lost."

She went to the door and carefully opened it a crack, peering out into the night. Liam watched from the table, one hand resting on his axe. He exchanged a look with Isaac.

"Sorry to bother you, ma'am," a male voice said loudly from beyond the door, "but me and my friends here were wondering if you could spare us some shetler for a couple hours."

Liam stood as he saw Kell visibly tense, her voice curt and direct.

"There's no room for all of you here, I'm sorry. I'm going to have to ask you to leave."

More clattering from outside. Footsteps. A lot of them.

The voice continued, unconcerned. "Where's your sense of charity? All we ask is for a couple of hours out of the wind. What do you say?"

Kell went to shut the door. "I'm sorry, but I just don't have the room."

But before she could close it, a hand shot out and grabbed the door, pushing it open and forcing Kell to step back.

"We won't be any bother," the man from outside insisted, "you won't even know we're here."

Isaac climbed to his feet as the man came into full view. He was a couple years younger than Liam, probably late twenties, early thirties. Dark hair fell to his shoulders, framing an angular face and a pair of sparkling blue eyes. When he spotted Liam and Avalice, he smiled, his teeth shining in the firelight.

"Looks like me and my friends aren't the only ones in need tonight," the man said from the doorway.

"Liam," Avalice whispered, her voice urgent.

Liam saw.

At the man's back were over twenty Profanes, each one sporting the broken chain insignia.

"The lady said there's no room," Liam said, stepping toward the door, keeping his hand on his axe. "I'm going to have to ask you to respect her wishes and leave. I'm sure you can find shelter further down the road."

The man shook his head, smiling. "Nah, I don't think that's going to work for us. You see, we've been walking for a very long time now and I swear, I'm about to keel over if I don't get some down time. Don't be sour about it. I know there's a lot of us, but we're a friendly bunch once you get to know us." He stepped into the house, the Profanes crowding at his back. He smiled at Avalice. "Don't you want to get to know us?"

Isaac stepped into view, joining Liam by the door.

The man blinked when he saw him. "Holy heavens, aren't you a big boy."

"I believe the lady asked you to leave," Isaac said calmly, bringing his sword into view.

The man whistled when he saw it, shaking his head. "Void below, but that's a big slab of steel. What do you have attached to it there? Are those rocket boosters?"

Isaac didn't move.

The man sighed and raised his hands. "All right, look. I don't mean to be rude, but we really do need some rest. So step aside and just relax, all right?" Without waiting for consent, the man strode past Kell and into the kitchen. The Profanes followed, filling the small cabin in a matter of seconds. Liam looked at Isaac and then at Kell. Unease rippled through his gut as he watched the new arrivals sprawl out in front of the fire, startling a very surprised Rezin as he came awake with a sputter.

The man, presumably their leader, went to the kitchen table and plopped himself down, a smile splitting his face when he saw the bottle Kell had retrieved.

"Are we drinking?" He asked, snatching it up. "I could use some fire in my stomach, that's for sure." He looked up at Avalice. "Why don't you fetch us some glasses, sweetheart?"

Liam felt Avalice tensing up, so he stepped forward before she could say anything.

"I'll get them. One drink and then you really need to go."

The man nodded, eyes shining. "Of course, of course. See? We're all getting along here, nothing to worry about." He looked up at Kell. "Well come on, old timer, have a seat and join me! I'd feel weird drinking without the host!"

Unsure of what else to do, Kell looked at Liam and then slid into a chair, folding her hands in front of her across the table. It was obvious she was just as nervous as Liam. Her eyes met his and then fell back to her fumbling hands.

"There anyone else here?" the man asked, leaning back in his chair as Liam fetched a couple of glasses.

Avalice stood where she was, eyes boring into the leader's. "None. Just what you see here."

The man nodded. "Good, good, good. Hope you don't mind if I have a couple of my guys check the back rooms, do you? I don't mean to invade your privacy here, but it's a real dangerous world out there, you know? Can't be too careful." He waved a hand and a pair of Profanes went to the closed door where Dekker was sleeping. They opened it and went inside.

Liam felt his heart begin to race, a nausea filling his entire body. Isaac's knuckles were white against the hilt of his sword, but he said nothing, waiting to see how things would play out.

Liam placed a couple of glasses down on the table and began to fill them from the bottle. The man looked up at him, beaming.

"You didn't have to pour for us, but who am I to dampen your manners?" He looked at the Profanes who lined the walls and filled the space in front of the hearth. "We got ourselves a regular gentleman here! Take note!"

A rustle came from the back bedroom and Liam heard Dekker cry out in surprise. The leader ignored the commotion and took one of the glasses, draining it in a single swill. As he licked his lips, the Profanes returned, dragging Dekker in their wake. The old man looked sick, his face flush, his feet dragging behind him.

His captors dropped him by the table next to their leader and crossed their arms. One of them nudged Dekker with the toe of his boot.

"This one was sleeping back there, sir."

The man sighed as if expecting this and turned to look down at Dekker. When he saw the old man's wrapped arms, he raised an eyebrow, bringing his attention back to Kell and Liam.

"You had a Transistor back there? And you didn't tell me?" He looked up at Avalice, disappointed. "You lied to me? Why would you do that? That's not how you make new friends. Come on now, you should know better." Without waiting for a response, he returned his attention back to the Profanes. "Did you search him for stones?"

In response, one of them chucked Dekker's sack of Rockflesh onto the table. The man took it, tsk-ing.

"And he was armed? Now I'm really alarmed. He could have killed us all." He looked directly into Avalice's eyes. "Don't you trust us?"

"I don't know you," Avalice responded, holding her ground. "And I don't appreciate men who barge into someone else's home uninvited. It sets my teeth on edge."

The man paused, surprise written across his face. "Oh my gosh. I haven't introduced myself, have I?" He slapped himself across the forehead with an open palm. "What an idiot." He stood and stretched his hand out to Kell. "I'm Desmond. It's a pleasure to meet you."

Liam felt his jaw clench and he shot Rezin a quick look. The bald man's face was slack, his mouth a thin line. He met Liam's eyes and caution rippled between them.

The man, Desmond, followed Liam's gaze over to Rezin. When he saw him, his smile faltered, as if he were seeing him for the first time.

"You have got to be kidding me," he whispered.

From the corner, Rezin brought his hands together. "It's been a while, hasn't it?"

Desmond didn't move, his eyes like ice. "What the *hell* are you doing here, Rezin?"

Rezin stayed where he was, his voice careful. "I've been looking for you, actually. I'm on my way to The Chain."

Desmond placed a finger down on the table. "And why the hell would you do that?"

"You know why."

Desmond stared at him for a long, pregnant moment. After a second, he threw his head back and let out a barking laugh.

"You are one of a kind, you know that? You just don't stop do you, Rezin? You just go and go and go!" His smile faltered. "But it's over, isn't it? Of course it is. It's all *over*."

Rezin remained silent, the fire crackling at his back.

Desmond's humor returned, along with his smile. "You may have been looking for me, but I have absolutely nothing to say to you so do me a favor and just shut up while I'm introduced to the rest of your friends. You can do that for me, can't you?"

"We're going to need to have a conversation, Desmond," Rezin said quietly, his eyes locking with the other man's.

"There is *nothing* I want to discuss with you," Desmond said sharply, his smile looking more like a gash now. "And if you can't keep your mouth closed then I'll get one of my friends to help you with that." As he said this, the Profanes pushed inward. Rezin appraised them and fell into an uneasy silence. Liam caught his eyes.

What had happened between these two?

Before he could speak, Desmond whirled back to Kell, "I'm so sorry we were interrupted. I really wasn't expecting to see an old friend here. I wonder what other surprises the night holds?" He laughed again, shaking his head. "I'm sorry, dear. What did you say your name was?"

Kell cleared her throat. "Name's Kell."

Desmond, smiled. "Lovely. And who are your other guests, Kell?"

The elderly woman raised her eyes and swept them nervously across the group. "The one with the axe is Liam. That's Avalice. The young man with the sword there is Isaac. And it seems you already know Rezin."

Desmond nodded, the Profanes appraising each and every one of them. The cabin felt crowded and overheated, a sense of tension hovering over the table.

"You all look like great people," Desmond acknowledged. "It's an honor to meet you. While I question the company you keep," his eyes fell on Rezin,

"I'm sure you just don't know any better." A scuffle came from beneath the table and Desmond let out a cry of surprise as Loo peeked up and began to sniff him.

"And a dog too!" Desmond exclaimed, pointing. "Look guys, they even have a dog! Do we have something to feed her? Bretton, grab that meat we cooked earlier from your bag and give it here!"

One of the Profanes dropped his pack and retrieved a piece of dark meat. He tossed it to Desmond, who offered it to Loo. The dog took it with enthusiasm, gulping it down with vigor.

"Good dog," Desmond said, grinning.

"What is going on here?" Dekker finally croaked from the floor, his eyes lost. "Liam, who are these people?"

Before Liam could answer, Desmond turned to him, one hand picking up the sack of Rockflesh.

"We're just a couple of travelers, same as you. I'm sorry my men were so rough with you. It looks like you've been through a lot recently." Desmond toyed with the sack's strings as he spoke, pulling them open to peer inside at the glowing stones. "But you have to understand, my men here don't like your kind." He stopped and then shook his head. "No, I take that back. It's not that they hate Transistors. They just hate *holy* Transistors. Men and women of the Church. It kind of goes against their whole thing. They're very anti-Creator. Isn't that right, boys?"

A murmur swept the room, all eyes on Dekker.

Desmond reached into the sack and plucked a single stone from the pile. He held it up and examined it.

"You see, they *hate* the Creator. They think he's responsible for the poison that fills these rocks. It's not personal, I hope you understand."

Dekker's face filled with remorse, his voice calm and even. "Well, just know that I will pray for each and every one of your souls. Whether you want to believe it or not, the Creator is the one responsible for saving us from the disease."

Desmond leaned forward, closing his fist around the Rockflesh, his voice going low. "Oh I wouldn't bet on that. There's a whole world of things you don't understand, but I'm not here to convert you. Clearly you're a devoted man, so I want you to answer this next question from the heart—do you think the Creator will save you again when the time comes?"

"If my purpose isn't fulfilled yet, then yes," Dekker said confidently, staring back at the man.

Without warning, Desmond reached out and grabbed Loo, dragging her toward him. The dog yelped in surprise, its paws scraping across the floor.

"And what about all the beasts that walk the surface of Tectonic?" Desmond continued, his eyes going dark. "Will the Creator save them as well? What is their purpose in all of this? Why must they suffer, too?"

Liam saw Kell's fingers dig into the table, eyes on her dog, fear filling her face. Avalice shifted where she stood, tense, hands tapping her leg with worry.

Dekker looked at the dog, his face softening. "All life is precious to the Creator, son."

Desmond smiled. "No it's fucking not."

Suddenly, the hand gripping Loo exploded with light, followed by a blinding wave of heat. The dog didn't even have a chance to cry out as its head was instantly vaporized, a splash of orange running down its body.

Kell screamed, surging forward as the animal slumped to the floor, dead. Desmond's arms burned red as he released the corpse, his eyes never leaving Dekker's. Liam heard movement behind him and turned, the tension shattering, and saw Isaac brace himself, his eyes ablaze with fury.

Liam knew what came next.

"Get down!" he screamed, tackling Avalice and taking them both to the floor.

CLICK.

The roar of Isaac's sword filled the cabin, a massive surge of heat and power that screamed through the air as its rocket thrusters were activated.

Liam collapsed on top of Avalice as Isaac swung at the Profanes, his sword taking four of them in its scorching arc. Blood exploded from their throats as their heads were cleaved from their bodies, the cabin erupting with commotion as the violence started.

Isaac twisted on his heels, the momentum of the rockets slamming his blade through the wall, sending splinters flying across the room in a splash of wood and gore.

Desmond sprung to his feet, screaming and pointing, his face as red as his arms. "Get them! GET THEM!"

The Profanes fell upon Liam's group, clubs and fists plowing into his body before he could stand and defend himself. He heard Isaac get body-slammed to the ground as a group rushed him before he could strike again. Avalice was snarling and kicking at anything that came near her, but there were simply too many of them for her to combat.

Something heavy smashed over Liam's head and he stumbled across the floor, desperately trying to break free and get a handle on the chaos all around him. He reached for his axe, but it was immediately yanked from his grip, a boot catching him in the ribs. Wheezing, he blinked away stars and looked up, vision blurry.

Avalice was being dragged across the floor by a pair of men, her face streaked red from a split lip. Her eyes met Liam's and he felt a fire ignite across his chest. Howling, he braced himself and stood, bucking his assailants off as he did so. Spinning, he searched for Desmond and saw him standing over Dekker with a boot on his throat. Snarling, Liam lunged for him but was stopped in his tracks as three Profanes collapsed over him once more. Swinging wildly, he managed to break one of their noses before his head was pressed to the floor, his arms pulled back behind him.

"GET OFF OF ME, YOU MONSTERS!" Liam bellowed, thrashing for control. In the madness he saw Isaac palm the face of a Profane and then smash his skull into the wall so hard that bits of bone splattered to the floor around him.

A shriek from Avalice pulled Liam's attention back to his wife, and he saw one of the Profanes bashing her across the back of the legs with a club while the others bound her hands behind her back.

"AVALICE!" Liam screamed, his body ablaze. He tried to pull himself up once more, but the Profanes had him pinned hard. He felt rope looping around his wrists, and his rage turned to panic.

He looked up, desperate, and saw Isaac fall beneath five Profanes, his knuckles as bloody as the faces that were trying to get at him.

"ENOUGH!"

Liam turned his head, feeling the knots around his wrists tighten miserably, and saw Desmond with his boot still on Dekker's throat.

But in his grip was a gurgling Kell, her face turning blue as Desmond tightened his hold on the woman's throat.

Desmond was panting, his eyes burning with anger, his knuckles white around the old woman's throat.

"No one had to die," Desmand growled, a trickle of sweat running down the side of his face. "We could have all had a nice quiet evening. But what did you do? WHAT DID YOU DO?!" He dug his fingers deeper into Kell's fragile skin.

"You lost your fucking cool, didn't you!?" Desmond roared, watching as Rezin and Isaac were bound. "And over what? A DOG!? Is that all it takes for you people to draw blood!?"

"I'll kill you for that," Avalice snarled around a mouthful of blood. "I swear to you."

Desmond looked over at her, his eyes wide. "The *fuck* did you just say?"

"You heard me, you monster."

Desmond shook his head in disbelief, shock written across his face. "You people just don't learn, do you?" He shook Kell violently, her eyes growing hazy. "I get to decide who dies now. Me. I'm *done* protecting you miserable, delusional bastards. You're just not worth it." His eyes found Rezin's. "And it makes me sick you think otherwise, *still*."

Isaac tried to stand in a sudden rush of adrenaline, but the Profanes on top of him pushed him back to the floor, a fist plowing into the side of his head.

Desmond took his foot off Dekker's throat and walked around the kitchen table, dragging Kell in his wake. He stopped and stared down at Liam and Isaac, then looked across the room at where Rezin and Avalice were held.

He wiped sweat from his forehead with the back of his hand, his voice dangerously calm, his eyes wild. "I mean, what are we doing here? What the hell is wrong with you people? The world's ending and you're spilling blood over an animal?" He looked at Liam. "I mean, if that's the way you want it to be, then I'll dance."

He suddenly yanked Kell around and slammed her face into the table. The old woman let out a shocked scream of horrible pain as her teeth scattered across the surface like bloody dice. Without waiting for her to recover, Desmond pulled her back up by the neck and threw her to the floor at his feet.

"What's wrong!?" he screamed down at her. "Don't you want to dance with me?!"

Kell pulled herself weakly across the floor, tears and blood streaming down her face. Her broken mouth pulled in desperate lungfuls of air.

"Please…" she gasped. "Stop…this…"

"Oh, shut up," Desmond mocked, standing over her. "This is exactly what's wrong with you people. You're *helpless*." He leaned down over Kell, his voice thick. "Helpless, delusional *children*."

He motioned to one of the Profanes and Liam watched in horror as his axe was handed to Desmond.

"Maybe now you'll understand," Desmond announced loudly to everyone in the room. "Maybe now you'll realize that we're all going to die soon and none of this actually matters. So allow me to collect the seven pounds of flesh you people owe me."

He raised the axe and brought it thudding into the side of Kell's neck. The old woman's body jerked violently as the blade connected, blood spraying from the wound.

Desmond snorted and yanked the axe back. Kell gurgled, still terribly alive, one hand outstretched to Liam, her face white with shock, her lips moving wordlessly.

"This is harder than it looks," Desmond mumbled, almost to himself.

Liam realized that he was screaming, that they were all screaming as they watched the frail old woman gush blood across the floor to pool around her trembling hands.

"One more for the road!" Desmond yelled, a smile erupting maniacally across his face.

He brought the axe down again, this time delivering the killing blow.

Liam screamed again, his throat raw, shock rippling through him like currents. He heard Rezin screaming at Desmond from where he was pinned, Avalice's cries rising with it.

Liam's stomach pooled with disgust and repulsion as the Profanes began to laugh, their victims secured, their dominance final.

"What do you want us to do with the rest of them?" one of them asked, motioning toward their bound captives.

Desmond's eyes swept over the beaten, bloodied group.

His smile grew.

"Do with them?" he asked quietly, resting the axe over his shoulder, his face stained with Kell's blood. "I think we should show them what it's like to live without the Creator."

Chapter 7

Rezin and Avalice were gagged and guarded in the corner, their limbs bound. Dekker and Isaac had been labeled as the biggest threats despite their capture and had been thrown down the trapdoor and into the crawl space. Kell's lifeless body had been tossed outside, along with the dog. Liam sat in one of the kitchen chairs, across from Desmond, his wrists tied securely to the wooden frame. Three Profanes stood at his back, watching him. Desmond stood at the opposite end of the table, staring daggers at Liam, that horrible smile still smothering his face.

"Not how you expected the night to go, huh?" he asked, hands planted on the table in front of him.

Liam met his gaze, his stomach in knots. He felt sick and terrified, the world spinning away from his control at an alarming rate.

Kell. Goddamn it, oh *Kell*.

Desmond shook his head, chuckling. "Don't feel like talking? Ah, I get it. This has all been rather traumatic."

"I've met your type before," Liam said, his voice shaking, the image of Kell's corpse ringing through his head. "And I've killed your type before."

Desmond laughed. "You know what, I bet you have. But this is my house now. And you? You're about to learn what it means to fuck with me. All of you are. So forgive me if I'm not quivering in my boots."

Liam leaned forward in his chair, his voice hoarse. "Who *are* you? Why are you doing this?"

Desmond walked around the table and leaned against it in front of Liam. "Me? I'm just a guy who's had enough. And all these cheery men here are my traveling pals, aren't you, boys?"

Ripples of laughter swept through the cabin as heads nodded.

A sudden voice cut through the air like a razor, silencing them. "You're supposed to be protecting these people, you coward."

The room went still and all eyes went to Rezin. The bald man sat propped against the wall, his face white, his eyes wide, like he was surprised he had spoken. His gag lay wet on the floor in front of him.

"Protect them?" Desmond asked, incredulous. "After everything I've been through? Have you gone mad? Have you gone absolutely *mad*? There's no stopping what's coming, you fool. Look around you. Look at this world. What have our efforts earned us?" He leaned forward, his voice going low. "I'm done playing the shield. I'd rather end us all on my terms. I'd rather be the executioner's axe for once."

Rezin shrunk into himself, his lips locking once more.

"So it's true?" Liam asked, straining in his chair, his thoughts fragmenting into madness. "You really want to destroy The Chain?"

Desmond seemed to relax suddenly. He sighed wearily and ran a hand over his face. "Heh. You all must think I'm crazy to try something like that. Not that it matters. You people have no idea how good you have it. How freely you all live. For the first time in my life, I'm doing exactly what I want. Does that make me crazy? I don't think so."

"Your madness was clear to me the second you walked in here," Liam said fiercely, trying to overcome his fear, to make sense of the insanity.

Desmond grunted and crossed his arms. "I think that's a little harsh considering you know nothing about me. What I've seen..." he trailed off, his eyes becoming empty voids. Shaking himself, he pushed away from the table and took his place at the head once again, his voice hardening. "Listen, I'm about to do some really awful things to you people, but I'm not *mad*. In fact, I think I'm one of the few sane people left in Tectonic. Am I trying to destroy The Chain? Yeah, you bet. Don't you know why, though?"

A silence swept the room.

"Of course not," Desmond continued, "Something tells me none of you have been given the truth." He looked across the room at Rezin. "You want to chime in here?"

"What is that supposed to mean?" Liam growled, cutting him off.

"It means that the Creator you people love so much isn't going to save you from what's coming. You notice how damn cold Tectonic has gotten over the past decade?"

"So what?" Liam challenged.

Desmond leaned forward, his voice low. "It's because Tectonic is moving again. Something is *pulling you up.*"

Liam felt his mind reel, his thoughts unraveling. "What?"

"How often do the sun splashes come now?" Desmond asked, his voice quiet. "How many times a year are you gifted a glimpse of sunlight? You are going *dark.* You are *freezing* to death. You are *starving.* Are you starting to get it? Nothing matters. My life, your life, your friends' lives, they are all meaningless because all of this will come to an end very soon."

"If we're so cursed," Liam ventured, "then why bother destroy The Chain? If you actually pull it off, then we're all going to plummet back down into the Void and we will *shatter.* If you're so convinced that existence as we know it will come to an end anyway, then why go through all the trouble of severing Tectonic from The Chain?"

Desmond's eyes turned to ice chips. "Because I will not let *them* have me."

Liam shook his head, confusion erupting across his scattered mind. "Who?!"

Desmond pulled himself up. "It doesn't matter. Even if I told you what's really going on, you wouldn't believe me. You haven't been over to that side of the world like I have. I will not waste my breath only to be doubted. But I can assure you—breaking The Chain is the better of the two evils. I may kill us all, but that is far more desirable than the alternative." His voice turned to a hiss. "The real evil isn't here in this cabin. It's up there in the sky."

"You've given up hope."

All eyes turned to Rezin once more.

"Hope?" Desmond asked dangerously. "Yes, I have given up *hope.* You of all people should know the Creator did not save us from the Void. We're damned to a fate worse than death. And so I'm going to take this disease, this curse that's been scattered across the world, and use it to my favor. Even now, I have hundreds working for me, gathering the infected, herding them toward the end. It won't be long now."

"What you're saying—" Liam started, but was cut off as Desmond sliced his hand through the air.

"Enough. I'm done talking. You invited us into this home and then killed four of my men. I may have a mission of my own, but that doesn't mean I'm going to let your actions go unpunished. It's time *someone* held you responsible."

"Just leave us," Liam begged, feeling a surge of sudden panic. "You've done enough, haven't you? If we're all going to die like you say, then there's no point in doing whatever you have planned. Just go. Please."

"Please?" Desmond said slowly. "Please? Seriously? Come on, I expected better from you. Aren't you supposed to be the leader here?"

"You've beaten us," Liam continued, voice straining. "Anything past that would be pointless. You yourself admitted this is all meaningless. Just leave us. We won't pursue you."

Desmond seemed to chew this over. "Meaningless? Probably. But I've been the spine of this goddamn place for a long time now and I've grown to hate how complacent you've all become. How you've done nothing with the gift you've been given."

"What gift!?" Liam yelled, leaning forward. "What are you talking about!?"

Desmond grinned. "What's the damn point? If you want to stop what happens next, then why don't you ask the Creator you people so fervently believe in? Go ahead. See what happens."

He looked over at Avalice and Rezin, that smile still twisting his lips. "No takers? Fine. Then let's get down to it, shall we?" He walked over to the pair, the Profanes stepping aside. Desmond looked down at Avalice and ran a finger across her cheek, toying with her gag.

"You're a pretty one, aren't you? It's been a long time since I've laid eyes on such a beauty." He grunted. "If you knew what I've done for you, you'd be begging for a piece of me."

Avalice just glared up at him, her eyes stained with tears.

"Don't you touch her," Liam snarled. "Like you said, I'm the leader here, so whatever you need to do, do it to me. I take full responsibility for your men's death. Just leave her out of this."

Desmond looked over his shoulder at Liam. "Does this one mean something to you? Hmm? Yeah, oh yeah, I think she does. I mean, just look at you.

Your hackles are raised, your veins are bulging, you look ready to absolutely annihilate me." He laughed and raised his hands defensively. "OK, OK, she's off limits. I got it." He went to Rezin next, his smile fading.

"Now you," he said slowly. "*You* I can't figure out. After everything, here you are, charging headfirst back into the fire."

"We have a duty, Desmond," Rezin said quietly, his eyes alive with vibrating intensity.

"Our duty is dead, you fool," Desmond spat, shaking his head. "I don't owe these people a fucking thing and neither do you. Clearly, they aren't worth it. None of it is. So now I'm going to take back what was stolen from me."

He crossed the room once more, going to Avalice to tilt her head up so that she was looking at him.

"You gotta stop with the angry eyes, love. This isn't my fault. Did your husband drag you into this? Do you resent him, now that you're trapped in here with me? With us? Who are you going to turn to now to protect you?"

Avalice growled something from behind her gag and Desmond chuckled. "Oh, hush now, no one wants to hear that." He looked over at Liam and then back to Avalice. "Do you love him? Is he a good man, your husband? Is he going to hunt me down if I let you go?"

Without waiting for a response, he suddenly reached down and roughly hauled her to her feet. "Come on, I have an idea. It'll make things better, I promise."

Heart racing, Liam watched as Desmond dragged Avalice over to the table in front of him.

"I don't want my intrusion here tonight to cause a rift between you two," Desmond said, throwing an arm around Avalice and looking down at Liam. "I couldn't live with myself. So I want to make sure you two are good."

"What are you talking about?" Liam hissed, the ropes cutting into his wrists.

Desmond pressed his cheek against Avalice's, despite her best efforts to repulse his advances.

"I want you to fuck your girl. Right now. Show me something good. Show me how much you people can love one another."

Liam felt his thoughts go blank. "What?"

Desmond closed his eyes, sighing. "I said, I want you to fuck your girl. Right here, right now, in front of us so that we can ALL see there's some good left in this world—that there's something left to protect. Show me the world you don't want to lose."

Liam shook his head, unable to believe what he was hearing, his heart plummeting into his gut. "You're *insane.*"

With lightning-quick ferocity, Desmond suddenly reached down and grabbed Avalice's crotch, a piece of Rockflesh appearing in his other hand.

"Call me insane one more time and I swear I will eviscerate her before your eyes. Go on. Try me. I dare you. *Do it.*"

"Desmond, STOP THIS!" Rezin yelled, his face in anguish.

Avalice was standing on her toes, her face twisted in pain as Desmond's hand dug into her, his eyes drilling hell into Liam's. A pained moan escaped from behind her gag as Desmond tightened his grip, waiting.

"I'm sorry!" Liam cried, surging forward in his chair, only to be pulled back by the Profanes. "Don't hurt her! I'm sorry! I'm SORRY!"

Desmond smiled and released Avalice, who shuddered, snot running down her face, tears finding her bloodshot eyes.

"Now," Desmond continued, still holding the Rockflesh, "do as I say and fuck her."

"Please…" Liam begged, his voice hoarse, the world falling away.

"If you don't," Desmond said firmly, "then I will let each and every one of my men here have a turn with her until she's so spent and broken that she'll beg to die. Do you understand? Do you want that?"

Liam felt tears roll down his face as he stared helplessly at his wife. His thoughts collided into one another, a terrible mixture of shame and anger and fear. He lowered his head and closed his eyes, lost in himself.

"That's right," Desmond said, "very good. No more talking back." He nodded to the Profanes at Liam's back. "Untie him. Go ahead, he's not going to do anything stupid." He paused. "But if you do, then I will have my men rape her without mercy. That clear enough for you?"

Trembling, Liam felt the ropes fall away. He rubbed his wrists and stared into Avalice's eyes, his own eyes red-rimmed and filled with despair.

Desmond released Avalice and pointed to the table. "Right here will do. Bend her over. You probably don't want to look her in the eyes while you do this, huh? I understand this isn't really the best way to do this, but we work with what we got, am I right?"

The Profanes pulled Liam to his feet and pushed him into Avalice, chuckling and crowding around the table. Their faces were filled with malice and hatred, a sickening glow that consumed Liam's world.

He took Avalice by the arms and stared down into her face, his voice shaking. "Sweetie…" he choked.

Avalice, her cheeks stained with sorrow, simply nodded and Liam felt his heart breaking.

"Get on with it already!" Desmond yelled, taking his place at the head of the table.

Liam tried his best to block out all thought. He tried to mute the snickers and smacking of lips that filled the cabin. He knew Desmond would do much worse to Avalice if he didn't go through with this.

A sob escaped his throat as he closed his eyes and positioned Avalice over the table, gently bending her over it. With her hands bound still, her cheek scraped roughly over the wood as she was aligned.

"I'm so sorry," Liam whispered to her. "I love you…I love you, Av."

Feeling his face burn red, he pulled her pants down. The cabin erupted in a cheer and Liam gritted his teeth, fighting against every instinct he possessed.

Wordlessly, he began to stroke himself, begging to just get this over with.

"You must not love her very much if you gotta get a head start like that," Desmond called from the head of the table, earning a ripple of laughter from his men.

Squeezing his eyes shut so tightly he thought they would burst, Liam finally felt himself go semi-hard. Sweating, he pushed himself into Avalice and felt her stiffen, her body rocking against the table.

"Yes! Yes! Go on now, give it to her!" Desmond encouraged, drumming the table from the other end. "Pretend we're not here and really plow that bitch!"

Keeping his eyes closed, Liam did as he was told, tears streaming down his face.

The Profanes cheered louder as Avalice was thrust back and forth across the table, her cheek roughly scraping against the surface. She was crying and her sobs found Liam's ears and he choked back his growing hysteria.

As he fucked her, the Profanes around the table began to masturbate. They stared down at the scene with intense lust, their hands stroking their exposed cocks, wicked grins plastered across their faces.

Liam dared to open his eyes and when he saw what they were doing, a fury emerged from the misery with such force that he almost stopped. But then he met Desmond's eyes.

"Don't you dare quit now," he said darkly, "don't you fucking dare."

One of the Profanes ejaculated then, dispersing his load across Avalice's back. And then another. And another.

Hyper-ventalating, Liam felt his mind consumed with a hatred so deep he thought he would drown in it.

Enough. Kill them all.

But before he could act on the sudden rage, he felt Avalice's hand squeeze his wrist. He looked down and saw her looking back at him, her eyes filled with the deepest of shame and pain. But there was something else there that made him continue in the act.

Resolve.

Smashing his teeth together, Liam pumped until completion, a horrible act that felt like the worst kind of betrayal.

When Desmond saw it, he clapped loudly, his face lit in elation. "Yes! What an absolute champ! Hey, everyone put your cocks away and give it up for these two! Come on now you nasty bastards, let's give 'em a round of applause!"

As the Profanes cheered and mocked, Liam stepped back and quickly redressed his wife before pulling his own clothes back up. Ignoring the noise, he drew Avalice up and embraced her, her face wet against his neck.

"We're going to get out of this," he whispered into her ear, chest heaving. "I'm going to take you to those falls, I promise. I promise…" he trailed off, his misery getting the better of him.

Suddenly he was yanked away from his wife, a crowd of Profanes jostling him back and tying his hands once more.

"I did what you wanted!" Liam gasped, eyes bulging and in a panic. "I did what you asked! Let us go! Just leave us alone!"

Desmond walked over to Avalice and grabbed her by the back of the neck, her knees threatening to give out, her eyes dim.

"I'm a man of my word," Desmond said, watching as Liam was secured. "I promised you that I wouldn't let my men touch her if you did as I said. And I won't." His hand tightened around her neck. "But I never said anything about me."

Liam felt a new terror seize him, a wave so dark and horrible he thought he would burn away.

"No! NO! LEAVE HER ALONE YOU BASTARD!" Liam screamed, thrashing and struggling against the mass of Profanes that held him.

Desmond forced Avalice to her knees, pulling her to the floor by her hair. "Don't worry, I'm a little more private than you are. I won't make you watch. I have to say, I'm impressed with your ability to perform. But it's also left me hungry. Like I stated earlier, it's been a while since I've seen a woman like this. Don't you think I deserve a little love?"

He looked at the Profanes at Liam's side. "Toss him down with the others."

"I'll kill you!" Liam howled, bucking and biting, catching a fist across the jaw. "I swear I'LL KILL YOU!" He felt like he was suffocating, like his chest was collapsing. His eyes found Avalice's, her expression numb and drenched in agony. "AV! Avalice! I won't let him do this! I WON'T!"

Desmond ignored Liam as he was dragged over to the trapdoor, his gaze finding a ghostly Rezin still huddled against the wall, his face white.

Desmond hunched down in front of the shocked man, his face grim. "Why didn't you protect them, hero?" When he got no answer, he motioned for the Profanes to take him away as well.

The Profanes obeyed and as Liam and Rezin were tossed down into the crawl space, Liam locked eyes with Avalice once more.

And he saw utter hopelessness.

Then he was tossed into darkness.

Chapter 8

L iam tasted dirt as he collapsed beneath the house, a cold wind slicing through the crawl space. Rezin landed heavily next to him, his knee catching Liam across the side. Blinking away tears, wrestling with panic, Liam fought with his restraints, a moaning hysteria echoing from his throat. He wriggled away from Rezin and rolled to his left, the latch above them closing with a grim finality. Panting, sweating, he bit his lip so hard he drew blood, a commotion rising above him. He could hear Avalice grunting and Profanes laughing, a combination that pulled him toward absolute madness.

"Liam?"

Liam looked behind him and saw Dekker and Isaac, both of them still bound and lying in the dark earth.

"Help me," Liam begged, wrestling with his ropes, "oh god, please help me Dekker."

"What's happening?! What have they done?" The Transistor asked, squirming to Liam's side.

The floorboards above them thundered as something slammed into them, the light from the hearth overhead filtering through the cracks to cast swaying shadows.

"Avalice, they have Avalice!" Liam cried, his chest roaring with horrible, frantic frustration.

"Creator help us," Dekker whispered into the dark, his voice laden with dread. "Oh no, Liam…"

"I can't...I *can't* let them do this!" Liam begged, his voice a choking plea. He looked past Dekker at Isaac, his eyes filled with dim desperation. "Help me, Isaac! Please!" He swung his eyes over to Rezin, "Can't you get free?! Anyone!? Oh no, please, no no NO!"

Feet stomped and crowded across the floor overhead, a chaotic filter of noise filling the crawl space as the mob watched whatever evils were being committed. Through the commotion, Avalice's pained grunts could be heard.

"STOP IT!" Liam shrieked, eyes bulging, "DON'T YOU HURT HER! DESMOND! DESMOND PLEASE! PLEASE!"

Desmond's laughter rolled down to them, a maniacal triumph of domination. Seconds later, Avalice's grunts turned to all-out screams.

"Oh no, no no no stop please *stop*," Liam wept, his whole body shaking.

"What the hell are they doing to that poor woman?" Rezin said, his voice cracking with disbelief.

"What do you THINK IS HAPPENING!?" Liam roared, eyes red and drenched.

Suddenly Isaac was at Liam's side, his body rolling through the dirt as best as he could manage. He looked into Liam's eyes, his voice gentle.

"Your friends are here, Liam. We're with you."

Liam stared helplessly into the young man's eyes as the terrible cries continued from above. They were so hauntingly familiar and foreign to him that he felt like his body was coming apart piece by piece.

"Grab that off the floor!" Desmond instructed from above, a patter of feet following his command. His voice was muted behind the unseen violence, and all Liam could do was shut his eyes and weep.

"She's got endurance, I'll give her that!" Desmond laughed, only feet above them but separated by what felt like miles.

And the talking continued, a stream of malice that knifed into Liam's gut with every expression.

"Hold her down! Her leg, you idiot!"

"How is she supposed to suck me off with all that blood in her mouth?"

"You doing OK, sweetie? Can you go another round?"

"You keep struggling and I'm going to bite your fingers off!"

"How about I put a baby in you?!"

"Shit, you're tight when you tense up!"

"In nine months I'll come back and see whose kid it is."

"What are the odds, boys!? Will it be mine or her husband's!?"

"I got an idea!"

"Hold her a second! Grab the poker!"

"Don't let her pass out yet!"

"Let's impregnate this cow!"

And then Avalice screamed so loudly Liam thought his skull would shatter, a plea of misery that absolutely gutted him to his soul. He lay there, in the darkness, shaking and shivering and weeping and praying for all of this to be over.

"I'm sorry, Liam," Rezin whispered, "I'm so sorry."

Liam fell into himself, his mind disappearing beneath the weight of his own horror, his eyes staring into nothing, his lips moving wordlessly.

Oh god, *Avalice*.

After what felt like an eternity, the noise from above quieted some. Avalice stopped screaming and it sounded like Desmond was finished with his sick games.

Footsteps clattered across the floorboards toward the hearth, and a muttering of conversation could be heard between the Profanes. Their show was wrapping up, the excitement dying.

"Leave her there," Liam heard Desmond say, "she looks like she's had enough. She's spent, just like the rest of this place."

Liam stared blank-faced and exhausted at the walls of the crawl space, his ears picking out the words but not really digesting them. His cheeks were stained with moisture that chilled beneath the wind, coming at him like a snake between the wood slats. His mind buzzed with a sick kind of hum, like his skull had been filled with bees.

"Liam."

He felt an elbow nudge him in the ribs.

"Liam, look."

Blinking, Liam turned to Rezin.

"Do you see it?" Rezin whispered, worming his way closer.

Liam followed the man's eyes and when he saw what Rezin was looking at, he felt a stirring in his chest.

It was a single piece of Rockflesh.

It glowed dimly from the dirt, a marble-sized piece that pulsed with power. Dekker and Isaac rolled over to see what was happening.

"Is that what I think it is?" Rezin continued, his voice urgently low.

Liam's eyes tore over to Dekker, and the Transistor nodded.

"We're going to get out of here," he said quietly, working his way slowly across to the orange rock. "We're going to save her, Liam. Just hold on." Rezin licked his lips in the cold as he watched Dekker position himself so he could scoop up the Rockflesh with his bound hands.

"It must have fallen through the floorboards during the commotion," Rezin whispered.

"Hurry," Liam croaked as Dekker's fingers closed over the rock. "Hurry, Dekker, *please.*" He suddenly felt his heart come alive again, a slow drumming that grew more intense as he watched the Transistor wince and roll onto his back, his bandaged arms filthy and bleeding through the gauze.

Dekker saw Liam watching him and his jaw tightened. "I don't care if I burn my arms away to ash. We're all going up there to save Avalice. We will not carry their sins with us, Liam. I promise."

Suddenly, a door burst open from upstairs, letting in a blast of frigid air that sliced through the floorboards. A panicked Profane could be heard panting, his voice loud and urgent.

"Desmond, there's Caps coming! They'll be here in a matter of minutes, we gotta go!"

Desmond's voice followed. "What? You're sure?"

"I saw them myself! A pair of vehicles!"

"Shit. SHIT." A pause. "I wonder if they followed us from Titan. Or perhaps they're looking for our guests downstairs?"

A different Profane now. "What do we do?"

Another pause. Then. "Let's get out of here. We don't have time to be dealing with them. We'll meet up with the others, just like we planned. By now they should have the last of the infected they were sent to retrieve. Once we make it to their camp, we'll head toward The Chain, just like we planned."

A clatter of boots filled the crawl space as the Profanes scrambled for travel.

"Let's move out!" Desmond ordered. "Leave the bastards below. Maybe it'll keep the Caps occupied for a while. Move! Go!"

Liam met Dekker's eyes as the cabin above them hurriedly emptied. "They're getting away!"

Dekker closed his eyes, the sound of the Profanes retreat echoing outside now. "I know, I know. Just give me a second, I'm sorry."

"Just do it already!" Rezin yelled, his voice frightened. "If the Caps find us down here—"

"Hush," Isaac said, gritting his teeth. "Let the man channel."

With Profanes fleeing and the Caps approaching, Dekker took a deep breath and his arms began to glow.

"Easy," Isaac cautioned, watching. "Easy now."

Dekker's face went white, his jaw clenched. After a moment, he snapped his eyes open and gasped, his ropes falling away as they were scorched. Immediately, he rolled over onto his back and released a stream of raw power from his open hand. The beam exploded through the trap door, showering the group with burnt wood.

Sweating now, Dekker climbed to his knees and quickly untied Isaac, who rose with fluid speed and climbed up into the main cabin, disappearing in an instant.

"Come on, come on!" Liam urged as Dekker worked his bindings next.

"Stay still," Dekker instructed, his voice rugged, the bandages around his arms falling away in smoking tatters as his fingers fumbled with the knots around Liam's wrists.

A moment later and the ropes fell free. Liam scrambled to his hands and knees, heart thundering, and climbed up into the open cabin.

Pulling himself up, he was almost immediately halted by Isaac, his shadow looming over Liam.

Liam raised his eyes, his voice trembling, his body aching. "What are you doing? Move!"

Isaac pulled Liam to his feet, blocking his view, his voice grave. "Liam…"

"MOVE!" Liam shrieked, pushing the young man aside, his chest heaving.

When he saw Avalice, he felt his body go cold, his limbs sapped of strength, his breath freezing in his throat. His eyes went wide and a scream began to rise from the darkest part of himself.

Avalice was on her back, stretched out across the table. She was naked and her skin was covered in bruises and cuts. Her eyes were closed and her head hung over the lip of the table. Patches of her hair had been ripped out, her nose was swollen beneath a break, her thighs were covered with dry blood.

"NO!" Liam screamed, surging forward, tears coming to life. "OH GOD NO AVALICE!" He reached her and cradled her head to his chest, his words coming out in a babble of pain and horror.

"What have they done to you!? Oh GOD what have they DONE!?"

Her eyes remained closed, but her chest rose and fell, her breath coming in rapid, shallow pulls.

"Baby, wake up!" Liam cried, cupping her face in his hands. "Oh please, please, baby, please wake up! I'm here now, it's over! It's over!"

Dekker and Rezin climbed from the crawl space and when they saw the state Avalice was in, their eyes went wide, their jaws going slack.

Liam turned to look at them, tears streaming down his cheeks. "Help me! Someone please HELP ME!"

Rezin was the first over to his side, his hands trembling as he examined her broken state. Dekker, his eyes laden with pain, joined Liam, his voice an empty thing.

"What have they done to you, child? Creator help us, what kind of *evil* is this?"

From outside, a distant rumble was heard.

Engines.

"Caps," Isaac whispered.

"Look at what they've DONE!" Liam howled, clutching his wife to him, the world disappearing.

Rezin suddenly stepped away from the table, his expression turning from horror to absolute repulsion. His eyes were glued to Avalice, a trembling hand pointing.

"Oh no...Liam...they've...they've..." he turned away, squeezing his eyes shut.

Tear-blinded, Liam looked at what Rezin was pointing at, wiping his eyes, sobs bubbling from his chest. When he realized what had shaken Rezin, when he saw it, he thought he would shatter, his mind pushed beyond the realms of sanity.

They had cauterized Avalice's vagina shut. The skin was blackened and raw, burning flesh mixed with angry pink. Her thighs were laced with inflamed stripes, a sickening trail that led up to her sealed organ. Pieces of her had been burned so bad that the skin had cracked, a nauseous smell rising from the welded folds.

Dekker turned away.

Rezin closed his eyes.

And Liam wept, hands balling in fury and sorrow.

"How could someone do this...?" he gasped from his knees.

The rumble of the engines grew louder from outside. Isaac, unable to look at Avalice, retrieved his sword from the corner of the room. He walked to the doorway and paused.

"I see them."

Liam remained on his knees, eyes wet. He stared blankly at the floor, shock rippling through him.

Rezin slowly walked over to him and placed a hand on his shoulder.

"No one should have to suffer like this," he said quietly. "They can't—" he paused, his voice sharp now. "Liam, her eyes! She's awake!"

It was like a bomb went off in Liam's head. He sprang to his feet, heart surging, and rushed to her side. He stared down into her fluttering eyes, his hands gently caressing her face.

"I'm here! I'm right here!" He cried, whispered, begged, watching as she slowly regained focus and locked eyes with him, her own laced with incredible pain.

"Put....it...." she whispered, her voice barely audibly around her swollen lips.

Liam leaned down, desperate. "What is it!?"

"They...put...Rockflesh...in..." she swallowed hard and winced, her teeth stained red.

Liam slowly stood up, an explosion of terrible dizziness rocking him where he stood.

"No...."

He looked down his wife's naked body, down to where the flesh was melted shut.

"Oh god...no...."

"Liam," Isaac said from the doorway, his voice like iron, his eyes trained on a pair of headlights from outside.

"What do I do?" Liam said numbly, his eyes blank, his voice shaking. "Oh god, what am I supposed to do!?"

Dekker was suddenly at his side, one hand trailing down Avalice's body. "I can drain it. But it will only be temporary. If the Rockflesh remains in her, then her body will grow around it, absorb it. She'll become infected." Dekker closed his eyes, his voice sick. "Liam, if she's to have any chance here, then we have to cut it out."

Doors could be heard closing from outside. Isaac gripped his sword, his voice rising in volume.

"They're coming. I need you, Dek."

Dekker looked at Liam, stared into his shell-shocked eyes. "We'll take care of the Caps. Do whatever you think is best."

The Transistor closed his eyes, keeping his hand over Avalice. Hissing, Dekker drained the unseen Rockflesh of its deadly power, the effort taking a visible toll on the old man. He opened his eyes, his tattered arms glowing and bleeding and burning, and followed Isaac outside without a word.

Liam was frozen in place, the weight of consequence thundering into his skull. Avalice let out a pained moan, her eyes fluttering, her arms reaching for him.

He took her hands and knelt by her, his voice dripping with gentle sorrow. "Listen, sweetie, listen to me. Please. You'll get infected if we don't...if we...if we don't hurry...do you understand?" He was crying by the time he finished, stroking her hair with a bloodied hand.

Avalice opened her eyes and looked into his, her voice a guttural plea. "Do...it. Don't let me...become...lost. Please. I want you...to do it."

Liam nodded, his vision blurry. "I know...I know, sweetie. But it's going to hurt. It's going to hurt a lot."

"Do...it."

From the doorway, the night beyond glowed as Dekker and Isaac met the Caps, the roar of combat following.

Trembling, Liam looked around and spotted his weapons in the corner of the room. He went to them and picked up his boot knife, along with his axe. The weight in his chest was almost too much to bear as he turned back around to face the table.

Rezin approached him and held out his hand, his voice unsteady. "Give me the knife. There are some things a man just shouldn't have to do."

Liam stared at him, his eyes lost.

"Come on, hurry, before I lose my nerve," Rezin urged, visibly shaken. "I hold some responsibility in all this. Let me help you, for once. Please."

Liam gave him the knife and went back to Avalice as Rezin positioned himself at the other end of the table. He wiped sweat from his brow, his face sick.

"I think you should probably hold her down," Rezin said, his voice strained.

Liam nodded and placed his hands on Avalice's shoulders, his voice as gentle as he could muster. "It'll be over soon, Av. I promise. Be brave. We're going to fix this, OK?"

Avalice gritted her teeth and simply nodded, her body tensing beneath Liam's grip. Rezin waited for Liam to give him the signal, and when he did, he lowered the knife.

And then he began to slice her open.

Avalice's reaction was explosive and instant. She arched her back and howled, her eyes bloodshot and bulging, the muscles in her neck straining. Liam, gasping, crying, did his best to keep her still, half-lying against her to keep her still.

"I know it hurts, I'm sorry, I'm so sorry!" Liam wept, fighting against her frantic thrashing.

Rezin's face had gone deathly white, his bald head streaking with perspiration. He blinked it away, breathing heavily, and pulled the tip of the blade down, opening her up. Blood spilled out across his hands as the skin cracked and came apart, releasing a torrent that had been welling inside.

"Hurry! She's DYING!" Liam screamed, Avalice's howls blaring into his ears and piercing through his skull.

Suddenly, from outside, a massive detonation filled the night and the body of a Cap came exploding through the wall. He struck the hearth, smacking wetly against the stone, and slid to the floor, dead. In an instant, another one came, airborne and windmilling as he flew through the cabin and crashed into the opposite wall.

His armor took the impact and after a moment on the floor, he slowly crawled to his feet, his mirror visor cracking and falling away to reveal a pair of furious, dazed eyes.

Rezin froze, the knife still inside Avalice as she screamed. Liam looked over his shoulder and saw the Cap coming for them, his hands bunched into fists, death on his trail.

Knowing he had only seconds, Liam made a split-second decision and released Avalice, his throat filling with a snarl. The sorrow he had been drowning in was replaced by a red-hot hatred, a need to channel his misery, his fury, into something physical.

He lowered his shoulder and met the Cap with a roar, lifting him off his feet only to slam him back down to the ground again.

"Avalice, no!" Rezin yelled from somewhere behind Liam.

A thud followed and out of the corner of his eye, Liam saw his wife fall to the floor, pulling herself away from Rezin's knife.

A fist plowed into Liam's jaw, bringing his attention back to the Cap beneath him. With blood on his tongue, Liam gripped the Cap's helmet and ripped it off, feeling his sanity drift away as hell crashed down around him.

With both hands around the Cap's throat, Liam bared his teeth and then sunk them into his victim's throat. He felt the man's windpipe collapse as his jaws snapped shut, bringing with it a tearing of flesh and a mouthful of foreign blood.

Panting, Liam spit out the mouthful of gore and sat up, watching as the Cap gurgled and clutched the hole in his throat. Without pause, Liam stood and dragged the man over to the hearth. Grunting, he lifted the Cap and shoved his head into the fire.

New screams filled the collapsing cabin as the man's face was cooked, his skin baking, then burning, then falling away in pieces.

"LIAM, HELP ME!"

Liam spun, feeling sick and high on adrenaline, the world rocking beneath his feet. From outside, he could hear the clash of weapons and the roar of flame. He could hear Dekker yelling. He could hear the wind roaring.

"Hold her! We're almost finished!" Rezin yelled from the floor, trying to keep Avalice still, the knife held loosely in one hand.

Snapping from his daze, Liam rushed them and skidded to his knees, his hands reaching for Avalice.

"I've got you, sweetie, I've got you! We're almost done!"

The roof of the cabin exploded in a wave of heat and light, a massive beam of raw power sweeping across it like a blazing spotlight. Liam covered Avalice with his body as pieces of wood rained down around them, the air singed and stinking.

Rezin, eyes wild, pulled Avalice's legs apart once again. "I can see the Rockflesh! I can get it! Hold her STILL!"

Panting, exhausted, Liam pushed Avalice down onto her back, his hands on her shoulders. She wriggled in agony beneath him, but it was enough. Barely.

Rezin, looking like he might vomit, slid the knife back into her vagina. Liam could hear the blade scraping against the deadly rock that had been shoved inside as Rezin dug at it.

"REZIN!" Liam screamed as Avalice bucked beneath him.

"I got it!" Rezin suddenly yelled, pulling away, "I GOT IT!"

In his hand was a piece of drained Rockflesh the size of a plum. It was covered in blood and bits of skin. After seeing it, Rezin threw it violently into the fire behind him.

Liam tore his eyes back to his wife, his hands stroking her deathly pale cheeks. "It's over! We got it out!" Avalice sputtered and her body slowed and then relaxed in his arms, her eyes fluttering and then closing as shock took her.

"Stay with me!" Liam cried, suddenly panicking. "Av! AVALICE!"

From outside, Isaac's voice roared through the night air with an urgency that chilled the cabin.

"LIAM! LIAM, IT'S DEKKER!"

"Goddamn it," Liam cried, swinging his eyes to the shattered doorway and then back. "Goddamn it, what is happening to us!?"

Rezin tossed the knife away and scooted away from the bloody wreckage, hugging his knees to his chest. His eyes were wide, like he couldn't believe what he had just done.

Liam looked back down at Avalice, choking on a sob. "Sweetie, *please…*"

Suddenly, Isaac filled the doorway, his body streaked with blood, his sword held firmly in one hand. He was out of breath, his chest heaving. He locked eyes with Liam, his voice like winter.

"Liam, get out here. Dekker's in trouble."

Rezin looked up from where he sat on the floor. "The Caps?"

Isaac shook his head. "Dead. But Dekker needs help. His arms…"

"Oh, no…" Rezin whispered, climbing to his feet, wiping his eyes. "Oh no, no…"

Isaac snapped his attention back to Liam, who was still cradling his wife. "Liam!"

Liam just stared down into Avalice's face, his shoulders shaking.

Isaac stepped toward him, his voice softening. "Liam?"

Liam looked up, his eyes lost, his body trembling. "She's…she's dead."

A silence swept the room, a horrible, fatal stillness, like the pause between lighting and thunder.

Liam slumped over Avalice, hugging her to him, and wept as the wind howled through the wreckage around them.

"My wife is *dead*…"

Chapter 9

No one moved inside the cabin, the terrible moment freezing them in time. Rezin, still hugging his knees to his chest, watched as Liam wept over Avalice. The ruined cabin howled with a bitter wind, but none of them seemed to feel it. He pulled his hands away from his knees and looked down at them. They were covered in blood. Wincing, he wiped them across his shirt, desperate to be free of it.

Gently, Isaac walked to Liam from the doorway, stooping down and then going to a knee. He reached out and touched Liam's shoulder, his eyes soft, his voice softer.

"I'm sorry..."

Liam remained where he was, a shaking mess, and held his wife to his chest. His cries echoed around them, mixing with the wind.

And Avalice remained dead.

Slowly, Rezin stood, feeling dizzy. He wrapped his arms around himself and approached Isaac carefully.

"Where's Dekker?" he asked quietly, Liam's muted sobs slicing like razors.

Isaac stood and backed away from Liam, his large frame seeming out of place in the cramped, blood-soaked cabin. His face drooped, and there seemed to be no energy in his voice.

"Outside. Can you help him?"

Rezin glanced at Liam, closed his eyes, and nodded. "I'll try."

Together, they walked out into the darkness, Liam's sobs following them into the chill. Rezin put a hand to his head as he witnessed the aftermath of the skirmish with the Caps, the violence staining the road before him. A pair of vehicles smouldered from the asphalt, the metal charred and melted. Bodies littered the ground, most of them missing limbs. As he walked across the hard dirt behind Isaac, he felt his boots splash across shallow pools of blood. The fire that still clung to the vehicles cast a dim light across the scene, painting a grim picture of the battle.

Isaac stopped and knelt down. Rezin, almost running into him, took a step back and saw what the young warrior was attending to.

It was Dekker. He was lying on his back, looking more like a phantom than a man. His chest rose and fell calmly, his eyes were open, but one look at him was enough to raise alarm. His arms were in ruin. One of them, his right, looked like it had been run over multiple times by a massive transport. Pieces of splintered bone popped through blackened skin. Fingers twisted and bent at unnatural angles. Deep gouges ran up to his shoulder, sluicing blood.

"It looks...worse...than it is..." Dekker said weakly, seeing Rezin's face.

Rezin took a knee and quickly began to tear strips of his shirt away. "What have you done to yourself?"

Dekker coughed, gritting his teeth. "We killed them. Isn't that right, Isaac?"

Isaac nodded, one hand touching the old man's leg. "Hush now. Let the man work. Save your breath."

"Don't know what I'm saving it for," Dekker whispered, or tried to at least. He ended up coughing violently instead, groaning as his broken bones shifted.

"The channeling," Rezin said, now wrapping the old man's right arm. "You've completely fried your limbs. Burned and broke it all the way down to the bone."

"Tell me something I don't know."

Isaac watched Rezin as he tightened the bandage, earning a sharp hiss from Dekker.

"Will he live?"

Rezin began to rip more of his shirt away, double-wrapping the limbs as best he could.

"If I can stop the bleeding, then yes. I think so. The thing about channeling is that when it reaches the level Dekker's at, the power that flows through him both cuts and cauterizes the flesh."

"Finally, some good news," Dekker muttered wearily, resting his head back.

Rezin finished with the wrap, wiping his hands across his pant leg. "Isaac, I need water. Hot water, but don't boil it. Can you manage?"

Isaac nodded and disappeared back into the house.

On his back, Dekker looked grimly at Rezin, his voice sudden and grave. "What happened in there?"

Rezin said nothing for a moment, his chest falling. Then, "She's gone."

Dekker seemed to hold his breath and then let it out in a hiss, his whole body deflating. He said nothing, letting the words wash over him in waves of disbelief. He stared up at the cloudy sky and then closed his eyes.

"Liam?" Dekker asked after a couple seconds.

Rezin looked down at his hands. "Alive. If you can call it that."

"She didn't deserve that," Dekker said quietly, the wind snatching his words away. "Neither of them did." His chest hitched. "Oh, Av…"

They said nothing more until Isaac returned, carrying with him a small bowl of water he had warmed over the fire. Rezin took it gently, their eyes locking in the dim light.

"Should we really leave him alone in there?"

"Let the man grieve," Isaac answered quietly. He ran a hand through his hair, his voice heavy and on the verge of breaking. "Let him say goodbye."

Rezin turned back to Dekker and began to gently pour the warmed water over the bandages.

"These wraps aren't exactly clean, and neither are your wounds. Hopefully this will stem—" he stopped suddenly.

Dekker was crying quietly. Tears rolled down his dirty face, carving trails in the grime. He squeezed his eyes shut, his bottom lip trembling.

Isaac stood and walked off, dragging his sword behind him.

In silence, Rezin continued to clean the old man's wounds and wash the blood from his body. When he was finished, he wandered over to the burning vehicles and huddled down next to the smoldering wreckage. The dying fire provided some warmth, and it seemed to be the only comfort left in the world. He glanced over at Dekker, a blanket now covering him up to his chin, and then swung his eyes across the clearing, trying to spot Isaac. The young man was nowhere to be seen.

With nothing left to do but wait, Rezin stared sorrowfully at the cabin. After some time, he heard commotion from inside. Like something was being tossed around. He stayed where he was, shadows of movement passing between the holes in the walls.

A couple minutes later, Liam walked out into the darkness, axe in hand and a pack slung across his shoulder. At his back, from inside the cabin, a curtain of flame began to spread and climb up the broken frame toward the roof. The wood was dry and the fire was hungry. As the blaze grew, Liam turned to stare at it, his figure outlined in the glow.

Pulling himself up, Rezin quietly walked to his side. The heat from the growing inferno felt good against his face as he stood in silence next to the grieving man.

Rezin cleared his throat cautiously. "Liam...I'm sorry. I'm really sorry."

Heavy bags clung beneath Liam's bloodshot eyes, his mouth pressed into a thin line. He didn't answer, his gaze trained at the fire. Pieces of roof began to collapse in on itself, the lumber popping and sparking.

"I tried my best..." Rezin muttered helplessly, an anchor in his chest.

"It's not your fault," Liam whispered finally, his eyes orange in the reflected flame.

Rezin ran his tongue along his bottom lip. "It's not yours either, you know. You do know that, right?"

"My decisions led us here," Liam said, the trees surrounding the cabin swaying in the breeze, fueling the fire. "Every choice I made brought us to this moment."

Rezin was silent for a moment, letting the wind do the talking. Crossing his arms, he tried again.

"I didn't know her very well, but it was clear to me that you two loved each other. As terrible as her end was, at least she left this world in the arms of the one she cared most about. That's better than some."

Liam's shoulders drooped. "They raped her, Rezin. They raped her and they shoved a bomb inside her. I don't think she was thinking about me when she died."

"I would like to believe that you were *all* she was thinking about."

Liam pressed his hands into his eyes. "It doesn't matter anymore."

"I'm sorry you've been handed this pain, Liam. I truly am."

Liam raised his eyes to the sky, his voice frail and weak. "How am I supposed to go on without her? What is the point to all this now?"

Rezin gently touched Liam's arm. "She would want the best for you, I think. Don't you?"

A wavering sob crawled up Liam's throat. "I was supposed to take her away from all this. I promised her—" he tried to collect himself, his eyes wet. "We were supposed to go back, just like before...oh *god*..." he covered his face with his hands and cried silently, lost in his grief.

Rezin kept his hand on Liam's arm and when the sobs subsided a little, he took another approach.

"How did you two fall in love?"

Liam wiped his nose and looked at Rezin, confused. "W-what?"

"How did your paths cross?"

Liam scrubbed his eyes. "I don't know. She saved my life."

"Saved your life?"

Liam nodded and struggled to get himself under control. "Of course she did. In more ways than one."

"Tell me," Rezin said gingerly.

Liam ran the back of his hand across his face. "I was working a job with Dekker, only our second one together. We were out in the wild and in trouble. We had run out of food and water. I thought we were done for. We were so far out, miles from the cities. She found us. She gave us supplies. She was kind to us. She was young, but it was clear she was capable of taking care of herself."

"So you three teamed up?"

Liam shook his head, eye wet. "No. Well, for a little while we did, until we got back to Maltor. Then we went our separate ways."

"Oh?"

"Back then, I was considering a life in the Church," Liam explained, his voice fragile. "That's how I came to meet Dekker. That's why I went to The Chain all those years ago. I needed to see it for myself. I needed to believe that we had been saved by some kind of divine intervention. I was trying to figure out where I belonged."

"And you decided it wasn't the Church?"

"When I crossed over the first time—when I reached The Chain and looked up into the heavens—I prayed to the Creator for guidance. I needed help. I *needed* direction. You know what I got?"

Rezin shook his head.

"Absolute silence."

"What did you do after that?"

Liam stared at the burning cabin. "I went back to Maltor and told Dekker I had changed my mind. I left the city and went to Titan to look for work. That's where I ran into Avalice again. She was arguing with a merchant about a bow. I walked up to her and got the merchant to lower his price. Not wanting to feel like she owed me anything, she said she'd tag along on the next job I had. We got married a year later. Eventually we found ourselves back in Maltor and I introduced her to Dekker. We've been working jobs together ever since."

Rezin smiled in the waning light. "I'm glad you have those memories, Liam."

Liam just stared into the blaze.

"What about Isaac?" Rezin asked after a moment. "What's his story?"

"I'll let him tell you that one," Liam said quietly. He wiped his eyes and looked over at Dekker. "How is he?"

"Not great. I'd be shocked if he ever uses his right arm again."

Wordlessly, Liam went to him and sat down, dropping his pack to the ground. He crossed his legs and laid his axe across his knees.

Dekker looked at him from beneath his blanket, his voice cautious and kind. "I don't even know where to start, Liam…"

"Then don't say anything," Liam whispered, the wind ruffling through his hair. "I know she meant a lot to you as well."

"She was like the last star in the sky," Dekker said quietly.

Liam looked down at him. "I heard you ruined your arm."

Dekker grunted. "I didn't care much for that one anyway."

"You're the only reason any of us are still here," Liam said. "You and Isaac." He looked up suddenly. "Where has he gotten off to, anyway?"

"I barely know where I am, nevermind him."

Liam ran his hands across his axe. He felt like someone had buried it deep into his heart and then ripped it away. His mind buzzed and his throat felt tight. Exhaustion blew through him like a hurricane and his chest felt like it was on fire.

"I don't even want to ask," Dekker said from the ground, "but where the hell do we go from here?"

Liam gripped his axe. "Do you really have to ask?"

Dekker tried to sit up, propping himself up on his good hand. "Listen, Liam—"

Liam cut him off, his voice sharp. "Don't even try to talk me out of it."

"I understand why you'd want to follow—"

"If you understand, then there shouldn't be an end to that sentence."

Dekker sighed painfully, his brows knit together. "I know you're in pain, son. Heaven help me, but I do. But chasing after that madman isn't going to solve anything. We're weak, Liam. We're scattered. You heard him yourself, didn't you? He's meeting up with more Profanes, which means we'd be even more outnumbered than before. We'd be marching to our death."

Liam's voice became a hiss. "I died back there in that cabin, Dek. Right now, I'm on borrowed time with a singular purpose. That son of a *bitch* does not get to walk away from what he did to Avalice. Do you understand me?"

"What chance do we have against him?" Dekker pressed. "We'd be wiped out. Adding to that, it sounds like the Profanes have been rounding up infected, which adds another element to the mix."

"Then we'll blow them up before they reach The Chain," Liam stated flatly.

"And how do we do that, exactly?"

"You're not dead yet, are you? Once your arm heals—"

"It's useless, Liam," Dekker cut in. "You and I both know I'll never be able to use it again."

"Good thing you got two, then."

Dekker exhaled wearily. "I appreciate your confidence in me, but in case you didn't notice, Desmond is also a Transistor. Not only that, but he's younger, faster, and has both his arms. Counting on me is a quick path to death."

"There are other ways to kill them," Liam growled, bunching his fists.

"If you don't—"

"Enough," Liam said sourly. "If you don't want to come, then I'm not going to force you. You've saved us more times than I can count. I wouldn't hold it against you. But I'm going." He patted the pack next to him. "I scrounged what supplies I could before I torched the place. I have Kell's map. I even managed to retrieve some of the Rockflesh that was in your pouch, the one Desmond found. So I'm doing this with or without you."

Dekker laid back down and closed his eyes. "All right, Liam. All right. I hear you. You win."

Suddenly Isaac bloomed from the shadows around them, his tall figure whisking across the ground. He looked down at Liam and Dekker, his face dark.

"Where have you been?" Liam asked, looking up.

"When are we going after them?" Isaac asked instead of answering.

"Oh, not you too," Dekker groaned.

Rezin approached the small group, wringing his hands together. Liam appraised him, his eyes hooded in darkness.

"Change of plans," Liam said to him. "We're going after Desmond. I don't expect you to come with us. The tablets you gave us were taken in the fire. I'd apologize, but I don't think I could stomach it right now."

Rezin bobbed his head. "You don't have to explain anything to me. I understand. I'd probably do the same if I were in your boots." He looked at the group. "But Desmond is headed toward The Chain with a mass of Profanes and infected, correct?"

"If what we heard is to be believed, yes."

"Then if it's all the same to you, I'd like to continue on with you."

Liam blinked, shaking his head. "Why? Why the hell would you want to come? What is all this to you, anyway? What's your history with Desmond? He seems to hold a lot of malice toward you, toward the whole damn world."

"I know," Rezin said quietly. "Our relationship is complicated. And I take some responsibility in the tragedy that came about here, so I'd like to offer any help I can."

Liam chewed this over for a moment before answering. "At some point, you're going to need to tell me more about him. About what happened between you two. If we catch Desmond before he reaches The Chain, then that's where we'll confront him. There's no guarantee we'll even reach The Chain."

"I know, I just want to help."

Liam sighed. "Fine. Creator knows we could use all the help we can get, anyway."

Dekker grumbled from beneath his blanket before pushing it aside. "Well, if everyone here is so eager to die, I might as well follow you all off the cliff." Isaac helped the old man to his feet, one hand on his shoulder to steady him.

"Just don't yell at me if I'm a little slow," Dekker muttered.

Rezin looked at Liam. "So where do we go from here?"

Liam pulled out Kell's map and studied it in the dying light from the fire. "We know Desmond is headed toward The Chain. If he's got all those Profanes with him—helping him herd infected—then he's going to have to go around the Red Ravine, just like us." Liam traced a finger across the map. "There's a marsh on the western side of the Ravine. It's between the mountains and is far enough away that we won't be exposed to the gases. That's our route."

"Well let's get to it, then," Dekker said, testing his legs.

"It's a miracle you can even move," Rezin observed.

"The Creator gives me the strength I need," Dekker said, keeping his dead arm close to his side.

Together, the four readied themselves and then began to walk down the dark road, the cabin flickering in their wake.

Trailing the pack, Liam looked over his shoulder.

"Goodbye, Avalice," he whispered.

As he left, the weight in his chest was almost too much to bear.

Chapter 10

For two days they marched. The winding road took them out of the forest and into the wild. The trees gave way beneath a gloomy sky, the ever-shifting mass of darkness floating overhead like a dead river of cloud. The landscape turned rocky when they reached the end of the road, the broken asphalt simply ending in a pile of scattered rubble. After checking the map, Liam guided the group onward, their path rising along the growing hills.

In the distance, past the approaching mountain range, The Chain could be seen. It grew closer with every step, the thin black line swelling into something tangible. The colossal links could be spotted now, unmoving and titanic in size, rising to the heavens and disappearing into the grim sky.

Dead grass and dry shrubbery peppered the rocky hills. The ground continued to incline as they approached the outskirts of the Red Ravine. Liam took them up and around a field of giant boulders, their climb growing more intense as the hours ticked by.

At the end of the second day, they had reached the foot of a mountain range. The great peaks stretched and curved from horizon to horizon, marking the edge of the basin that was the Red Ravine.

They spent the following day traveling across treacherous foothills, parallel to the mountains, daring not ascend any further. Liam knew what lie just over the summits of the shadowy peaks. He had seen it once before.

A great hole, swathed in gases, that plummeted straight down through the core of Tectonic, all the way to the dead world below.

As the fourth day approached, the sky never changing despite the hour, Liam consulted the map once more. After chewing it over, the details of Kell's cartography growing thin, he informed the group that it was time to ascend.

"If I'm reading this right, then we've passed the edge of the Ravine and these mountains continue onward south. Most of them seem to be impassable, but here—" he pressed a finger to the map, "here there's a marsh between two of the peaks. It seems to be the only way to the other side. Unless we want to walk another ten days south?"

"I'd rather not," Dekker said wearily. The old man was holding up surprisingly well, but there had been a time two days prior that he had to let Isaac carry him. Despite his initial protests, he finally caved and let the young warrior hoist him onto his back, the strain of his injuries slowing him to a crawl.

Rezin peered at the map over Liam's shoulder. "Why would there be a marsh between the mountains? That seems extremely uncommon, doesn't it?"

"Things are changing," Liam said, storing the map away and swigging down a mouthful of water. "Maybe it's not a marsh at all, but that's what Kell's markings appear to be. Is everyone ready to climb?" he looked at Dekker. "Do you need Isaac's help again?"

"I'll be fine, but ask me again in an hour," the Transistor said, lifting his eyes to appraise the towering peaks before them. They cut into the inky heavens, the rocky slopes appearing as inviting as an axe to the throat.

"Let me have a sip of that water," Rezin said, holding out a hand. Liam passed it to him and then checked his pack. "We only have a little left. Hopefully it'll rain soon."

"Yes, wouldn't that make for a nice climb," Dekker muttered, still staring at the sharp rocks above.

Rezin capped the bottle and Liam stashed it away. He looked at Isaac as he shouldered his pack.

"You doing OK? You've barely said a word the past couple days."

Dekker grunted. "Yes, he's usually such a chatterbox, isn't he?"

Isaac just gazed up the slope, his face impassive.

"All right then," Liam said, checking to make sure his axe still hung at his hip. "Let's get this over with. Dekker, if you need to stop at any point, then say something. This will be the worst of it, physically. Once we make it up, we just have to make it across the marsh and then down into the other side."

"I'll be just fi—"

Dekker was cut off as a sound erupted from the sky. It was impossibly loud, a massive wave of noise that dropped from the clouds and crashed into their ears.

It sounded like a horn, a deep, singular, wailing note that echoed down and across the mountains toward them. The blast only lasted a handful of skull-rattling seconds before dying out, the shadow of its call shaking the earth beneath them.

"What on earth was that…?" Dekker said shakily as he lowered his hands from his ears. They were all staring at where the sound had originated, wide-eyed and in shock. The sky remained a swath of black ink, the clouds marching along in the wind as if nothing had happened.

"Did that come from The Chain?" Liam whispered, still shaking the impact of noise from his head. He swung his eyes to Rezin.

"Have you ever heard anything like that before?"

Rezin's face was white.

Dekker dug a finger into his ear with his good hand. "Think I'm down an arm and an ear. Void below, but that was loud."

"We shouldn't stick around here," Isaac said quietly. "Whatever that was, I doubt it signals anything good."

Liam continued to stare at Rezin and then finally snapped out of his trance-like state. He clapped the bald man on the shoulder.

"You OK?"

"I'm fine." Rezin said uneasily. "I think Isaac is right, though. We should be off."

Staring dreadfully at the summit before them, the four lowered their heads and began to climb.

Soon they fell into a weary rhythm. The going was slow and the hours seemed to stretch out before them like melting wax. Liam felt the fatigue of the past few days bleed through his muscles and it wasn't long before Dekker had to tap Isaac on the shoulder.

Liam had no clue where the young man got the strength to carry him, but without blinking, Isaac crouched down so that Dekker could clamber onto his back with a muttered apology.

It took half the day to reach what Liam guessed was the midway point. They all took a breather and passed around the dwindling water supply. The going was brutal, the uncharted slope littered with massive rock structures and shale. More than once, Rezin had slipped and almost split his head open or gone tumbling down the side.

After an hour, they continued upward. Liam's legs burned and Rezin was sweating heavily despite the rising winds. The cold was growing relentless and the exposure was beating them down almost as much as the incline. It was getting harder and harder to breathe the closer they got to the top, each pull of air a little more shallow than the last. Only Isaac seemed unaffected by the conditions, but Liam guessed that even he was suffering, despite his outward appearances.

As the day came to a close, the exhausted party finally crested the summit and turned south to stare down the spine of ridges before them. Sitting snugly between their peak and the next, was a kind of dim flatland. It was covered by a thick fog and rested just a couple miles from where they stood. Glowing orange light could be seen in the mist, the wispy tendrils clinging to the mountains that marked its border.

"Doesn't that look inviting?" Dekker mumbled. He turned around and faced north, the jagged peaks looking like black bone.

"Guess it makes sense now why we have to go through the mountain marsh," Rezin whispered, his breath trailing in the wind.

Liam turned as well and saw a dangerous, sharp ring of cliffs that plummeted down into certain death. The north face of the mountain appeared to have been scraped away, leaving a smooth slope that conjoined with others along the range.

And hovering in the far distance was the roof of the Red Ravine. An orange smog clouded the heavens, a diseased pollution that seemed to exhale from below, filling the natural basin created by the mountain range. Massive spires of twisting neon rock rose out of the smoky aura, giving the illusion that great horned monstrosities lie hidden beneath the coat of wafting gloom.

"So that's what the end of the world looks like," Dekker whispered in awe.

Rezin shifted, a sudden wind smacking them all across the face. "Perhaps it's best if we get off this mountain. I know we're hundreds of miles from it, but I would rather not play with fate right now. Those gases look eager."

After taking one last glance into the distant abyss, the four turned and began to scale down the south side of the mountain toward the bizarre marshlands. The going was easier on the legs but hell on the knees. The rocky slope was thick with loose gravel, causing them all to check their balance every few steps. Dekker made the descent on his own but would occasionally reach out and grab onto Isaac's arm so he didn't fall.

As they trekked down toward the marsh, Liam continued to study it. At the moment, they were above it, giving him a clear view of its entirety—or at least what he could see of it through the mists.

From what he could tell, it appeared to be at least a dozen miles from end to end, the exit walled on either side by those impossibly steep cliffs.

Orange bulbs pulsed through the fog, a sign of further contamination and mutation. Liam prayed that when they passed through the marsh, none of the Rockflesh would explode, filled to capacity by the all-encompassing disease.

About halfway down, Rezin stopped suddenly and pointed to the far end of the marsh.

"Look! Are those...torches?"

Everyone slowed and trained their attention to where he was pointing. After a moment, Liam saw them. At first, he thought it was just a cluster of Rockflesh in the mist, but upon further inspection, he saw that the lights were flickering and moving away from them.

"That must be Desmond and his Profanes," Dekker said darkly, catching his breath. "Can't think of anyone else who would risk such a dangerous excursion." He blinked. "Besides us, of course."

"Do you see that?" Rezin continued, straining his eyes. "Trailing behind them?"

It took a second, but Liam eventually spotted what he was talking about. It was a second cluster of orange, a gloomy dome of light in the fog, and this time there was no denying what it was.

"He's taken the infected as his prisoners," Liam said. He set his jaw. "It seems our assumption was correct. He's going to use them to blow up The

Chain."

"That seems incredibly risky," Dekker said. "How does he know they won't detonate before then?"

"He probably had the Profanes round up anyone who showed early signs of the disease," Liam stated grimly. "It certainly would eliminate a lot of the risk, considering how long a journey it is. By the time they reach The Chain, most will have advanced to the later stages."

"And will be in prime shape for maximum impact," Rezin finished, shaking his head. "Those poor people."

"Come on," Liam said, beginning to descend once again. "We're almost to the marsh and he can't be more than ten miles ahead of us."

"Only ten miles," Dekker muttered, wincing as he followed.

They continued on, the sky starting to grumble and then spit rain. Despite the urgency of their trek, Liam was forced to slow his pace. The rocks began to shine beneath a slick coat of moisture as the drizzle opened up across the range. They pulled their hoods up and pressed onward, the dim sky barely doling out enough light to see the path ahead.

After an hour, the ground began to level out. They had descended down into the space between the mountains, a wall of towering fog rising before them. Winking between the thick mists were pockets of orange, appearing as if electric lights guided their way.

The ground had slowly changed from loose rock to damp earth, with sprouts of wet grass and mud mixing beneath their boots. As they headed toward the fog wall, Liam looked around him, up at the twin peaks that bordered the march ahead. The sharp mountain summits seemed to dwarf them now and he realized just how far they had come, the stretch of bland rock deceptively distant.

"I feel like I'm walking through soup," Dekker said as they breached the fog.

"Visibility is going to be a problem now," Liam said, feeling the mist cling wetly to his skin as he crossed over. "I want everyone to stay close. I have no idea what we'll find in here or what lies ahead. I don't want any unexpected surprises."

The world became noticeably muted inside the expanse of gray, the air uncomfortably still and stagnant. As they splashed through the mounting sludge, a terrible smell invaded Liam's nostrils, causing him to wince. He checked the map once more and saw the last of Kell's notes.

"There anything of use on that parchment?" Rezin asked, wrapping his arms around himself as the rain continued to lazily fall around them.

"Seems to be only two things," Liam said, walking around a large brown puddle. "The first is to stay along spires of Rockflesh. It seems as if they lead across to the exit."

Rezin eyed one of the glowing fangs, the surface appearing bloodshot with orange disease.

"Can't say I'm thrilled about that," he said softly. "What else does it say?"

Liam looked up. "It says to keep quiet."

Dekker looked at Liam sideways. "Well doesn't that just fill my soul with optimism?"

Liam put the map away and hefted the pack on his shoulder, feeling how much lighter it was now. "Let's just get across as quickly as we can. Isaac, if Dekker starts to slow, are you good to carry him again?"

Isaac nodded, his eyes sifting through the dense blanket of stinking smog.

Dekker looked up at him, noting his unease. "Stop looking so nervous. When you're nervous, I'm nervous. And when I'm ner—"

"Dekker," Liam called.

The Transistor looked over at him.

"Shut up."

"Right, yes…"

They pressed forward, the soggy earth stretching out before them and disappearing from sight. The puddles they splashed through began to grow in size, getting deeper as they traversed the wetlands. The drizzle continued, taking its time to soak them. Bits of greenery began to pop up, long reeds of bending grass and stiff clusters of unknown plant life. Liam guessed that this bowl between the mountains was where most of the rainwater gathered, an isolated basin that evolved over time into what it was now.

It wasn't long before they were forced to take wide detours around bodies of deep, stinking water. As they skirted around these, Liam kept his eye on the surface of the pools, half-expecting something to come lunging out at them.

The ground turned even more muddy, slowing them and pulling them to the earth. The natural towers of Rockflesh began to space out the deeper they waded in, and more than once they wandered blindly between them, only hoping that they were headed in the right direction.

After an immeasurable length of time, Liam suddenly slowed, raising his fist to stop the others behind him. Something stirred in his gut and he cocked his ear, listening.

Rezin squelched over to his side, his voice hushed. "What is it?"

Liam felt his stomach squirm. "Do you hear that?" He whispered.

After a second, they all heard it. It was a low whine, a muted, single note that held no echo in the fog.

Rezin swallowed hard and nervously licked his lips. "What on earth was that…?"

Dekker and Isaac joined them, waiting for the sound to repeat. A few seconds ticked by and then it did. It was the same chilling note, with a slight rise in pitch as it died. In the fog, it was impossible to decipher just how far away the source was, the murky haze swallowing up any sense of distance.

"That almost sounded like a child, didn't it?" Dekker whispered tensely.

"Void below, don't say that!" Rezin exclaimed, his eyes going wide. "My skin is crawling enough as is."

"What do you want to do?" Dekker asked, shooting a nervous glance at Liam.

Before he could answer, the whine came a third time. It made the hairs on the back of his neck stand up. It really did sound like a child, one that was in distress.

"We don't really have a choice, do we?" he said as the sound died once more. "Let's go. Isaac, keep that sword handy though, all right?"

They continued inward, the group now on edge. The strange noise didn't repeat, and Liam hoped that whatever it was had moved on.

The ground grew soggier and they eventually had to stick to plates of random rock that jutted from the sappy soil to progress. It was slow going, but once they made it through the worst of it, the earth firmed back up enough to traverse it once again.

As Liam adjusted his hood, the fabric hopelessly soaked through now, he came to a stop, his boots splashing. He squinted in the swirling fog, his eyes locking on something ahead of them.

"There's something there," he whispered as Isaac came to his side. "Do you see it?"

Isaac nodded.

"Is that a...person?" Rezin asked quietly, the dark shape pulsing in the muck a couple dozen feet ahead of them.

Slowly, they crept forward, the mists clearing a little. As they reached the shape, Liam felt his pulse quicken...

"Oh, hell," Dekker muttered as the group circled around the edge of a muddy pool.

Standing at the center, waist-deep, was an infected. A thick band of Rockflesh glowed from the woman's neck, her hands helplessly digging into the sinking mud as if trying to escape its clutches.

"Hello...?" she called, her eyes ablaze, his skin slick with rain and fever.

Liam crossed his arms from the edge of the bog, assessing the stage of her infection. Isaac stood behind him, a statue of silence. Dekker and Rezin's face dropped in despair as they watched the young woman struggle to free herself, each movement pulling her deeper into the squelching pit.

"Help...me..." she whispered, her eyes finding and then losing them as madness ate away at her mind.

"She must have been a straggler," Dekker observed, his voice laced with sympathy.

Liam raised his voice, calling out to her. "How long have you been stuck here?"

The woman snapped her head in Liam's direction, her eyes rolling wildly in their sockets. "Have you seen...where am...how do I...get home?" she called, her thoughts tumbling over one another.

"Desmond," Liam continued, "how long ago did he and his Profanes leave you here?"

The woman coughed, the patch of Rockflesh flaring around her throat. "Profanes? Death cult...hate...Creator. Want to die. Desmond wants...everyone to die."

The woman began to cry. "Where's Rin? Where did she go...?"

Dekker walked to Liam's side and reached into the pack, pulling out the small pouch of Rockflesh. When Liam saw what he was doing, he reached out and grabbed the Transistor's wrist.

"What do you think you're doing?"

"I'm putting her out of her misery," Dekker said.

"You're in no condition to waste your energy on her," Liam came back.

Dekker jerked his hand away. "Where's your heart? Look at her! She doesn't deserve to die like this!"

"Maybe so, but I'm not letting you channel. You're just getting your strength back, I don't need you exerting it without a good reason."

The woman's voice cut into their argument, a rising, pleading thing. "Please...help me! I'm dying...I think I'm dying..." she tried to wade forward but was sucked down deeper, the bog rising to her chest now

"Void help us, don't make her suffer," Dekker said.

"Stay put," Liam hissed.

The woman's face twisted with a kind of lost panic. "Bad...bad things coming. Coming from the sky...it's going to come from the sky..."

"What is Desmond so afraid of!?!" Liam yelled.

The woman looked at him, her face clearing for a split-second of all madness. "You've heard them, haven't you? Heard them calling to one another... so loud..." the mud rose to her chin.

"OK, enough, this ends now," Dekker said, sinking his hand into the pouch.

Before he could go any further, Isaac was suddenly before them, a knife in hand. With a quick flick of the wrist, the blade whistled from his fingers and buried itself into the woman's forehead. The force of it snapped her head back, paralyzing her expression forever as the last of her sank down into the mud.

Stunned, Liam and the others watched in silence as she disappeared from sight, the bog eating the rest of her and digesting her down from sight.

"We done here?" Isaac asked before turning away.

"Yes, can we please get out of this place?" Rezin said somberly, hands clutching his cloak, his knuckles white.

Liam eyed the pouch of Rockflesh in Dekker's hand. "Better keep that with you, just in case."

"You sure?" Dekker muttered. "Wouldn't want to waste my energy..."

"We're moving," Liam said, starting forward once again. The group followed. As they moved their way across the wet stones and soggy earth, Liam began to feel a mounting sense of claustrophobia. The fog barrier was starting to get to him, the wet, muted air pushing its way down his throat, filling his lungs. He pulled his hood off his head and kept his eyes moving as quickly as he feet. He tried to push his dread aside but couldn't shake it.

Something was out there watching them.

After a couple minutes of tense progress, Liam's ears picked up distant footsteps, lots of them, splashing through puddles, announcing some unseen presence. It came from all around them, but it was impossible to tell just how far away they were. Everyone else seemed to hear it as well, an air of tension seeping between them.

The further they went, the more urgent the footsteps became, a swirling, sprinting paranoia that pulsed with every beat of Liam's racing heart. He felt his shoulders tense, his axe brandished and ready for whatever came out of the fog at them.

A whooping cry froze the blood in his veins, a shrill, frantic thing. He exchanged a glance with Isaac and he nodded. It was the same sound as before, the one that sounded like some kind of child. Dekker clutched a piece of Rockflesh in his hand, ready and waiting to absorb its power the second it was needed.

Suddenly, stumbling from the cloak of fog before them, a man emerged, a groan escaping his lips as he collapsed to the ground.

Liam stifled a cry of surprise and stepped back, the squirming body crawling toward them with a sick kind of desperation.

"What is that?!" Rezin half-yelled, his eyes wide.

The man looked up at them, and to everyone's surprise, they saw that he was a Profane. He pulled himself up on his knees, his muddy clothes bearing the symbol of the broken chain. He reached out to them, his voice shaking and pleading.

"Save me...please!" he cried.

Suddenly the footsteps came back with a vengeance, as if dozens of unseen people were sprinting in circles around them, just outside their field of vision.

"Liam, his arms," Isaac said quietly, pointing to the Profane before them.

Liam looked and then grimaced, a new horror emerging.

It appeared as if something had gnawed on the man's arms, the flesh torn and bitten down to the bone. Strips of muscle glistened with blood as he raised them to the group, his eyes streaming with terrified tears.

"They ate me," he wept, his whole body shaking. "They forced me down and then they ate me..." He suddenly shuddered violently and then collapsed, never to rise again.

A roar erupted from the fog, an animalistic snarl that chilled the blood in Liam's veins.

"RUN!" Liam yelled, not waiting to see what was coming.

In a panicked splash, the four of them bolted for the next spire of Rockflesh, their boots churning in the mud as they fled. The whoops and whistles began to escalate around them, a haunting sign that whatever was out there was communicating and coordinating an attack.

They managed to get a hundred feet before they came.

Liam saw them first, a rush of bodies that charged from the fog. His heart crawled up his throat as they drew close, their features coming into focus. He gripped his axe and readied himself, calling for Isaac at his back.

The shapes fell on them, at least six in the initial assault. They were human, but barely so. As they hooted and screamed, weapons raised, Liam saw that they were wearing cloaks of flayed skin, a disorienting detail that he found difficult to track. Tied to their arms were other severed arms, creating a fleshy armor embedded with bone. It made them look as if they were mutants, some sort of altered human race. Their faces were smothered with dried mud, making them appear as if they were wearing masks. Their eyes were wide and white, bulging from the caked earth and filled with hunger. They wielded an array of swords and axes, remnants of previous victims.

Liam crouched and blocked a wild lunge as they reached him, his axe clanging against a rusted broadsword. His attacker, a woman with six arms tied to her own, shrieked in a rage and spun, slashing for his throat. Liam ducked and jammed the head of his axe up and into her jaw, breaking a mouthful of teeth in the process. Stunned, the woman staggered back giving Liam a chance to chop at her chest, collapsing her rib cage in a brutal blow.

Dekker spun in place, Rockflesh glowing in his hand, trying to spot a target. Isaac grabbed him and Rezin and threw them behind him.

"Don't!" Isaac growled, seeing Dekker preparing to channel. "Not unless you must!"

"We're being attacked!" Dekker yelled, the growing mob swarming for them.

With no time to argue, Isaac spun toward the wall of cannibals, his sword turning to a blur of iron death. His blade found its mark, the massive edge cleaving through four of the attackers at the chest. Blood exploded from severed torsos, and body parts rained down around them.

"Keep moving!" Liam howled, "We have to get out of this damn marsh! MOVE!" He deflected a spear that was thrown at him, the long, wide blade narrowly missing his left eye. Two more cannibals came screaming from the fog, headed right for him.

Cursing, trying his best to run, he backpedaled and caught a downward strike from a long sword. Grunting, he shoved the axe aside and spun with the momentum. He backhanded his attacker across the face and then sunk his blade, one-handed, into the man's throat. The second cannibal fell on him before he could pull his blade free. A short dagger came soaring for him and Liam winced as he felt a line of pain drawn across his arm. He dropped his axe and let out a pained gasp, his eyes snapping to the weapon and its wielder. Before another blow could be delivered, Liam grabbed the cannibal's wrist and broke it, bending the bone to the side with a vicious twist. Howling, the man dropped the dagger, giving Liam a split-second to retrieve it. He did so in one quick swoop, then stood and plunged it into the man's neck, bringing forth a geyser of blood.

Behind him, Isaac was fending off the majority of the assailants as best he could, all while still trying to run. His large frame shielded Dekker and Rezin as they all splashed through the mud, breath heaving from their lungs as the foggy shapes continued to pour from the mists.

"We have to be close, hurry!" Liam called, waving them on and retrieving his axe. He rushed back to help Isaac, who had a pair of cuts along his left shoulder where his armor ended. Four more cannibals charged their group, their skin-cloaks fluttering, their teeth bared.

Isaac stepped into them and swung, muscles straining with effort as his sword arced out before him and crunched through the attackers in an explosion of gore. One of the cannibals dove under the deadly blow and rolled up in front of Isaac, knife in hand, eyes alight as he stabbed toward Isaac's exposed stomach.

Liam's axe plowed into the man's jaw, severing it from his face. Teeth and blood erupted from the impact, and Liam saw the man's tongue go flying off into the mist.

Panting, Isaac righted himself and faced the next wave. Liam, gasping, did the same, his body drained. Facing them were twelve more cannibals, all clicking their tongues and snarling at them. They formed a semicircle around Liam and the others, more careful now that they knew their victims could fight back.

"There's a lot of them," Isaac said quietly between breaths.

Liam looked back at Dekker, who was standing as if frozen by Rezin.

"Be ready. I don't know if we can shield you two from all of them. If they rush us all at once, I want you to—"

His words were cut short as a deafening roar came from the fog at the cannibal's backs. The cannibals immediately silenced, their posture changing in an instant. Liam, wincing beneath the wave of sound, looked at Isaac, feeling dread seep into his chest. Isaac set his jaw as the roar sounded again.

Suddenly, the ground began to rumble beneath their boots. Crying out in unexpected fear, the cannibals dispersed in an instant, clambering to get ahead of their peers and away from whatever new hell approached.

Liam swallowed hard.

It sounded like something *massive* was coming their way.

"Dekker, Rezin, GO!" Liam yelled, grabbing at their cloaks and shoving them ahead toward the next spire of Rockflesh.

"You need me!" Dekker protested, skidding in the mud. "I can fight, my arms are fine!"

The ground quaked.

"No, they're not! Let us take this one!" Liam argued, his boots vibrating. They could now hear something of great size sprinting through the marsh right for them.

"Liam—"

Isaac stepped forward and pushed Dekker, his voice low and urgent. "Please, Dek. We'll meet you on the other side of the marsh. Go."

Hissing between his teeth, Dekker looked at them both and then, after a moment of indecision, he left, followed in tow by Rezin. As they disappeared into the fog, Liam turned to face whatever was coming, a looming shadow now beginning to emerge from the thick mists.

"Probably could have used him," Liam muttered, heart dancing in his chest as he squeezed his axe.

"Just stay with me," Isaac said calmly. "I feel like I'm going to need you."

Another roar shattered through the air, followed by a sudden shape that came thundering from the fog, headed straight for them. When Liam saw what they faced, his blood ran cold.

It was an absolutely massive alligator. It stood at least seven feet tall, its long, wide snout gaping to expose a set of knife-sized teeth that surged straight for his head.

"LOOK OUT!" Liam screamed, diving to the side. Isaac dove in the opposite direction as the beast bulldozed the spot where they had just been standing. Its legs were the size of tree trunks, its scales clothed in mud and dried blood. Its long tail snapped out like a whip as it spun back around, almost taking Isaac's head off.

"It's infected!" Liam screamed, pulse roaring in his ears.

He backed off, trying to form some plan of attack, his eyes trained on the massive monster's tail. It was riddled with Rockflesh, the tip hosting a great bulb that flickered dangerously. Orange veins spider-webbed up toward the creature's backside, the infection still taking root across its body.

The alligator raised itself to its full height, its eyes glowing neon orange, and hissed menacingly at Liam, its jaws snapping.

Liam took another step back, the creature towering before him, its body thick with natural armor, leaving little room for a wounding blow.

The creature lunged for him, teeth exposed. Liam ducked and slid away from it, raising his axe as he did so. He felt a rush of air blast past him, and his axe glanced harmlessly across its thick legs.

Arms vibrating from the strike, Liam sprung back to his feet and wiped sweat from his eyes. The alligator spun around, snapping its tail at Liam. The strike caught Liam across the shoulder and he went flying backward, feeling as if his arm had turned to stone, a heavy pain shooting down his body. With a grunt, he splashed into a shallow pool and gasped, head pounding.

The alligator approached, focused on its injured prey. Its shadow loomed over Liam as he struggled to stand, his balance failing in the sinking mud. A second before his head was bitten clean off, Isaac whirled into the fray with all the force of a raging tornado.

His sword came crashing down over the beast's head, the sharp blade crunching across the monster's eyes. Its flesh remained intact, but the sheer weight of Isaac's weapon was enough to stun it for a moment, allowing Liam a panicked retreat.

"Is it broken?" Isaac breathed, nodding toward Liam's injured arm.

Liam shook his hand, already feeling the numbness leaving. "No, it just went dead for a second."

Isaac backed up, both hands gripping his sword, his eyes trained on the recovering alligator. "We're not going to last long if we don't put this thing down soon. We've got speed, but this thing outmatches us on every other front."

The monster crouched and hissed at them, its gaping jaws widening.

"That thing's tail is like a bomb waiting to go off," Liam panted, circling their foe, his words rushed. "If it strikes out with enough force, it's all over for us."

Isaac jumped back as the beast snapped at him. "I'll worry about that; you just wait for an opening!"

Liam held his axe out in front of him, his shoulder throbbing. "Here it comes!"

They dove in opposite directions once more, the ground slowing their movement to a maddening pace. This time, the alligator went for Isaac, its body changing direction in an instant. It was like watching a river suddenly change course and smash into an embankment, the violence like an overflowing force of nature.

Isaac managed to get himself into position a second before the creature's jaws closed. Isaac stopped the attack with his sword, the long blade held horizontally. The alligator's teeth slammed down around it, like a horse around a bit, and Liam saw Isaac's veins begin to bulge as he held the creature in place.

"LIAM!" Isaac yelled, his boots sliding backward in the mud as the alligator pressed him.

Liam charged, pulse roaring in his ears. He timed his slide between the creature's flickering tail, a prayer on his lips as he leapt into a skid. The tail missed him by a fraction and then he was plowing, feet-first, beneath its hindquarters. Mud sprayed his vision as he swung out and up, his axe finding its mark and drawing a thick line of blood where the creature's back leg met its soft underbelly.

Immediately, the alligator went down, its body crashing around Liam like a mountain collapsing. Its jaws snapped at the open air, coming together like crunching metal, and it rolled onto its back, blood sluicing from the wound. Its tail came around and partially caught Liam across the ribs, the breath leaving his lungs as he went sprawling.

Without waiting, Isaac sprang forward and planted a boot on the creature, using it as a platform to leap into the air. Liam blinked mud away and saw the young man somersault forward, his blade spinning like a wheel of death.

CLICK.

The explosion of the rocket thrusters was instant and loud enough to rattle Liam's teeth as he watched Isaac come roaring down like a guillotine. With the boosters activated, Isaac's sword met the base of the tail with all the force of an avalanche. The blade sunk through the meat with a squealing clash and cleaved the thing off in a single stroke. Blood fountained from the stump as the flesh parted, coating the ground in a viscous ooze.

Holding his side, Liam hauled himself to his feet, watching as the now-dead tail twitched and rolled away, the Rockflesh intact.

Knowing this would be their only chance, Liam charged the upturned, wounded beast while Isaac twirled and brought his sword around once more.

They struck together. Their weapons met the beast in its guts, the sharpened iron sinking deep into the soft belly. Without a moment's pause, Liam wrenched his axe away and brought it down a second time, feeling his injuries howl in protest. The alligator hissed angrily, still gushing blood, and tried to roll away, but Isaac smashed the flat side of his blade against the animal's head, dazing it for a moment.

Leaping up onto its exposed stomach, Isaac raised his sword and plunged it deep into the creature's meaty throat, burying half the blade in the process.

"MOVE!" Isaac commanded, twisting the hilt and diving away. Liam jerked himself back, half falling, and watched as the boosters activated once more.

The massive weapon moved on its own, traveling down the length of the alligator's stomach as it jettisoned forward at an incredible velocity. It parted the meat with ease, splitting the creature's stomach open in a wave of death. When it reached the severed stump, the thrusters died and the sword went end-over-end, landing with a thud, point down in the mud, inches from where Liam stood.

The animal writhed on its back, its insides leaking out and across its gutted body. Blood pulsed and gurgled from the death blow in absurd volumes, its body draining of its life force.

Isaac and Liam stood tense, panting, and watched to see if the great beast would rise from the incredible blow.

It didn't. It's jaws slowed, the snapping of its teeth growing weaker and weaker until finally the daunting beast grew still.

Neither Isaac nor Liam said anything for a moment, the rush of battle still raging through their veins. Liam's shoulder and side ached miserably as he lowered his axe and finally breathed.

"I...I think it's dead," he exhaled as some of the tension drained from his inflamed muscles.

Isaac slowly sat down on the ground, and then wordlessly, he laid back.

Liam limped over to his side and sat, wiping blood and grime from his face.

"You OK?" he asked, still trying to calm his heart.

From the ground, Isaac closed his eyes. "Just give me a minute. *Shit.*"

Chapter 11

L iam and Isaac trudged through the marsh, shoulder to shoulder. The mist seemed to be thinning, a hopeful sign that the exit was near. The spires of Rockflesh continued to guide them forward, and Liam wondered if perhaps the cannibals had erected them in some archaic attempt at cartography.

His shoulder and side throbbed from where the alligator had struck him and he marveled that none of his bones had been shattered. Even so, he found breathing a laborious task now, each pull of air feeling like a knife to the ribs.

Isaac seemed to be no worse for wear, but the young warrior was skilled in the art of hiding his injuries. His sword was slotted across his back, cleaned of mud and dripping blood. After the battle, he had discarded his cloak, the fabric soaked through and tattered. He strode now without it, his dark hair damp with moisture.

"Dekker and Rezin shouldn't be too far ahead," Liam said, breaking the silence.

"If the cannibals didn't get them," Isaac responded quietly.

"Pretty sure that damned animal chased them off," Liam said, scanning the clearing mists. If they were attacked again, he wasn't sure he had the strength to lift his axe.

"Thanks for saving my skin back there," Liam said, splashing through a puddle.

Isaac just grunted.

"Can't count how many times you've pulled me out of the furnace since we started working together," Liam continued. "I think you've saved all of us at least a dozen times over. Me, Dekker, Avalice—" the words died on his lips, a sudden shadow reemerging.

He slowed, her name burning his throat.

Isaac noticed the sudden change and slowed as well, turning around. His face looked weary and tired, dark bags clinging beneath his eyes.

"Liam?" he asked quietly.

Liam swallowed hard, her sudden memory lunging for his chest. It wasn't like he had forgotten about her, but he had just been so preoccupied with traveling this mountain and staying alive and—

"I'm OK," Liam whispered, his thoughts swirling.

A lump formed in his throat, the pain coming so quickly that he was almost devoured by it. It was like turning around to find an arrow whistling through the air, straight for your heart.

Liam gritted his teeth.

The arrow plunged deep into his chest.

Isaac looked at him, his eyes gentle. "I miss her, too."

Liam took a steadying breath and then continued to march, thoughts of Avalice dancing through his fatigued mind. He bathed in them, each one bringing memories of joy, followed by the terrible realization that he would never be able to create new ones with her. It was like stepping off a cliff and then blacking out, only to reawaken and see that you were still plummeting toward certain death.

"I haven't really thought about her since we left the cabin," Liam admitted, boots sloshing through the mud, Isaac at his shoulder.

Isaac said nothing, letting Liam speak.

"With everything that's been happening, I was just so focused on getting us all through these mountains safely," Liam muttered, a knot in his chest. He hated that. Hated that someone had put that there and buried it deep to burn away at him.

Desmond.

"She should still be here with us," Liam said, his voice cracking. "And it's hard to remember she's not."

"Liam?"

Liam stopped and turned to see Isaac staring at him.

"What?"

"What are we doing here?" Isaac asked quietly.

Liam blinked, surprised by the question. "Doing?"

Isaac stepped toward him, his voice soft. "Where are we *going*?"

Liam opened his mouth but couldn't seem to wrap his tongue around the words.

"You know I'd follow you straight into the Red Ravine if you asked," Isaac continued, "but...where does the end lie with you?"

Liam finally found his voice and shook his head. "We're going after Desmond. I thought I made that clear back at the cabin. Are you suddenly having second thoughts? Is that it?"

Isaac grunted. "No. I want to see him dead just as much as you. But what about Dekker? He's not like you and I. He has...hope."

Liam examined Isaac's face, unsure if he had ever heard him express himself so openly. "Dekker chose to come with me. Just like you did. He's free to leave whenever he wishes."

"Dekker loved Avalice," Isaac said, his voice low, "and I know he hates what was done to her. But he doesn't cling to anger like you do. He believes in forgiveness. This journey, if any of us make it out alive, is going to change him. This is death for the sake of death."

"What are you saying?" Liam asked carefully.

Isaac looked off into the mist. "I don't know, Liam. I guess I just wish things were different. I wish we could all come out of this whole. But even now, I can see the pieces falling away. And that hurts." He shifted his weight and then met Liam's eyes. "That's all."

Liam looked down at his hands, saw his nails caked in blood and dirt. He let Isaac's words roll over him like a dark tide and realized that the young man was right.

"When I encouraged us to go on this journey," Isaac continued, "I was of the same mindset as you. I wanted us to execute Rezin's request and then step away from all of this. I wanted us to take a break. I wanted you and Avalice to be happy, together, in safety, if only for a little while." His eyes fell to the ground. "And I'm sorry for that. I'm sorry I played a part in all of this death." He balled his hands into fists. "Sometimes I feel like that's all I'm good for."

"Hey," Liam said gently, going to his side. "Don't go there. You've been nothing but a friend to Avalice and I. I know Dekker loves you like a son. You're more to us than a blade. Don't you ever forget that."

"I miss her, Liam," Isaac whispered.

Liam felt his eyes well up. "I miss her too, Isaac."

A wet breeze blew between them, and their eyes fell away from one another. Silently, they continued their trek through the final stretch of the marsh. After a couple of minutes, Liam looked across at Isaac.

"You know, a couple days back Rezin asked me what your story was."

Isaac kept his eyes ahead.

Liam looked away. "When he asked, I realized that even I didn't fully know. I remember coming back to Maltor with Avalice after we got married, and we ran into Dekker again. But you were there with him. I asked Dek who you were and he just said you were someone who needed help."Liam felt a small smile cross his lips. "That was enough for me. I just accepted it and soon realized that I was better off not asking. You were young then, just a teenager, but I could tell you didn't want anyone prying into your privacy. You stuck with Dekker and kept your mouth shut. You never complained and proved yourself extremely useful when we went out on jobs. Dekker seemed happier when you were around, despite your almost constant silence." Liam sighed. "And so I didn't implore any further. As the years went on, I just kept the questions I had about you at arm's length. Soon, I began to think of you as a friend. You became one of us. Just another lost soul trying to make his way through this miserable world." Liam glanced over at Isaac. "But the questions never left."

Isaac was silent for almost a full minute before he spoke. When he did, his words came out slowly, as if he were unearthing something long dead.

"Dekker saved my life."

Liam stayed silent and let the young man continue.

"When I was young, my father caught me doing something he didn't approve of," Isaac said, his voice almost a whisper. "He found me...fooling around...with someone he thought I shouldn't be fooling around with. I grew up in Titan and the slums we lived in were a bad place. But I made friends. Mostly boys." He looked at Liam knowingly and then cast his eyes back to the ground. "When they caught me, my parents were enraged. My mother just as much as my father. They told me that I was an abomination. That I was unnatural. Even in the slums, amongst the lowest of the low, they were still so *ashamed* of me."

"I'm sorry," Liam offered quietly.

"My father dragged me into the alley behind our house, looking for my friend. My friend was there, along with some others." Isaac took a long breath. "And then he beat me in front of them. Beat me within an inch of my life. I can still remember how scared I was. He had never done anything like that before. It was like he had turned into someone else. As he beat me, my friends just watched. They were in shock. They were terrified. I remember hearing someone crying, begging my father to stop. He didn't until I lie broken at his feet, trembling, bruised, and bleeding. I think he thought I was dead because he left me there and went off to drink at the inn." Isaac took a moment and visibly gathered himself. "While he was gone, I managed to crawl back into our hut. My mother was there and she seemed surprised to see me. I lay on the floor and cried, begging her to help me. Do you know what she did?"

Liam just shook his head.

"She locked me away in the cupboard until my father got back. I could hear them arguing, trying to figure out what to do with me. I laid there in that cupboard for what felt like an eternity. I prayed to anything I thought would listen." Isaac stared into the distance. "It was in that cupboard that I realized the Creator didn't exist. Or that if he did, then he couldn't see me there."

"How did you get out?" Liam asked gently after a moment had passed.

"My father finally dragged me out. I remember begging him for a cup of water, but it was like I didn't exist. I was dead to him." Isaac shook his head. "Never understood how someone could treat their own like that."

"That's terrible," Liam said, feeling his stomach twist. "You didn't deserve that."

"I know. But back then, I felt like I did. Like somehow I *was* an abomination. I was ashamed of myself and felt guilty that I had made my parents so angry. I blamed myself. I hated myself. I felt like I was a burden on my parents' existence. And so...I left. I ran away that night. I know they heard me leave and they didn't do anything to stop me. I bummed around Titan for a while, but none of my friends would talk to me. I think they were afraid of my father. I guess that was the point." Isaac's voice grew weary. "So I left Titan and made my way to Maltor. Don't know how I managed. When I got there, I felt just as lost as when I had left. I remember sitting down in the mud, amongst the bustle of the city, and feeling absolutely invisible to everyone who passed me, as if they could see my shame. That's what I believed—that everyone was like my father. I decided that night that I was going to kill myself."

"But you didn't," Liam said quietly.

"No. Dekker found me. I remember looking up at him and seeing his old, weathered face. It surprised me, not because he saw me, but because there was such *kindness* in his eyes. He scooped me up, told me everything was going to be OK, and took me to the local Church. He bathed me, fed me, and gave me a bed to sleep in. He never asked questions, never even asked my name. He was always just...there. Helping me when I needed it. I don't think I even spoke the first week I was there until one night he came to my side and asked if I would like to pray with him. He told me that the Creator loved me and that He would like to know that I was OK." Isaac exhaled, as if releasing a great weight from his chest. "I broke down into tears, like a dam had been released. I curled up in his arms and sobbed and sobbed and asked him over and over again why he was being so kind to me. Dekker stroked my hair and comforted me. He told me that we all deserve kindness. That my life was worth something." Isaac paused. "That night, I devoted myself to something. I told myself that I was going to get as strong as I could so that I could protect this person who harbored such unimaginable love. And that's exactly what I did. When you and Avalice returned to Maltor, I wasn't sure what to expect. Dekker told me he was leaving with you on a job but that he would return. The thought of being away from him, that he might die without me, was overwhelming. I didn't even give him a choice. I was going with him. And so I did. And here I am."

Isaac met Liam's eyes. "Like I said earlier, I will follow you into the Red Ravine if you ask. You and Avalice and Dekker are the closest thing I ever had to a loving family." Isaac stopped and stared hard at Liam. "But I cannot bear the thought of Dekker dying for something he's fought against his whole life."

Liam said nothing for a moment, the impact of Isaac's confession striking him like a hammer to the chest.

"I know he made this choice of his own accord," Isaac pressed. "All I ask is for you to remember this conversation. Remember how much he means to me. Please."

Liam stepped toward the young man and placed a hand on his shoulder, his voice soft and assuring. "I understand, Isaac. And I promise that he means the world to me as well. I know this journey has been a terrible one, but I *will* see it to completion with everyone still breathing. Desmond took the most important thing in the world away from me. I want him dead for that. I want it so badly. But if what we heard was true, then this man is a threat to the rest of us as well. Yes, this is about revenge, but it's also about saving the few remaining Dekkers in the world, too."

Isaac stared at Liam and then his eyes softened some. "I believe you."

Taking his first breath in what seemed like hours, Liam nodded. "Then let's be on our way and find the old bastard."

Together, they turned in silence and continued. After a few minutes, they reached the edge of the marsh and left the fog, along with the haunted memories it had revealed.

Chapter 12

They found Dekker and Rezin only a half-mile beyond the marsh. The two men were sitting on a ridge waiting for them. When they saw Liam and Isaac, they rushed down to them.

"Thank the heavens," Dekker said as he slowed before them. "For a while there, I was actually worried."

"Well, I wouldn't want that," Liam said, giving the old man a tap on the shoulder. "How are you?" He looked at Rezin. "Did you run into any more trouble?"

Rezin shook his head. "No. I think that beast scared the cannibals off. Drove them back to whatever holes they live in."

Dekker pointed to the ridge. "We found ourselves a nice spot with a good view. Figured if we were going to die up here, we might as well go out surrounded by some kind of beauty. You want to see?"

"Sure," Liam said, "but hold up. How are you feeling? You've been pushed hard these past couple of days."

Dekker threw a wink at Isaac. "Listen to him, worrying about his elders." He extended his arms. "Rezin here was kind enough to apply fresh bandages. I'm a little sore and more than a little tired, but I'm on the up and up."

Isaac gave Rezin an acknowledging nod.

"What about you?" Dekker asked, examining Liam and Isaac. "How'd you two fare? You're walking, which is better than I had hoped."

Isaac placed a hand on Dekker's shoulder. "We're fine. Why don't we have a look over that ridge?"

Dekker snapped his fingers. "Ah, yes! It's right up here, follow me."

As they scrambled up the slight incline, a bitter wind whipped through the gloomy sky, causing Liam to shiver. He walked slowly, letting Dekker and Isaac go ahead of him. He scanned the world around him and saw a sprawling cavity of mountain and rock all around them. The landscape dipped down across the slope before him, spinning toward a vast plain at the base of the mountain. Sitting only a couple miles from the foot of the slope was The Chain. The massive links hung from an ink-stained sky like a pillar holding up the roof of the world. It stretched down from the dark clouds and plunged into the earth, disappearing beneath a basin of broken rock. There was no sign of Desmond or his infected.

Liam felt a hand on his arm and he turned to see Rezin looking intently at him.

"What is it?"

Rezin's face was unnaturally serious as he spoke, his tone a grave whisper. "We're getting close to the end here," he said, casting his eyes toward The Chain. "And I believe things are going to accelerate at a pace we can't predict."

Liam narrowed his eyes in confusion. "What is this all of a sudden?"

Rezin's grip tightened on Liam's arm. "When the time comes, I'm going to need you to trust me."

Liam shifted in the rubble. "What are you talking about?"

"This march does not end where you think," Rezin continued. "There will be things that I need to do once we get closer—things you won't understand. But I need you to believe in me. I know we don't know one another very well, but I think I've earned some loyalty. I understand that you have your own mission now and it is just as important as mine, but I'm going to need you before this is all over."

Liam pulled himself away from Rezin and kept his voice low. "You're being incredibly vague. Maybe it's finally time you told me what's really going on here between you and Desmond."

"If I told you why I really wanted to come to this place, the real reason I hired you..." he trailed off for a moment before continuing. "There's just no way for you to understand until you see it. If I told you now, you'd think I was mad."

"I think you should give me a chance," Liam said evenly. "If you're asking me to do something for you, then I should know what it is."

Rezin ran his hand across his bald head and stared up at The Chain. He looked at it for a long time before he spoke.

"Do you believe in the Creator, Liam?"

Liam blinked, the question an unexpected one. He shook his head. "No. I don't. I have no idea what really happened to Tectonic all those years ago, but I don't think there's some almighty being up there looking out for us."

Rezin stepped forward, his voice razor-thin. "What if I told you that I was the Creator?"

Liam's face went slack and he stared at Rezin, waiting to see some crack in his expression. When it didn't come, he snorted and jerked his head from side to side.

"Rezin...I'm sorry, but there's no way you're the Creator."

Rezin smiled grimly. "You're right, I'm not. But I'm the closest thing the world has to it."

"So what does that make you then?" Liam asked incredulously.

Rezin's eyes went dark. "I'm a pilot."

Dekker's voice cut through their conversation. He called down to them from the ridge while waving his arms.

"Hey you two, get up here! You're not going to want to miss this!"

Liam studied Rezin for a hard moment. "This conversation isn't over."

"Just don't mention any of this in front of Dekker," Rezin said, slowly leaving Liam for the ridge. "He still has faith there's a Creator and I don't want to take that away from him. Not when our end is so near." He pulled himself upward and then looked back. "As awful a person as Desmond is, he is right about one thing."

"And what would that be?" Liam asked, now striding up the ridge with Rezin.

"Something beyond the clouds wants us dead."

Before Liam could press him any further, Rezin climbed the rest of the way, leaving Liam behind. Mind spinning in confusion, he could only follow. He pulled himself up the rest of the way and brushed his hands against his pants as he stood shoulder-to-shoulder with the others.

"Impressive, isn't it?" Dekker said, shooting Liam a look.

Liam let his eyes travel to the edge of the mountainous horizon and felt his thoughts fall away.

The range ended abruptly about twenty miles south of them, but it wasn't just the mountains, it was everything. It was as if a butcher's cleaver had been brought down across the world and severed the rest of the landscape away. Snaking from the empty space were hundreds of thousands of smoke trails, all wafting lazily up from the edge of the world. They were all a million different shades of green and looked like shooting stars falling in reverse. Beyond the wall of color, sitting just above where the phenomenon ended, between the horizon and wall of black clouds, was a wide line of dim blue sky, dotted with a smattering of barely visible stars.

It was the most beautiful thing Liam had ever seen.

"It's something else, isn't it?" Dekker whispered, smiling softly.

Isaac, arms crossed, shook his head. "I never thought I'd get to see the edge of Tectonic."

Dekker clapped him on the shoulder. "It is as stunning as it is terrifying."

"Those tails of green," Liam said, pointing to the array of wisping lights. "What are they?"

Dekker shrugged. "Beats me. Probably fumes from the Void below us. They just look like that because of the sky behind it—throwing the light and all that. I mean, have you ever seen a blue sky like that?"

"Not even in a sun splash," Liam said in awe. He glanced over at Rezin and saw that his back was turned, his eyes on The Chain.

Turning back, Liam felt his heart sink as he gazed at the spread of beauty before him. "I wish Avalice could have seen this."

Dekker smiled, a hurt, loving thing. "As do I. She would have loved it."

Liam turned away, hiding his face from the old man.

Dekker shuffled over to Isaac, giving Liam a moment.

"What do you think, kid?"

Isaac's eyes absorbed the colors like ink to paper. "I think we're a long way from Maltor." He looked down at the bandaged Transistor. "A long way from Titan."

Dekker nodded, his eyes shining. "That we are, son. That we are."

Liam stood away from the rest, with thoughts of Avalice swirling around his head. He stared down the mountain slope toward The Chain and tried to center himself. He found it more difficult than anticipated, the pain of his recent loss burning away in his chest. He shut his eyes and focused his breathing, the dull throb of his heartbeat echoing in his skull. Avalice's face rose in his mind's eye and he clung to it, wishing he wouldn't. Not yet. Not before this fight was over.

Rezin walked to his side, his gaze running down the steep mountainside. Liam looked at him and for the first time since meeting the strange, timid man, he realized that he had no idea who he was standing next to.

Liam cleared his throat. "What you said back there—"

Rezin cut him off, pointing toward the base of the mountain. "Liam, look."

Liam did, forcing his questions back down his throat. He squinted in the gloom. When he saw what Rezin had spotted, he felt the burn in his chest ignite into an all-out blaze.

"Desmond," Liam whispered, his eyes tearing as a frigid wind tore across the summit.

Rezin nodded. "He's close. Looks like most of the infected made it through the marsh." He grunted. "Unlucky for us. How many Profanes do you think are down there with him?"

Liam trained his eyes at the distant group, a bubble of orange light, a dome making its way down the final stretch of the mountain.

"I don't know. Forty?"

"I'd estimate the same," Rezin said, nodding. "If we don't hurry, then they'll make it to The Chain before us." Rezin looked at Liam sharply. "I don't need to remind you what will happen if he carries out his insane plan."

Isaac and Dekker joined them, and once they saw Desmond's group, Liam noticed Isaac's face visibly tighten.

"They've already made it so far," he whispered, eyes glued to the orange glow of torchlight and Rockflesh.

Dekker's eyes grew hard. "They've almost made it off the mountain. Liam, once they do, it's a straight shot to The Chain. It's right there. They're going to reach it unless we slow them down somehow."

Liam touched the axe at his side. "Even with the diseased slowing them down, they're going to beat us." He bunched his hands into fists. "Even if we ran and managed to not break our necks—we wouldn't make it in time." His teeth came together. "God *damn* it."

Dekker reached for his pocket and pulled out a cluster of Rockflesh. He looked at Liam and cocked an eyebrow.

"You think an avalanche of stone would slow them?"

Liam looked at Dekker's fistful of glowing poison. His stomach tightened.

"Do it," Rezin urged, nodding. "It's the only hope we have. We all know what the consequences are if we fail here."

Isaac stepped between Rezin and Dekker, shaking his head. "No. He's still too weak. This one is on Liam and me."

Rezin snorted. "Unless you sprout wings and an army of angels, I don't think you two are up for it."

"We'll be fine if we—"

"Isaac."

The young warrior turned around to see Dekker smiling patiently at him.

"You've already shouldered so much. You and Liam both. Let me do my part. I'll be OK."

"We can handle this—"

"No, you can't." Dekker pressed. "And that's OK. You need to let me help. It's what I want. You understand?"

Isaac closed his mouth and his eyes fell to the ground.

Dekker tapped him on the arm. "Just watch my back, all right?"

"Right."

Liam walked to the edge of the ridge with Dekker, the wind scourging the naked rock field that littered the landscape.

"You sure you can do this?" Liam asked, trailing a path down to Desmond with his eyes.

"Only one way to find out," Dekker muttered. "I'll try to aim the blast away from us."

"I'd appreciate that," Liam muttered, taking a step back, Isaac and Rezin crowding his side.

The old man closed his eyes and muttered something that was lost in the wind. After a moment, the light in the Rockflesh vanished.

Dekker snapped his eyes open, teeth gritted, and raised his right arm. Heat and light exploded from his palm as the Transistor channeled, blasting warmth across the dead mountain.

A pillar of pulsating orange streaked across the rocky slope from Dekker's open hand and detonated a hundred yards away, erupting across a wide cluster of massive boulders. Eyes bloodshot, Dekker guided the raging beam diagonally across the mountain, sending a shower of broken rubble airborne. The result was immediate and devastating. As Dekker ceased channeling, the mountain groaned and shifted, a great, crunching roar filling the air in its wake.

"Back off, back OFF!" Liam yelled, feeling the ground rumble beneath his feet.

The four scrambled away from the precipice as the avalanche began, a tumbling wall of power that gained in density and momentum as the mountainside collapsed. Massive boulders and great sheets of shale collided with one another, falling and spreading and breaking downward. Liam stumbled as the destruction splintered outward and grew, widening with every second that passed.

The wall of debris hurled itself toward Desmond's group. Even from this distance, and with the world rumbling beneath his feet, Liam saw the party below pause, the roar of the avalanche heard. As soon as the impending violence was spotted, the cluster of bobbing lights dispersed, fleeing for safety.

"Watch your footing!" Rezin yelled, half-falling as the mountain continued to split apart.

"Over here! This way!" Dekker called, waving.

But before anyone could move, a thin beam of light soared toward them from Desmond's location. The orange beam exploded into the mountainside, a dozen feet below them, and then was swept to the side, carving a massive trench in its wake.

Something huge collapsed beneath them and Liam felt himself slide downward, the wide plate of rock he was on now starting to come away like a sheet of ice.

"He's channeling!" Dekker yelled, frantic. "GET AWAY! RUN!" But then he was sliding as the ground swelled and began to fall away.

Isaac raced for the Transistor as the mountainside crumbled all around them. The young warrior swooped to Dekker's side and yanked him out of the way as a cluster of rubble exploded past where he had just been standing.

He collapsed on top of the plate of rock Liam and Rezin were on, the entire thing slipping down the steep slope like a broken sled.

Now, with the four of them on the same plate of rock, Liam could only brace himself, the world beginning to race by. He reached out for Rezin and their hands met, pulling themselves together. Isaac, still clutching Dekker, stumbled and crawled his way over to them, the wind whipping across their faces.

"HOLD ON!" Liam screamed into the whistling gale. "JUST HOLD ON!"

They all gripped one another as their fragile vessel slid down the mountain at an alarming speed.

Heart racing, Liam watched as the brunt of the avalanche collided with the majority of Desmond's group, extinguishing their lives in a brutal wave of roaring power. Rock dust flowed down the shaking mountainside, joined now by the gases released from the crushed infected.

At least a mile away, the sheet of rock Liam and the others were on bounced violently, and Dekker screamed as he bit his tongue, blood spilling out from between his lips. Isaac pulled him close and hugged him in a protective crouch.

Head pounding, Liam turned and traced their trajectory, everything happening at breakneck speed. Eyes watering, dust choking him, he saw that they would come to a stop at least a mile from Desmond's group and the toxic gas. Even now, he could see that the avalanche had not taken them all and knew that their cover was blown.

"We've almost reached the bottom!" Rezin yelled, crouching on all fours, eyes alight with fear. "Brace yourselves!"

As soon as the words left his lips, the rock plate skipped violently across some dead foliage and smashed through a series of small rises, sending rubble zipping backwards. Liam spun and shielded his face, feeling his back ignite with pain as tiny fragments pelted him, bouncing off his leather armor and biting his arms and legs.

With a great, groaning roar, the plate of rock bounced off a sharp rise in the landscape and sent them spinning toward the foot of the mountain. The rock slowed some, the decline finally leveling out, but the shift in momentum caught them all off guard.

Sliding toward the edge, Liam, from his stomach now, managed to find a handhold and clung to it for his dear life. Vision blurring, he looked to his companions. Rezin was on his back, spread-eagle, managing not to go careening off, but only by a fraction.

Liam turned his head and felt his heart stop.

Isaac and Dekker were gone.

Fear for his friends exploded up his throat, but before he could act on it, the rock vessel crunched into a rise of boulders and came to a jarring halt. Liam felt himself go airborne, the world spinning, his teeth smashing together.

He landed on his shoulder hard and rolled across a wide plain of dirt. He bounced across dead underbrush, his body howling as he connected with a strew of smaller rocks. He tasted blood on his tongue as he came to a rolling halt. He panted, out of breath, bloody, and covered in dust. The world shuddered and his head thundered. Blinking, he coughed violently and felt his side hitch in pain.

Struggling to get his bearings, his vision became obscured as a vortex of swirling particles swept over him, causing him to cough again as dirt and debris flooded his nostrils.

Chest heaving, he managed to clear his vision and crawl to his hands and knees. He had no idea how he was alive or what stroke of luck he had been gifted, but he was grateful for it. Squinting, he spotted Rezin not too far away, the right side of his face covered in blood and grime.

Wheezing, Liam forced himself upright, eyes smothering his surroundings as the dust settled.

Dekker. Isaac.

He tried to call out to them, their sudden disappearance horribly foreboding, but fell into a fit of hacking coughs instead. Stars exploded across his eyes and he went down on one knee. He could hear Rezin calling his name as he wandered closer, but his voice was faded and muted.

Slowly, Liam collected himself and looked up. When he did, he felt his heart sputter with unexpected fear.

Striding across the destroyed mountainside was Desmond, backed by at least ten Profanes and twice as many infected.

They were headed right for him.

Chapter 13

Liam knew he was in trouble before Desmond even reached him. Rezin wasn't doing any better, his eyes dazed and confused as to what had happened, the dust still settling around them. Liam spat a wad of slimy blood from his mouth and searched for his axe, all too aware that his enemy was approaching.

"Rezin!" he croaked, half-falling toward the older man. "Run! Get out of here!"

From a dozen feet away, Rezin looked at him as if seeing him for the first time, his eyes wide. A cut ran down the length of his cheek, coating his face in blood. He blinked when he saw Liam and stumbled toward him.

Desmond and the Profanes reached him first.

They knocked him to the ground, snarling, furious. What remained of Desmond's group appeared to be in poor shape. The avalanche had done its job and these few remainders wore the evidence across their faces.

"Of course it's you!" Desmond yelled, his voice thick and fatigued. "Who else would it be but Rezin and his rabble?"

He kicked Rezin in the ribs, knocking him back to the ground as he attempted to stand. The Profanes stared down at the beaten man with a lustful violence. The infected stayed behind, looking scared and lost, their mutated flesh pulsing with disease. They huddled as one, pack-like, with their arms around one another as if they were lost children.

Liam pulled himself up, finding his voice. "Leave him alone!"

Desmond cocked his head to the side and appraised Liam's fragile state, a sneer twisting his lips. "Well, if it isn't the shameless lover! The phoenix has risen from the ashes to seek his revenge! How's your lady doing these days? I don't see her. Don't tell me she died? Not after I went to all that trouble!?"

Liam curled his hands into fists, the mountain still groaning around them. "Where's the rest of your army? Don't tell me I buried them?"

Desmond strode toward Liam with a look of dark amusement, pulling half the remaining Profanes with him. The others stood watch over Rezin, who looked on in discomfort.

"Did you really come all this way to kill me?" Desmond asked, planting himself in front of Liam.

"There's a lot of reasons I came," Liam said, trying to ignore the pain. "But yeah, that one tops the list."

Desmond snorted. "How noble. You strike me as a man who follows his emotions straight into trouble." He twisted his head and appraised his dwindling numbers, along with the fidgeting infected. "I'd say you found it. Problem is, I'm still standing and you're outnumbered. Not exactly how you saw this going, did you?"

"The avalanche missed you, but I'm still breathing," Liam said. "Which means I haven't failed yet."

Desmond shook his head. "She must have been quite the girl for you to follow me this far. Speaking of which, where are the others? The big guy and the Transistor? Don't tell me they died, too?" He snickered. "Didn't expect me to fire back, did you?" He rubbed his arms, which were inflamed, the skin an angry red. "You gotta think ahead, you know. Otherwise you end up in situations like this."

"If you kill me, at least I'll die for her," Liam spat.

"Kill you? I hadn't thought of that. I have some important things to attend to here at The Chain, but I gotta say, now that you've planted that seed…"

"You don't have to do this," Rezin said suddenly, his voice cutting through the tension. "There is another way, Desmond."

Desmond turned around slowly. "Seriously?"

Rezin got to his feet, wincing. The Profanes stepped toward him, but Desmond waved them off.

"You of all people should know the necessity of what I'm doing," Desmond said darkly.

Rezin wiped the blood from his face. "You're a coward."

Desmond's eyes turned to cold slits. "Excuse me?"

"There is a way to fix this," Rezin said. "But instead, you've chosen to run. You're terrified to face them so you've decided to destroy The Chain and kill us all."

Desmond shook his head slowly. "You can't seriously be suggesting what I think you are."

"What the hell are you two talking about?" Liam cut in, wincing as his ribs flared with pain.

Rezin looked at Liam. "I told you I was a pilot, remember?"

Liam nodded.

Rezin pointed at Desmond. "So is he."

"*What?*"

"Shut up," Desmond growled. "There's nothing left." He pointed a finger to the sky. "Not after what they did to us."

"Who!?" Liam yelled, confusion and exhaustion colliding.

Rezin looked at Liam, his voice low. "The Old Horns."

"Don't talk about them," Desmond hissed. "Don't you dare draw their attention to us, not now."

"I can't let you kill the last of humanity," Rezin said. "There's still hope for us if you'll help me. I can't do it without you."

"I won't die like the others," Desmond snarled. "You saw what was done to them. Where they *went*. It's a miracle you and I were able to escape at all."

"We're the only ones who can fight back," Rezin said sharply, stepping toward Desmond. "We're the last of the pilots. We carry with us the entire fate of Tectonic. We can't fail them. We *must* not fail them."

"I'm not going back up there," Desmond said from between his teeth. "And I'm not going to listen to any more of this. I'm taking these last infected I've managed to keep alive and we're going to blow up The Chain and I'm going to save us from *them*."

"You have a duty, goddamn it!" Rezin yelled suddenly, his whole body coming alive. "You can't just run from it! You signed up to protect Tectonic in case they ever came back!"

"They weren't supposed to come BACK!" Desmond yelled, veins bulging. "But now that they have, now that I've seen what they're capable of..." he stood panting, face red. "Fuck, Rezin, they consumed *everyone* like they were *nothing*! What chance do you think we have against that kind of power!?"

"We weren't ready," Rezin pressed angrily. "We didn't even have a chance to fight back this time. Hell, you and I barely made it to the pods! But we're ready now. We have the codes. We can activate it. You know there's a station down here, don't you? That's the whole reason I came all this way! Not to kill you, but to go BACK! We have to KILL them!"

Desmond was shaking his head before Rezin even finished. "Enough...I'm not going to listen to this shit any more. Call me a coward if you want, but I'm *saving* everyone from a fate worse than death."

He waved to the Profanes. "We're taking them with us. Find something to bind their hands with and hit them if they do anything stupid. The rest of you, round up the infected back there. They look ready to blow at any moment and I don't want to set off a chain reaction, so be gentle."

"Why don't you just kill us?" Rezin growled as the Profanes advanced. "We're all dead anyway."

"Why?" Desmond asked sarcastically, turning to stare at The Chain. "Because you're the only person left alive who gets me, Rezin, despite your obvious contempt. We're the last link to the old life and I want you standing with me when it all ends. Not because I give a shit about you, but because you *owe* me this. We've been through hell and together we're going to sink this ship." He shot a look at Liam. "You're lucky I like you. Not too many sons o' bitches would have hunted me down like you have. It'd be a shame to just kill you in cold blood like this. Consider this an apology for killing your lady. I actually do feel a little bad about that, you know. But if you had been exposed to the things I've seen...well...there's no telling how you'd handle it. I tend to get a little...riled up sometimes. Call it PTSD or manic or whatever you want. I don't really care. Just behave and I'll let you see the end of this as well. The more the fucking merrier." He clapped his hands loudly. "All right, let's move out!"

When the Profanes finished tying him, Liam was pushed along with the rest of them. He felt like he should fight back, lash out, do something, but he knew it would be a death sentence, at least right now. He still had time to find his moment.

And yet, his mind was reeling, confusion exploding through his senses. He had no idea what Rezin and Desmond were talking about, what they had supposedly survived, and what their importance really meant. What were The Old Horns? What had happened? Where were Rezin and Desmond really from? As he was herded along, now joining the ranks of the infected, he could only guess. He stared ahead at the looming Chain and wondered if he'd live long enough to get an answer.

They were only a couple miles away from the base of The Chain, the landscape a grim plate of broken rubble and dead oaks. The air smelled of dirt and dust, each breath an inhalation of earthy decay. The sky pulsed overhead, the thick cloud cover oozing grim darkness. Liam stared up at it, tracing the colossal links of iron that hung from the heavens.

Just what the hell was really going on here?

Rezin stumbled to his side. He was breathing heavily, but his face was a mask of stone. His eyes shifted from side to side, warily appraising the infected that jostled along all around them. Their skin burst with orange Rockflesh, grotesque mutations that held a reminder of their approaching death.

The remaining Profanes intermingled throughout the group, watching the prisoners with a careful eye. They looked exhausted, their faces angry, but troubled as if they weren't exactly sure what was going on, either. As Liam trudged along, he wondered just how much they understood.

Carefully, he nudged his way over to one of them, a man with long blond hair.

"Do you all really want to die so badly?" he whispered under his breath.

The man looked at him, as if shocked he had spoken.

"I don't know what's going on here and something tells me neither do any of you," Liam pressed, stepping away from an infected that bumped into him.

"Keep your mouth shut," the Profane muttered, as if swatting away a bothersome insect.

"Desmond wants to plunge Tectonic back into the Void," Liam continued, figuring he had nothing to lose. "You can't want that, can you?"

The man shook his head, his blond hair spilling across his eyes. "This pilgrimage started out as a rebellion against the Creator. Nothing has changed."

"There is no Creator!" Liam hissed. "Haven't you been listening?!"

The man smiled, but it was really just a show of teeth. "Believe what you want. Desmond holds his own theories, and frankly none of us care. The important thing is how this all ends. He is going to free us from the Creator's grip. Whatever delusions he suffers don't matter. None of us care if he thinks he's some kind of traveler from the stars. You've seen how he is. He isn't right in the head." He snorted. "None of us are. Not while the Creator continues to hold us in his grip. Not while he forces us to inhale his vapors."

Liam closed his mouth, unsure how else to continue. He walked a couple steps ahead to Rezin's side, watching as Desmond led them toward The Chain.

"You have to start making sense of all this," Liam said quietly, staring at the infected ahead of him.

Rezin looked sideways at him and for a moment Liam wondered if he was going to get shut down. But after a moment, the older man sighed and his face softened into something more tired.

"I don't even know where to begin, Liam. So much has happened that has been hidden from you people."

"What does that even mean?" Liam said in a low voice. "Who am I to you? Who are any of us to you?"

"You were the ones we chose to save."

"Save from what?!"

Rezin kept his voice to a whisper. "The Old Horns."

"That's the second time you've mentioned them, but I still have no clue what that means. Just who are you, Rezin?"

"I'm part of a colony that was selected to preserve the human race," Rezin said grimly. "There were two hundred of us when we launched all those years ago. I wasn't part of that group, obviously, but I was birthed from a tube sometime during our excursion."

"*What?*"

"Before the Void became what it is now, we were a thriving race," Rezin said carefully. "We had cities, oceans, and technology that would seem like magic to you. We were at the peak of our existence. There are records I could show you that you would laugh off as fiction because your mind wouldn't be able to process them. Tectonic is all you know; it's all anyone here knows. The Creator never existed, but my people did. And we saved *everyone* from the First Exposure."

"I don't follow," Liam said, confusion sparking through his mind like electrical shocks. "Saved us from what? These Old Horns you keep mentioning?"

Rezin nodded. "We didn't know what they were or when exactly they would arrive. We spotted something on our radars along the outskirts of known space." He looked at Liam. "Imagine a large looking glass that can see past the stars. That was just the tip of our capabilities."

"Right," Liam muttered, feeling dazed.

"We could see that whatever was out there was coming closer and everything in its wake simply vanished. As you can imagine, this sent us into a panic and so we started to build. We worked without rest, frantically coming up with some kind of way to save humanity if the anomaly continued to move closer. And it did. Slowly. Terribly so. But there was no doubt that it was coming."

"Void below," Liam whispered, trying his best to make sense of the chaotic pieces.

"It wasn't called the Void back then," Rezin said. "It was called Reactus. That's where my people originated from. The land before the Void. My home. Your home."

"This isn't possible," Liam hissed, keeping a careful watch on the Profanes in case they were listening.

"It's all true, whether you believe it or not," Rezin said. "The brilliant minds of Reactus built a station. A vessel. They called it Upper Heaven. It took the better part of thirty years, but they got it done. After its completion, they selected two hundred of the most advanced minds to board and sustain the vessel prior to launch. This population would be responsible for maintaining Upper Heaven. Scientists, biologists, doctors, engineers...they would all work together to keep the human race alive and out of harm's way. Labs were constructed on the vessel with the sole purpose of growing new humans in case the population started to dwindle, a fact that was almost a certainty. That's how I, along with many others including Desmond, came to be." He stopped suddenly, as if the history was draining him. "You see, Liam,

The Chain wasn't cast down by some Creator. It was built to save you."

"How...?"

"The space station Reactus built, Upper Heaven, lifted the continent of Tectonic using The Chain. It was the only slab of land in which this insane plan was possible. We...*they*...didn't even know if it would work, but it did, miraculously."

"Upper Heaven *lifted* Tectonic away from Reactus?" Liam sputtered. "Like...like some kind of crane?!"

Rezin nodded grimly.

Liam shook his head. "But the people of Tectonic, the ones living there before they were hauled up..." Liam said, overwhelmed. "How could they agree to something like that?"

"They were given fair warning and they made sure the continent had the means to survive after Tectonic was lifted from Reactus."

"Hell..."

Rezin looked up at The Chain, closer than ever. "Mere weeks after liftoff, the Old Horns arrived at Reactus. There is video footage of the attack taken from Upper Heaven's holo scopes." He looked apologetically at Liam. "Sorry. It's hard to remember the technologies known down here."

"What are they?" Liam whispered. "The Old Horns?"

Rezin shook his head. "I don't really know. Wanderers of the cosmos. Beings from another realm. Dimensional titans. Humanity didn't have time to study them once they made themselves visible. But when they did, it was all over." Rezin's eyes grew dark. "They annihilated Reactus in a single day. They just...*leaned*...and then everything started to break apart and vanish."

"Why didn't you fight back?!" Liam asked.

Rezin grunted. "Humanity tried. You see, Upper Heaven wasn't the only thing Reactus built. There were three other constructs that were mechanically birthed into existence. Three massive weapons capable of immense destruction. Two of them were left on Reactus to fight the impending threat. Upper Heaven took the third."

"What kind of weapons were they?"

"They were vehicles, mechs of colossal size."

"What happened to them?"

"The two left on Reactus were piloted and launched during the Old Horns attack. It was a desperate plan, but it was all we could muster given the time we had. We even managed to kill one of them. The Red Ravine is a result of that battle. Even though Tectonic was being shuttled away, a blast from the fight reached the underbelly of this continent and ripped a hole in it. Unfortunately, that same blast traveled all the way to Upper Heaven and the space station was struck. Not critically, but enough to anchor us. At least that's what the records tell."

"Clearly, the mechs weren't enough to combat the Old Horns," Liam said, mind straining.

Rezin shook his head. "The two mechs were destroyed. The annihilation of Reactus followed just hours later."

Liam's brow furrowed. "But why didn't the Old Horns destroy Upper Heaven and Tectonic? Surely they could have, if what you're saying is true…"

Rezin smiled darkly. "Indeed they could have. Upper Heaven only had a couple weeks of a head start. We weren't that far away. But I think they grew cautious of us. We had killed one of them, after all." He looked at Liam. "There were four in total—the Old Horns, I mean. A loss of one of their own might have rattled them, if that's even possible. Whatever the reason, they've waited three hundred years to return. Perhaps the initial battle drained them of their power." He paused and drew a heavy breath.

"In the meantime, we had no choice but to leave the Tectonic below to evolve on its own. The rest of the population, the ones above at the other end of The Chain, struggled to find hope in the devastation. We began planning, charting courses through space that would never come to be. Like I said, Upper Heaven was damaged as well during the battle for Reactus and it left us stranded. Our resources were limited and we struggled to repair the massive damage while also maintaining our link with The Chain. All contact with Tectonic was lost. We were crippled and mute. And so, Tectonic eventually evolved into what it is now—a primitive shell of a past long dead."

Liam's head was throbbing. "I don't understand, though. If this is true, then what happened? What changed? Why are you *here?*"

"Because the Old Horns have returned to finish what they started," Rezin said miserably. "They just appeared out of nowhere. It wasn't like before when we saw some ominous smudge on our radars. They simply came. And when they did, they began to destroy Upper Heaven without warning. It was a miracle Desmond and I managed to get to the escape pods and launch down here to the surface. But we were separated and so I immediately began to seek him out so that we could get back. But this place was so foreign to me. I knew I couldn't survive, and so I sought help. I met people that were patient with my lack of knowledge. Eventually, I came to understand this relic of a place. And when I did, I knew I needed to get back to The Chain, back to the heavens."

"Why? If the Old Horns have returned and are now the ones holding The Chain, hauling us up to be annihilated or eaten or whatever, then why bother? You yourself said Upper Heaven was destroyed!"

Rezin nodded. "It was, but the mech wasn't. The one Upper Heaven took with it. It's still up there. And Desmond and I are the only two pilots I'm aware of that can get back to it and fight against these abominations. You see, before we lifted Tectonic from Reactus, we installed hidden stations down here that would enable us to get back to the mech if need be. Right now, we're walking toward one of those stations."

Liam shook his head. "But you said the other mechs were destroyed after taking out only one of these dimensional walkers. Why do you believe in the powers of this one remaining machine when you're so outnumbered?"

The corners of Rezin's mouth twisted into a smile. "Because of the three, this one is the most powerful. The two left on Reactus—we named them Mach Zero and Yuet—were inferior but still immensely capable." His voice grew low. "But the remainder, the one still hovering up there around the debris of Upper Heaven—that was the last one built, and it contains the might of our evolution. It possesses a cannon of sorts, unique to its design and immensely powerful."

He turned and looked at Liam, his eyes laden with shadow. "We named this machine Final Sky."

Chapter 14

L iam felt sick. Sick and overwhelmed at what he had been told. It was almost too much to bear, too much to process and accept. It made his skull creak beneath its severity.

The sky groaned along with him and thick clouds rolled past, reminding Liam of the darkness of death. They had reached the base of The Chain, and he knew it wasn't far off. They had come such a long way and left so much blood in their wake. It weighed heavy on his mind, like an anchor pulling him to the earth.

The revelations Rezin revealed clogged his mind. More death. More hopelessness. It was almost too much to digest, as if he were trying to fit a boulder down a bottleneck. The history had drained him. Made him feel small. Exhausted, Liam pushed it all away, allowing his mind to recoil.

Thoughts of Avalice replaced the dread, and he welcomed them. He thought about the way her eyes softened when she looked at him. The way she made him feel safe when everything around them was crashing down. He needed that now more than ever. But she was gone. And now Isaac and Dekker were missing as well. Dead.

Liam flinched at that. No. He refused to believe they were gone. They had simply been tossed away during the mountain's collapse. They wouldn't have died. They couldn't.

Please.

"We can't let him do this," Liam whispered, staring ahead at Desmond, who had begun shepherding the infected around The Chain, positioning them with the help of the remaining Profanes.

Rezin looked at him, their hands still bound behind their backs. "The hidden station is only a hundred yards away at most. If I can get to it…"

Liam continued to watch the infected, lost and cursed to certain doom. They looked to Desmond with a kind of hopeless confusion as he led them around the great iron links. There were dozens still, more than enough to cause catastrophic damage.

"Can The Chain even be broken?" Liam whispered, keeping his voice low so the three Profanes guarding them wouldn't hear.

"We wouldn't be here if it couldn't," Rezin said grimly. One of the infected began to shamble out of line, breaking its formation, and was met with rough hands, dragging it back. Liam prayed the woman wouldn't explode as Profanes punched her in the stomach, being careful not to strike the exposed Rockflesh.

"We have to do something," Liam hissed. "Did you spot Dekker or Isaac after they disappeared?"

Rezin shook his head, a trickle of sweat running down his face. "No. I'd be shocked if they survived."

"Don't say that."

"Sorry."

"They wouldn't die. Not like that. Isaac wouldn't allow it."

"You act like he had a choice."

"They'll come."

Rezin pursed his lips. "I wish I had your faith."

Liam shut his mouth and watched as the last of the infected were put into place. A few of them were crying and calling out to loved ones, their minds clouded by the disease. Others simply stood like cattle, their eyes blank. The Profanes slowly backed away from the linked circle, keeping a watchful eye on their victims.

Desmond strode toward Rezin and Liam, a grin plastered across his face. He stopped beside them and appraised his work, dusting his hands on his pants.

"God, but do I hate touching them," he said loudly. "Feels like poking at a nasty boil or something."

"Those are human beings," Rezin said flatly. "The same as us. The same *people* as us."

Desmond sniffed. "No, they're not. They're children that *we* saved. They're toddlers that we have looked after all these years, completely unaware of the sacrifices made for them."

"And what luxury we've lived in," Liam cut in. "You were born in complete safety, high above us, long after all of that," Liam spat. "I sure as hell wasn't."

Desmond stared hard at Rezin. "Sounds like someone's been running his mouth."

"He deserves to know the truth. He got me here."

Liam met Desmond's eyes. "Despite your violent cowardice."

Desmond turned and slapped him across the face, causing Liam to gasp. "Don't you *dare* undermine what's been done for you. Do you know what you people did after you were hauled away from Reactus? You destroyed your records. You erased your history. There's a reason Reactus is called the Void now. It's because your ancestors decided it would be better to spin a hopeful fable about a Creator instead of remembering the tragedy the rest of us went through."

"Look, Desmond," Rezin said, "you and I have been through hell. We witnessed an event no one else alive has seen. I know it's changed you, and it's changed me as well. But we can beat them, you know we can. I just need your help powering Final Sky. That's it. Just give me a chance to fight back. Please."

"I am not going back up there," Desmond said with iron in his voice. "I won't chance looking at them again."

"I'm scared, too," Rezin said, "but we have a duty. A chance to punch back. Don't you want that?"

"Of course I do," Desmond snarled. "What the hell do you think we're doing here? I'm not letting those monsters take the rest of us. I'd rather we all burn. I'd rather we all cut our throats and drop dead. Because I am not letting them toy with us anymore." He stepped toward Rezin. "Because that's what they're doing, Rezin. They're fucking with us. They're clinging on to that Chain and pulling us up a foot at a time until they decide we're ready to be consumed and sucked down those swirling vortexes. I'm not letting those bastards get what they want. Bunch of chicken-shit animals, hiding up there behind the clouds…"

"They're not hiding behind them," Rezin said flatly. "You are."

Desmond punched Rezin in the mouth hard enough to flatten him. He towered over the bleeding man, shaking, his eyes red hot.

"If you don't keep your tongue behind your fucking teeth, I swear I'll rip it out and watch you choke to death in blood. Just because I've let you live this long doesn't mean I have to keep honoring that. The only reason you and your friend are still breathing is because I respect what you've done to get here. Don't fucking test that." He leaned down, his voice a hiss. "You've seen how *manic* I can get." He stood and swung his eyes over to Liam. "And so has your girl. So shut up and behave if you want to go down with the ship like the warriors you claim to be."

Without another word, he turned and motioned toward one the Profanes. "You! Grab one of those poor saps and drag their ass over here. It's time we lit the fuse and were done with this!"

Liam began to feel a very real sense of panic as he watched a Profane drag one of the infected away from the others. It was a man with a gray beard. His eyes constantly shifted from side to side, as if he had no idea where he was. The left side of his face was covered in sprouting Rockflesh, a cluster of glowing disease that pulsed each time he drew a frantic breath. The man was pushed to his knees in front of Desmond who stared down at him.

"You should be honored you know," Desmond said, placing a hand over the man's head. "You are the match that's going to set this world free. Do you have anything you'd like to say?" Desmond chuckled to himself. "As if you even know what's going on. Look at you. You're a mess." He looked at Rezin and Liam as if expecting something. "Do either of you have anything you'd like to voice? Any more pathetic attempts to stop this from happening?"

Rezin flexed his arms, testing the ropes he was bound with. "Maybe cut us free before you do this? I'd at least like to die a free man."

"I'm afraid that's out of the question," Desmond said, hand hovering over the man before him. "Don't want you doing anything rash here at the end of all things." He looked at Liam. "And what about you? Got anything? One last threat perhaps? A snarling declaration of revenge? God, but I'm glad I haven't killed you yet. Your face, right now, is worth the fucking hassle."

Liam shifted in his restraints, the Profane at his back placing a firm hand on his shoulder as he did so. "Whatever happens to us next, I hope it hurts. I hope it hurts and you get the worst of it."

Desmond sniffed, amused. "Not bad. Not bad at all." He turned away from them and looked up at The Chain, his face draining of emotion. His eyes lingered on the dark clouds where the massive links vanished. When he spoke, his voice was calm.

"Never thought I'd make it this far."

And then he gasped, his whole body tensing as he drained the man before him of his power. The infected shuddered, his eyes bulging and gaining clarity. The orange glow from his face disappeared and was pulled up Desmond's arm, the skin immediately flaring red as it held in the power. The Profanes began to back away, exchanging worried looks. It was as if their dreams were being brought into reality, only to realize that perhaps this was a nightmare instead. One of them closed their eyes and began to tremble.

"Now or never," Desmond whispered, the air shifting around him. He brought his hand up and aimed it at the circle of infected surrounding The Chain.

"Desmond, DON'T!" Rezin cried suddenly, lunging for him.

But before Desmond could release the power he held, an ear-splitting sound detonated from above. It was colossal and it was instant, a massive wave of noise that blasted down from the heavens above them. It filled Liam's head and threatened to split his skull in two as the enormous blast resonated in a deep, low tone across the fractured earth. It drove everyone to the ground, hands held against their ears as their senses were assaulted. Liam and Rezin could only shut their eyes and grit their teeth, their hands squirming in their restraints.

As the first booming eruption faded, another began. It sounded as if a massive pair of horns were being blown, the shockwave so deep Liam could feel it thudding into his chest. Horribly, he peeled his eyes open. When he did, he looked up into the sky.

And his heart skipped a beat, his face going pale. He opened his mouth, but no sound came out, or if it did then it was lost beneath the rumbling avalanche of sound.

Coming through the clouds, *leaning* down toward them, was a monster unlike anything known. The surface of its titanic body was colored a deep red, almost black. Its torso was smooth and broad, filling the gap in the clouds and expanding beyond. It looked slightly humanoid, the skin stretched over countless ribs, rising toward a long, thin neck that supported a flat, rectangular-shaped head. In the madness, it reminded Liam of a blacksmith's anvil. There were no eyes, no ears, no nose. The head was completely featureless except for a vast, swirling vortex of twisting color. It was like staring into the depths of a whirlpool, the slow spinning circle sparking with yellow electric bands that danced and shuddered across the gaping expanse. Black and orange streaks lined the vortex like a palette of mixing paint. They twisted and spun in a nauseating circle, pulling Liam's eyes inward like an optical illusion.

Disappearing into the vortex, confirming every fear Liam held, was the other end of The Chain. It was as if the monster was slowly, terribly slurping it up, inching them closer to whatever horror lie beyond.

Liam stared up at the abomination, terror paralyzing him in place. He could hear the Profanes screaming and fleeing, fear overwhelming their resolve.

The monster, this Old Horn as Rezin had called it, continued to lean down from its celestial platform. As it did so, something else emerged from the ceiling of cloud. It was an arm, a thick, bulging twist of red and black bone. It appeared almost as if it were made of wood, the movement emitting a massive groan, like a great oak creaking in the wind. A hand followed, bursting through the smog. It had four fingers, each one shimmering, as if casting off a vermillion mist. The hand reached for The Chain below itself and the fingers closed around it, the sound like the crack of bone.

From his trance-like state, Liam suddenly heard Desmond screaming. He turned and saw that he was running toward the infected still standing at the base of The Chain. His arm was raised and he took aim, a last act of desperation.

But a second before he could release his final devastation, the cosmic monster above them flicked its hand, the one gripping The Chain. The speed of it was both terrible and shocking, the reaction immediate.

The Chain shuddered and rippled downward like the crack of a whip. Liam's eyes went wide as he followed the rolling curl of iron all the way to the bottom where it smashed outward, sending the infected airborne as the shockwave hit them.

They didn't stand a chance. The force of the blast was so immense that they were sent soaring miles in every direction. A few of them exploded, sending puffs of disease down across the world, but they were so far away that their death held no threat.

"NO!" Desmond screamed, skidding backward as a wave of air hit them all, sending them tumbling to the earth, bouncing and rolling painfully away.

Liam cried out as he was flung, along with Rezin, the rock and hard dirt rising to crash into them as they were tossed. When he hit the ground, he immediately tasted blood as he bit his lip, the impact jolting him. He skidded across the dirt and came to a thudding halt, gasping and blinking and dazed.

In the chaos, he could see Desmond on one knee, his body still pulsing with power. He was screaming up at the cosmic titan, his face filthy and red and filled with rage. Blood covered the side of his face, his veins bulging in his throat as he bellowed up at the Old Horn. Refusing to accept defeat, he raised his arms and released a stream of searing power from the palms of his hands. It arched across the dirt-stained sky and struck The Chain, enveloping an iron link in a wash of heat and fury.

But The Chain held fast.

"NO!" Desmond screamed, the skin on his arms splitting with blisters. "NO NO NO NO YOU DON'T GET TO HAVE ME!"

He scrambled to his feet, shaking, eyes wide, staring up at the abomination. Liam coughed and fought to stand as well, twisting on his sides and cursing his bindings. Rezin was next to him, looking dazed.

"Get up!" Liam yelled, his voice wavering.

Rezin got to one knee and then rose, almost falling over in the process. He hacked up dust and spit out a mouthful of blood, blinking away an almost certain concussion.

"We have to get to the station!" he yelled. "We don't have much time!"

The air around them had begun to pick up, a wind spraying rubble across the world like a sheet of hail. Liam raised his eyes to the heavens and the

FINAL SKY · 165

horrific being above let out another earth-shaking bellow, a rolling exhale of sound that struck their ears like a hammer.

"SHUT UP!" Desmond was screaming. "STOP IT!"

Slowly, the blanket of cloud began to part even more, the veil of black pulling away to give way to what lie behind it.

"Oh no…" Liam whispered, his voice a dry rattle. "Oh god, please…"

The sky filled with two more of the cosmic horrors, each of the heavenly nightmares flanking the one holding The Chain. They were visible from the waist up, the horizon still rolling with inky black. Their anvil-shaped heads were consumed by the same otherworldly vortexes—swirling, bottomless wells that sparked with cracking electricity.

They leaned down as one, filling the sky with their haunting presence. From his hurricane of thought, a single one rose to the surface with stark clarity.

Have they been here this whole time, gathering their strength to strike again?

"Liam! LIAM!"

Liam turned to the voice and saw Rezin jerking his head.

"Follow me! HURRY!"

Lost in confusion and terror, Liam did as he was told. Rezin led the way, rushing in an all-out sprint toward Desmond, who seemed to be frantically searching the earth for more Rockflesh or fallen infected—anything to strike out again at the towering behemoths overhead.

"Desmond!" Rezin screamed into the roaring wind. "Desmond, you have to help me!" They skidded to a halt in front of the crazed man, the three of them seemingly alone to face the mountainous titans.

Desmond spun, his eyes wild as if lost to madness, and faced them.

"Help you!?" he screamed, his voice carrying in the gale. "It's OVER, Rezin!"

"Cut us free and stop being such a goddamn COWARD!"

In response, Desmond cocked his fist back and plowed it into Rezin's face. Rezin toppled over, the air alive with swirling debris.

Snarling, Desmond raised his boot and was about to stomp the dazed man, but Liam lowered his shoulder and bull-rushed him. He plowed into Desmond and they both went sprawling, saving Rezin from the staggering blow.

Coughing, his whole body aching, Liam rolled onto his back, fighting against his insistent restraints, knowing he had seconds before Desmond was on him.

"You just don't know when to quit," Desmond growled, pulling himself up to stand over the two men. His hair whipped wildly in the wind, the sky groaning and creaking and splitting apart.

"I've let you live long enough," Desmond rumbled, falling over Liam, his hands going for his throat. "I think it's time you joined that dead bitch of yours."

Liam gasped and squirmed beneath Desmond, the madman's fingers tightening and squeezing the air from his lungs. He bucked and kicked frantically, but Desmond was like a boulder, his face twisted in a rage.

Gagging, heartbeat thundering in his ears, Liam knew that he was about to die. And it terrified him. He tried to speak, call out, but Desmond's grip was firm and final. His eyes burned down over him with hatred and conviction.

As the darkness began to grow around the edges of his vision, something changed. Relief was suddenly roaring down his throat, his stream of oxygen returning in a whooping heave of hungry air. Blinking away stars, Liam looked up and saw that Desmond was being hauled off of him.

It was Isaac. He looked like hell. His armor and shirt had shattered and torn away, exposing bloody skin and bruised muscle. He yanked Desmond away, one hand firmly gripping the back of his neck, the other plowing into his ribs, his knuckles scuffed and bloody.

"Get off of me!" Desmond roared, spinning to deliver an elbow to Isaac's chest.

Isaac released him and doubled over, only to stand a second later, his face blazing with a hatred so intense his eyes went dark.

He took one step toward Desmond and punched him in the mouth, putting everything he had behind it. Desmond went sprawling, a tooth ejecting in a spray of red. He fell hard to the earth, catching himself at the last second to save his skull from splitting open against the rocks.

Isaac circled him, panting, his hands balled into fists. When he spoke, his voice joined the rising violence roaring around them from the skies.

"Get up. Get the *fuck* up."

Desmond slowly pulled himself to his feet, shaking the stars from his eyes. He looked at Isaac and tested his jaw.

"You again," he growled, shaking his vision clear. "Thought you were dead."

Isaac stepped toward him once more, raising a fist as he did. This time, Desmond stepped underneath the blow and landed one of his own. It caught Isaac beneath his jaw, and Liam could hear his teeth click as knuckle met flesh.

The punch staggered him, but any lasting effect vanished a moment later. He lunged for Desmond, fists flying. He planted a flurry of blows across his body, each one doubling Desmond over, his eyes bulging, the air hammered from his lungs. He raised a hand, as if to block the vicious assault, but Isaac swatted it aside. He grabbed Desmond by the collar and ripped him toward him. He slammed the crown of his head into Desmond's nose, breaking it in an instant, the crunch of cartilage accompanied by a geyser of blood. Isaac released him, letting the blow sink the bloody man back to the ground.

Chest heaving, Isaac stood over the beaten man. He leaned down and pulled a knife from his boot and then planted a knee in Desmond's chest.

"This is for everything you've ever done," Isaac said darkly, flipping the hilt so that he could stab the stunned man in the throat.

"Isaac, wait!" Rezin yelled. "You can't kill him! STOP!"

Isaac looked over at him, his face caked in grime and dried blood. "Look at where he's gotten us!" he yelled, his voice hoarse. "You've seen what he's done! You were there every step of the way!"

Rezin hobbled over to them, jerking his head toward the titans in the sky. "Do you see them!? DO YOU!?"

Isaac looked past Rezin, up into the gaping cosmos that held the trio of nightmare creatures. If they frightened him, his face held no evidence.

"Please!" Rezin said. "I need him to fight them! We're all dead if you kill him!"

Isaac shook his head slowly. "I don't know what you mean. I have no idea what's going on or what those things are, but it looks like we're all going to die here in a couple minutes anyway. Let me at least bury this bastard."

Liam leaned down, his arms straining behind his back, and met Isaac's eyes. He kept his voice low and urgent. "Listen to me, Isaac. We don't have time to explain everything, but things aren't as they seem. Rezin isn't who we thought he was. Hell, everything is upside down right now and I don't fully understand it myself, but what he's saying is true."

Isaac stared hard at Liam. "Don't you want this animal dead?"

"Of course I do," Liam spat, "and once this is over, I want to be the one to bury that knife in his heart, but this goes beyond that. I will never ever forgive him for what he did to Avalice, but it seems like he'd suffer more if we kept him breathing, just for a little while longer. Can you do that? For me?"

Isaac held his gaze for a second and then nodded. "Fine. OK, Liam." He got off of Desmond and twirled his finger. "Here, hurry, let me cut you both free."

"Thank you, Isaac."

Once Liam and Rezin were free, both vigorously rubbing their wrists as the ropes were severed, Liam bent down and grabbed Desmond by the collar.

"You're going to help Rezin whether you want to or not, but first I really need to do this."

Liam slammed his head Desmond's nose, crushing the cartilage with a sickening crunch. Desmond screamed and recoiled as blood exploded from his face, the wind streaking it across his face as the gale continued to rise around them.

"Get up," Liam snarled, jerking the whimpering man to his feet. "If you don't cooperate with Rezin then I'm going to do that again." He stepped into Desmond, their faces inches apart, Liam's breath hot and furious. "Don't think of this as mercy, either. I'm going to murder you one way or another. But there are a lot of ways to kill a man, and I'm an imaginative person. You took away something precious from me, and I have a lot of ideas on how to repay you for that. So shut the fuck up and fall in line." He looked up at the Old Horns, their presence a chilling image against the rumbling sky. "Whatever these things are need to die, and you're going to help."

Rezin took Liam by the arm. "The station is hidden just a hundred yards from here. We need to move."

"Hold on," Liam said, the wind blasting against his beaten body. "Isaac, where the hell is Dekker? Did he make it? Is he alive?"

Isaac nodded and pointed to a rise only a couple dozen feet away. "He's alive, but he's in bad shape. One of his legs is broken and he's barely hanging on. If he channels, he dies. His body wouldn't be able to take it, so I set him down over there."

"I need to speak with him before we go," Liam said. "Rezin, just give me a moment."

"Liam, time is run—"

"Just fucking WAIT!" Liam yelled, trotting away toward where Isaac had pointed.

He found the Transistor propped against a large rock, his clothes in tatters. His leg jutted away from his knee at an odd angle, and his right arm was coated in blood, the skin split. When he saw Liam, his tired eyes warmed, despite his condition.

"Good to see your face, son," Dekker rasped, his lips cracked and dry. "Creator above, but it's good to see you."

Liam knelt and took the old man's hands in his own. "I thought we lost you in the avalanche."

"Ah, it'll take more than a couple rocks to bury these old bones," Dekker said, then coughed. His hand came away bloody. He looked down at it and sniffed. "Must be the dust in my lungs…"

Isaac appeared and knelt down opposite Liam. He looked worried and his eyes met Liam's.

"We can't move him like this, Liam."

"I know."

Dekker ignored them and craned his head back to look up at the all-consuming titans in the sky. The vortexes continued to spin, the lighting cracking across the colored pits.

"Don't really know what's going on or what those things are," Dekker said dryly, "but I'd guess that we'll all be in a bit of trouble."

"Listen to me," Liam said quickly. "Rezin knows a way to fight back against those monsters. I don't have time to get into it, but I believe him. I'm going to go with him and help him. There's a lot of things that we believed in that just aren't true, and it'd take a very long time to detail it out."

Dekker sighed, wincing. "I won't pretend to know what is happening or what those things are, but it's clear something terrible is about to take place. If any of us make it through this, I'm sure we will have a nice long sit-down and discuss it over a couple glasses of booze. But right now you need to do whatever it is you need to do. Don't worry about me. I'm not going anywhere."

Isaac cleared his throat. "I'm staying with him, Liam. I want to help you, but I'm not leaving him. I won't."

Liam nodded once. "Of course. I wouldn't ask you to."

The sky rumbled as a wave of creaking sound blasted down over them, the Old Horns shifting and leaning as a boom of thunder exhaled from the clouds.

"Do what you must," Dekker said, gripping Liam's hands firmly. "And take care of yourself, son."

Liam smiled down at the old man and suddenly felt immensely sad. "I will. This isn't the end. I *will* see you again." He looked at Isaac. "Thank you for getting me this far. I love you both like brothers. Watch over one another until I return." He stood, voice heavy. "And look for me in the sky."

And then without another word, he left them.

Chapter 15

Liam caught up to Rezin and Desmond as they made their way across the rocky plain. Desmond was still mopping blood from his face, his expression brimming with hatred. The air seemed to scream around them as the weather worsened. The Chain rattled from the heavens, sending out massive waves of metallic noise. The Old Horns remained frozen where they were, horribly leaning down from the sky like children peering into a toy chest. Lightning lashed out violently, followed by rolling thunder, great booming explosions that rattled Liam's head.

Panting, he came to Rezin's side, who had a death grip on Desmond's shirt, jerking him ahead of them. He looked at Liam, his face coated in dust.

"We're not far now!" he yelled over the gale. "Do you see that rise over there? The one with the cluster of dead trees? That's where the station is! We just need to get inside!"

"How can you be sure?" Liam yelled, giving Desmond a push.

Rezin shielded his face from the swirling dust. "When I lived in Upper Heaven, before it was destroyed, the first and last thing I did every day was to study the map of Tectonic in case something like this ever happened. If you knew that one day you might be in trouble, wouldn't you make sure you were prepared?"

"I suppose I would."

"Trust me, it's there."

"What's going to happen once we get inside?"

Desmond was the one who answered, coming as a snarl from over his shoulder. "We're all going to hell, that's what. We're going to be sucked up to Final Sky and pulled into those vortexes, just like everyone else we've ever known. Isn't that right, Rezin?"

"Shut up."

"But we won't die, will we?" Desmond continued. "Don't you remember the transmission we got?!"

"We don't know what that was," Rezin said, giving Desmond's shoulder a shove to keep him moving. "It could have been anything."

"What's he talking about?" Liam asked as more lightning lit the sky.

"It was nothing," Rezin growled, rubbing grit from his eyes. "A glitch in our coms."

"Coms?"

Desmond laughed, but it sounded sick. "A glitch!? Are you serious!? Liam, we heard voices! Voices from people LONG dead. They were TALKING to us through our tech!"

An icicle slid down Liam's spine. "What's he talking about, Rezin?"

"Don't listen to him," Rezin said firmly. "We don't know what we heard or where it came from. Could have been some old transmission."

Desmond let out another sickly bark. "As if! They were begging to DIE, Liam. All of them, howling and pleading for someone to just kill them."

"That's enough!" Rezin yelled.

"I don't know where the Old Horns take you, but I can promise you that once you're through the vortexes, there's something on the other side waiting. Something far more terrible than those monsters in the sky."

Rezin stepped forward and punched Desmond in the back of the head. "I told you to shut up! What good is this doing us?!"

"He should know what he's walking into," Desmond said, scowling.

Liam grunted and shoved Desmond ahead. "Since when have you ever cared about my well-being? I may not know what's going on, but I trust Rezin a hell of a lot more than a violent maniac like you."

Desmond flashed his teeth, stained red now from his broken nose. "You'll eat those words before this is over."

Liam reached out and grabbed Desmond, jerking him close, his voice a hiss. "You want me to keep breaking your face?"

Desmond fell into silence as the trio marched quickly across the remaining distance. When they reached the rise, nothing more than a slope of rock that held a handful of dead trees at its crest, Rezin stopped.

"It's somewhere in this area," Rezin said, getting down on his hands and knees at the base of the rise. "Look for a square box. It's probably covered in dirt, so it might be hard to spot." He swept his hands across the ground, the wind sending clouds of grit across the land.

Liam, not quite sure what to expect or see, began sweeping his boot over the ground, hoping something would stand out. After a couple minutes, Rezin began to grow frustrated as he widened his search.

"Don't stop, keep looking!" he yelled as The Chain clinked loudly at their backs. "I know this is the spot! This is where the maps indicated! It HAS to be here!"

Liam began to doubt as he continued to drag his boot along the ground. He could see Rezin visibly beginning to panic, his strokes becoming more and more frantic.

After a minute, Desmond groaned and pointed. "For god's sake, it's right there, you idiots."

Rezin and Liam both looked to where he instructed, and Rezin gasped. He scrambled over to the tiny rise, toward a perfectly square object in the dirt, no bigger than a fist. He brushed dust away from the surface, revealing metallic plating.

"He's right, this is it!" Rezin yelled, his fingers prying at the odd shape. "Stand back a little! I'm not quite sure where the entrance is located and I don't want you falling in and breaking your legs. Goddamn it, back up, Liam!"

Liam pulled Desmond away from Rezin as he flipped the metal box open on its hinges, revealing another square box about half the size. Without hesitation, Rezin pushed it. Almost instantly, the ground began to rumble.

"It's opening! Look!" Rezin yelled, excited, bounding to his feet as the dirt began to shift. Amazed, Liam watched as the earth seemed to peel away, opening up to reveal a small staircase that led into a dimly lit metal room below.

"Grab him and follow me!" Rezin instructed, racing down the stairs without waiting.

Liam took Desmond by the arm, but the injured man didn't budge. He stared hard at Liam, his face grim. When he spoke, his voice was barely audible above the gale.

"Listen, I know I've done a lot of bad things to the people you care about, and I'm sorry. Really, I am. I shouldn't have done that. But if there's any humanity left in you, then please do not make me go back up there to face those things."

Liam leaned forward, his voice like the crunch of gravel. "Just because I'm in the dark about all this doesn't mean I don't know how to hate someone. And Desmond, I fucking *hate* you. All I want is for you to suffer for what you've taken from me. So thank you for giving me that. At least I know that if we die up there, then I'll die doing the one thing you're still afraid of. Now move."

He shoved Desmond ahead of him and down the stairs, their boots clinking down the metal steps. When they passed below ground level, the earth slid back over their heads, sealing them inside, encasing them in the strange electric glow of the hidden room.

Liam kept one hand firmly on Desmond as Rezin scurried around the small interior. Electric bulbs blinked overhead, casting a thin light across the walls. Each wall was lined with whirring machinery and flashing panels. Rows of buttons and switches filled the metal space, and Liam watched as Rezin bounded between them, pushing and pulling them in some kind of sequence that was lost to Liam. At the center of the room was a hollow ring, just wide enough to stand in. As Rezin continued to maneuver, the ring began to hum and come alive, slowly spinning in place.

Above, the ground began to rumble.

"OK, I've marked the coordinates and established a link to Final Sky," Rezin said, out of breath. "Thankfully, it's still receiving and hasn't been destroyed, but it's been knocked off course."

"What does that mean?" Liam asked.

"It means we still have a chance, but we're going to have to work for it," Rezin said, still pushing buttons, the room filling with a low hum. "When the Old Horns destroyed Upper Heaven, they must have thought we all died, leaving Final Sky to carom off into space. It's still in range, but barely."

"My head hurts," Liam muttered.

Rezin stopped in front of Desmond and Liam, his face taunt and pale. "I'm going to go through first. After I'm gone, send Desmond next. You go last. I'll be waiting."

Liam eyed the whirring metal ring with unease. "What's going to happen to us?"

"Think of this like a door, except the exit is hundreds of miles from here. You won't feel a thing, I promise."

"Don't do this," Desmond said, almost to himself. "You don't want this, Liam."

"Shut up."

Liam looked at Rezin and nodded. "OK. I'm trusting you. We'll be right behind you. Do whatever it is you're going to do."

Rezin nodded and clamped a hand down on Liam's shoulder. "Right. See you on the other side."

Taking a deep breath, Rezin stepped away from them and into the ring. He closed his eyes and grit his teeth. After a moment, the metal ring rose from the ground and seemed to pull up a curtain of red light with it. When it reached the height of Rezin's form, Rezin vanished.

It happened in the blink of an eye and Liam gasped, taking a step back.

Desmond turned to Liam. "Don't become his pawn. We can still leave. He can't follow us now."

Liam, still dazed by Rezin's disappearance, shook his head, distracted. "What...? No. Shut up."

"We're all going to die," Desmond pressed. "If we go up there, then we're choosing the absolute worst way to go."

Liam centered himself again, watching as the metal ring returned to the floor. He grabbed Desmond by the back of the neck and shoved him forward.

"I'm going to rip your goddamn tongue out if you keep using it."

Desmond stumbled into the ring, tripping only to right himself once more. He looked hard at Liam.

"You're a fool, Liam."

And then the ring activated once more, rising upward, bringing with it a glow of red. Liam stared into Desmond's eyes, unflinching, until he vanished.

Alone now, Liam collapsed against the wall, breathing heavily. His mind felt like it had splintered into a thousand pieces. He clutched his temples and squeezed his eyes shut. The world above groaned and rocked and screamed down at him, the floor shaking.

"What the hell is going on?" he whispered. "What the fuck is all this?"

He opened his eyes and looked at the ring as it returned to the floor. He knew that on the other side was a world he could never understand. The mystery terrified him, but he knew Rezin needed his help. Even though he didn't understand the assault of information that had been leveled at him, he knew that the Old Horns were real and that Rezin needed him to complete his mission.

"What am I doing here, Avalice?" he whispered into the empty room. He imagined her standing next to him, smiling into his beaten face. Liam grinned sadly.

"God, I miss you."

And then he stepped forward into the ring. As he did so, he realized that he was shaking. He forced the fear out as best he could as the circle of metal began to rise around him.

"Here goes nothing."

A moment later, everything went dark.

Liam felt his entire body tense up and become weightless. Walls of black pressed in around him, filling him with a horrible sense of claustrophobia. He opened his mouth but found that he couldn't sense it. He couldn't sense anything. He tried to touch his face, but his arms weren't there. He tried to move, but his legs were lost in the terrible void. All he could do was blink with eyes that didn't seem his own as his mind filled with a colossal sensation, like he was falling at a tremendous speed.

Right as terror seemed to overwhelm him, the world rushed back in a hurricane of sound, color, and sensation. He felt like he had been dropped, his boots hitting solid ground, clinking loudly, his legs turning to jelly. He went sprawling across a metal floor, a wash of white filling his vision, dazing him.

Panting, sweating now, he could hear movement all around him. Voices. They sounded underwater. As he regained himself, his vision clearing, he realized that it was Rezin, screaming his name.

"LIAM, HELP ME!"

Liam dragged his eyes up, feeling like he was going to vomit, and saw that Rezin was on the ground in front of him with Desmond on top. Desmond was pummeling Rezin, drawing blood, his face encased in a snarl.

Liam pulled himself to his feet and half-lunged, half-fell into Desmond, the world still a dizzying palette of cold white.

He plowed Desmond off Rezin and fell on top of him, quickly focusing and finding his strength once again.

"Get off me!" Desmond yelled as Liam's weight pressed him to the floor, a fist hammering into Liam's side.

Liam reached for Desmond's throat and clung to it, choking the man where he lay and also steadying his swaying vision. Gagging, Desmond thrashed and drummed his feet against the white metal floor, his eyes bulging. Liam waited until his senses cemented some and then released his grip from Desmond's throat. He sat up on the man and then delivered a single blow across his already broken nose. It was hard enough to knock some of the fight from him.

"You idiot," Rezin said, staring down at Desmond, wiping blood from his lip. "You're already through, what's the point in fighting now?"

"You going to behave?" Liam asked, his voice a rasp.

Desmond clutched his nose, panting. "Whatever. Keep beating on me if you want. I'm not going to help you."

"Oh yes you are," Rezin said, helping Liam to his feet. "You have a lot of bones for Liam to break. You decide how many stay intact."

"Fuck you."

Liam booted him in the side, Avalice's face still present in his mind's eye. Desmond grunted and held up a hand.

"Fine. Help me up, you damn gorilla."

"Get up yourself."

As he did so, Liam looked around, taking stock of where he had landed. As he swept his eyes around the space, he began to feel like an intruder on some unknown world.

"Easy, Liam," Rezin said, watching him carefully. "I know this is a lot."

"This is crazy," Liam whispered. "I had no idea…"

They were in a small room, the walls covered in machinery, much like the room they had left. A door stood at the far end, leading to some unknown corridor, a green light blinking across its surface. Opposite the door, in front of Liam, were a handful of stairs that led to a raised platform that held four metal chairs that had been bolted to the floor. Tubes and neon wires twisted around the chairs, dangling from the ceiling to plug in at the base. Everything was white and cold and metallic. The space itself was fairly wide, but all the foreign machinery made Liam feel claustrophobic.

But all that wasn't what blew him away.

It was the window, a massive thing that stretched across the space in front of the four chairs. Liam climbed the handful of stairs and stepped past the seats to stand before the window, his heart racing.

The expanse of space sprawled out before him. Hundreds of millions of stars coated the inky canvas like candles in the night. In the far distance was the sun. Its light was swallowed up by the ebony jaws of night that seemed to hold it in its grip. Hanging below them, at the bottom of the window, were the Old Horns. Their backs were turned to Liam, their massive bodies seemingly frozen in the vastness of the cosmos. Liam pressed his face to the window, eyes wide, and saw that the monsters were engulfed in darkness below the waist, as if they had risen from a colossal cloud. The swath of darkness they rose from danced with the same electrical energy that sparked across the vortexes, now hidden from sight.

"I can see Tectonic," Liam whispered in awe. "It's so...broken."

"Doesn't seem worth saving from this vantage point, does it?" Desmond grunted, holding his nose.

Liam didn't answer, enthralled by the display. Tectonic was just barely visible, a flat stretch of distant earth absorbed by clouds, only seen from over the Old Horns shoulders. He could see The Chain, rising up from the murky surface to disappear into one of the vortexes, as if it were a piece of food being slurped down.

"As much as I'd like to give you more time to take this all in, we need to hurry," Rezin said, pushing Desmond up the stairs toward one of the seats. "Liam, I need you over here."

Liam continued to stare down at Tectonic. It looked like some kind of fragmented vessel that had been left to drift across some terrible, endless ocean. The surface was so...dark. It made Liam shiver, wondering how such a grim thing could hold the remains of humanity in its arms.

"Liam."

Liam turned, shaking the images from his head. He walked to Rezin's side and looked down at the chairs.

"What are these?"

"We're in the cockpit of Final Sky," Rezin said, shoving Desmond down into one of the metal chairs.

"This...is what we're going to fight the Old Horns with?" Liam said, spinning.

"This machine is much larger than what you see here," Rezin said, pulling a harness over Desmond, locking him in place with a click. "I don't have time to give you the tour, but this is just a fraction of this place's facilities. We're in the head, if you will. This mech, this machine, it's far more powerful than you could ever imagine. Once we get it started, you're going to need to sit down and strap yourself in. See how I did Desmond here?"

"Wouldn't want you splattering your brains all over the walls now, would we?" Desmond said, showing his teeth in a sick smile.

Liam had the urge to slap that smile off his face, but instead he looked at Rezin. "What do you need me to do?"

"Once I spark the first phase of the engine's ignition, there's going to be a panel that comes down from the ceiling in front of Desmond. It's a retinal scanner."

Liam shook his head, lost.

"It'll read Desmond's eyes," Rezin said, seeing Liam's face. "One will come down over my seat as well. I need you to make sure this bastard unlocks the second override. It takes two of us to override the safety locks—a precaution we put into place in case a pilot went rogue. That happened once while we were building the second mech back on Reactus. Thankfully, he only managed to start the engines and release the cable locks before he was stopped. After that incident, the engineers changed it so that two pilots were needed."

"Aren't we lucky?" Desmond spat, slumping miserably in his chair.

Rezin stared down at him. "You don't have to make this difficult. Once we get going, I'm more than capable of operating the cannon and limbs. But it'd be a lot easier if you'd just cooperate and held me with the thrusters."

"Never was your forte," Desmond mumbled.

"Will you help me?"

"We'll see," Desmond said, his eyes turning to slits. He looked over at Liam and that smile returned. "How's it feel to rely on the enemy? Makes the pit of your stomach all woozy, doesn't it?"

This time, Liam did slap him. It wasn't hard, but it was enough to wipe the smile from the man's face. He wanted to reach down and throttle the bastard, really make him die miserably, but he knew he couldn't. Not yet.

Rezin walked over to the seat in front of Desmond and took his place, securing himself in. He pulled a panel toward him that was on a hinge and began inputting commands, his fingers dancing over the blinking buttons.

"Feel like I should say something," Rezin muttered quietly. Instead, he finished logging in some flashing sequence and then leaned back in his seat.

After a moment, the flooring beneath Liam's boots began to rumble. It was low at first, nothing more than a minor tremor. But it continued to grow until he felt it in his knees. He steadied himself next to Desmond, his hand on the chair for balance.

Something in front of Rezin craned down from the ceiling, a small arm that held some kind of glowing screen. Rezin leaned forward once it was eye level and a chirp followed.

"He's next!" Rezin said, his fingers back to work over the control panel.

Sure enough, a similar panel descended in front of Desmond and Liam gripped the back of the man's head, pushing him toward it.

"I remember making your girl do something like this," Desmond said sickly as his eyes were engulfed with a phasing light across the small screen.

Liam felt rage explode up his throat and he gripped Desmond's hair even harder, every ounce of him screaming to slam his face down into the floor.

"Careful, tough guy," Desmond said, wincing. "Wouldn't want to hurt humanity's last hope now, would you?"

"Just do your fucking job," Liam growled, releasing him as the panel ascended back into the ceiling.

The room began to shake even more and a great, groaning creak echoed from somewhere below them. The stars outside began to sway ever so slightly, and Liam could feel the air around him heating up.

"We're up!" Rezin called excitedly. "Goddamn it, we're actually up! Liam, you're going to want to sit down now before we really light the fire here. Make sure you strap in, too."

Liam quickly sank into the chair next to Desmond, his pulse thrumming. He found the strap over his shoulder and secured it across his body, quickly glancing over at Desmond, who was smiling at him.

"You look like a bird without his wings up here," Desmond chuckled, his lips twisted at the corners.

Liam steeled himself. "And you look absolutely terrified."

The smile fell from Desmond's lips. "You would be, too, if you knew what was coming."

From ahead of them, Rezin's voice rose. "Here we go! We're moving! This is it, Liam! Hold on!"

Liam closed his eyes and gritted his teeth as the room began to shake violently, the roar of some monstrous engine blaring below them, filling the cabin with an intense heat.

Final Sky swiveled and the Old Horns filled the window.

182 • ELIAS WITHEROW

Chapter 16

Isaac collapsed against the rock next to Dekker, his body throbbing with pain. The wind threw dirt across his exposed torso, causing the ruins of his shirt to flutter like tiny flags. He leaned back against the boulder and stared up at the trio of monsters above them, the sky creaking beneath their presence. He had no clue what they were or where they had come from, but The Chain rose to disappear down one of those terrible vortexes, and that was enough to finalize his sense of dread.

"What the hell are we looking at?" Dekker asked at his side.

Isaac said nothing, the air screaming as electricity danced and sparked between the three towering titans. They continued to lean down upon the world, their bodies shuddering and vibrating, sending tremors rumbling beneath the earth. He knew he should be afraid—that he was likely witnessing the beginning of the end, but he found that he wasn't. He was just too tired.

"You still with me, son?" Dekker asked, looking over at him.

"I'm here," Isaac said, squinting as grit whipped across his face. "Just too exhausted to care what happens next."

Dekker patted his leg. "I suppose most folks would be running in terror right now."

"What's the point?" Isaac said, letting his arms hang loosely at his sides. "We can't fight that."

"Rezin seems to think we can."

"I think there's a lot about this world we don't understand."

"Maybe we were never meant to. Maybe this is how the Creator intended everything to end."

Isaac smiled sadly at the wounded man. "I'm glad I'm here, Dek. With you."

Dekker grinned, wincing. "Don't make an old man blush when he's dying, son. It's disrespectful."

Isaac stared up at the growing chaos, the clouds splitting and unfurling in great rolling waves to make way for the looming creatures. "I never did thank you for what you did for me all those years ago."

"And you don't have to," Dekker said, sounding tired. "You're a good kid, Isaac. You deserved a better hand than you were dealt."

Isaac looked down at Dekker, his face softening. "You've been the only consistent good thing in my life. That means something to me."

"It breaks my heart to hear that," Dekker said, leaning back to stare up at the monsters in the heavens. "But thank you, Isaac."

The two fell into silence as the wind continued its assault across the world. In the distance, tornados began to touch down, roaring across the earth left to right. Isaac let them carry his eyes, watching as Tectonic continued to tear itself apart.

Above them, the Old Horns began to vibrate with a heightened intensity. Their vortexes spun faster and the thunder came at quicker intervals now. The monster in the center, the one gulping down The Chain, slowly spread its arms, as if reaching for each horizon. The other two mimicked its posture, stretching into the far corners of space. As they did, the sky sounded off once again, a trio of blaring noise that echoed like low horns.

When the blasts faded, Dekker took a deep breath, as if bracing himself.

"Looks like they're getting ready to strike."

Isaac watched the heavenly monsters, searching his mind for any sign of fear. All he discovered was exhaustion and a sense of finality.

"Maybe they're the reason Tectonic has suffered so much," Dekker said quietly, despite the wind. "Maybe this terrible disease is their doing." Dekker wrapped his ruined arms around himself. "And if it is, then I bet they're about to do it again."

Isaac let his eyes climb the sky, but when he did, he paused. He gripped Dekker's leg and pointed.

"Look."

"What is it, son?"

"There, coming through the clouds. The light. Do you see it?"

Dekker raised a hand, squinting. When he saw what Isaac was pointing at, his eyes widened. "Creator above…"

It was a streak of blue light, as if a comet was roaring toward the Old Horns, leaving a trail of power in its wake.

"Is that a machine?" Dekker whispered.

He leaned forward, finding his energy once more. He and Isaac watched as the massive construct soared directly for the Old Horns, the details of its shape coming into focus.

At this distance, it appeared to be some kind of colossal vehicle, its design resembling that of a human if they were cast from metal plating. Its bulky legs trailed behind itself as it rocketed through the heavens, propelled forward by a great engine rising from its back, spitting great spumes of fire as it fueled its trajectory.

One of its arms hosted a massive blade, a hundred feet long, while the other sported some kind of barrel, thick and bristling with charging power, the end glowing blue. The head was a wide, stocky thing, resembling some kind of helm.

"It's going to strike," Dekker said, breathless. "It's going to attack those things!"

A moment later the great machine struck, fire exploding from exhaust ports as it adjusted its aim. It swung its massive blade across the stars, the sound finally reaching them in a wave of collapsing fury.

The arm blade sliced through the back of one of the Old Horn's necks, immediately releasing a spray of orange light from the wound. The light erupted like blood from a severed artery, washing the cosmos with neon color that fanned out in every direction.

The monster arched its back, surprised by the unexpected assault, and howled, a bellowing eruption of noise that shook Isaac's skull.

Letting the blow carve a path across the sky, the great machine flew past the monster, spinning as it did to aim its other arm at the thing's face. A single heartbeat passed, and then an explosion of blue light filled the heavens as a beam of white-hot power was released.

The pillar of energy struck the monster and blasted its head back in an eruption of earth-shattering violence. Isaac and Dekker slammed their hands over their ears as an avalanche of screeching wails rained down over them, a tremendous death cry accompanied by a shock wave of neon color. Blue and orange mixed and fought and blew past one another, painting the sky in dual strokes of stark, violent beauty.

The light faded a moment later, and when it did, Dekker gasped.

"Are you seeing this?" he whispered. Isaac nodded, unable to find the words he sought.

The Old Horn was headless, its body slowly rising now from the dark cloud from which it had birthed. Its corpse hovered where it had fallen, a long stretch of motionless horror. Dekker could see what the bottom half of the creature—now on its back, dead between the stars—looked like.

He had expected legs, but what he saw instead was a tangle of tentacles, each one of the massive appendages grasping an absolutely massive crystal filled with pulsing orange energy. As the neon spray lessened from its headless corpse, so did the light in the crystals, finally winking out and going dark.

"What the hell are these things...?" Dekker whispered, his voice not quite steady. Isaac kept his jaw locked, his hands gripped into fists. He watched in amazement as the machine spun once more, its engines flaring, readying to strike out at the remaining two Old Horns. The great construct was bigger than anything he had ever seen here on Tectonic, its bulk at least half the size of the monsters above. Its arm blade was coated in orange, and as it activated its boosters, the massive weapon left a trail of color across the sky, like a paintbrush dragged across a black canvas.

Groaning, the two living Old Horns turned to face the fast-approaching threat. As they did, the one holding The Chain in its maw jerked Tectonic with it, sending Isaac and Dekker sprawling. It felt like an earthquake, like the mountains around them were splitting apart in a roar of protest.

As they went tumbling across the rocks, Isaac reached out and grabbed Dekker, pulling him close and shielding him with his body. They rolled to a stop as the Old Horns squared up against the howling machine.

Eyes filled with swirling dust, Isaac looked up, feeling Dekker cough into his chest as the old man struggled to find his breath.

The Old Horn without The Chain swung an immense arm at its attacker, its speed shocking. As it did so, its flesh split apart to release a swarm of shrieking light, all howling toward the mech. It was like watching a great mass of orange fireflies set ablaze and shot out at a terrifying speed.

The machine in the sky rolled on its side, boosters roaring as it swung to avoid the incoming assault.

But it wasn't enough. The lights hit the mech like bombs going off, each one bringing a tremendous explosion of noise. The effect was instant, the peppering of power blasting across the surface of the airborne apparatus with dazzling ferocity. Pieces of blackened plating shattered from its figure, filling the sky in a junkyard of debris.

Despite the violence of impact, the mech survived. It changed course with a blast from its main engine, sending fire streaming out behind it. The arm without the blade was powering up once more, a dim blue light starting to flicker from the end of the barrel. As it charged, the blade extended outward and the machine swooped toward its attacker.

It struck, weapon first, the wide edge of the sword carving a long slice across the Old Horn's torso. The wound glowed orange and then erupted in a spray of neon, sending color into the outskirts of space.

The machine passed by its victim, but it didn't make it far. The Old Horn shot a hand out and grabbed at the metal legs, catching one of them, anchoring it where it hovered. The creature's skin burned beneath a thruster as the mech creaked to get away, but the monster held fast, bringing it to its chest to grip it with both of its long hands.

Metal could be heard groaning as the Old Horn began to squeeze, its massive square head staring down at its prey. Electricity leapt from its gaping vortex and spider-webbed down the machine's surface, blackening its white surface.

"Oh, no," Dekker whispered from under Isaac, his eyes wide. "Oh, please no…"

Isaac kept his eyes on the struggling machine, fighting not to shatter beneath the monster's vice-like grip. In horror, he realized that the monster was slowly raising the mech toward its vortex.

"It's going to eat it," Isaac said, his voice low.

The mech let out a burst of fire from its main engine, releasing an exhale of scorching power across the creature's hands. It was just enough to free the mech's arms in a squealing wail of metal.

The colossal blade stabbed upward, another booster activating at the elbow for increased power. The strike plowed into the monster's throat, sending a gurgling eruption of electricity out across the heavens. An instant later, the mech shoved its cannon into the wound alongside the blade.

The blast was massive. The Old Horn's head evaporated in an instant as the beam of power released, sending a pillar of blue light straight through the monster's flesh. Orange neon birthed out of the darkness, sending a spray of light into the corners of the cosmos. The grip around the machine fell away and the now-dead nightmare slowly rose from the cloud to expose its tentacles and fading crystals.

"They're doing it," Isaac whispered as the world shook. "Hell below, they're actually doing it."

But the machine shuddered violently as it rose, great plumes of dark smoke mixing with the red fires of its engines. One of its legs had been completely crushed, causing the whole mech to stumble awkwardly as it retreated to regroup.

And as it did, the last monster, the Old Horn that held The Chain, raised its arms outward toward it.

"No, no, no, NO!" Dekker yelled, lunging up, voice hoarse.

The Old Horn's skin split apart, releasing millions of screaming lights, all soaring directly for the wounded machine in the sky.

Chapter 17

Alarms blared all around Liam. The lights in the cockpit had gone from cold white to an angry red. The enclosed space was sweltering now, and sweat poured from Liam's face as he clung to his seat while the massive vehicle, Final Sky, shook violently. The assault on the Old Horns had come viciously and without mercy. Rezin clung to the controls before him, screaming at Desmond a stream of commands as they fought to keep the shuddering machine under control.

"The left leg is gone!" Rezin yelled, clutching the display before him. "Desmond, divert power back to the main engine and get us back on axis! NOW, GODDAMN IT!"

Desmond was hunched over his own panel, his face white and coated in a thick layer of smoky grime, his eyes shifting wildly as the stars spun beyond the wide windshield.

"We got two of them, but Final Sky is FUCKED if we don't get back on axis!" Rezin yelled, slamming his fingers down over his display. The machine groaned all around them, and Liam could feel the world spinning, taking the stars with it. He felt like he was going to throw up, the speed at which they were soaring causing his stomach to plummet. The metal chair was slick beneath his palms as he struggled to piece together what he had just seen. Everything had happened so fast, their attack shocking him in its effectiveness. Somehow, they had killed two of the great titans, their bodies now floating beyond the expanse like they were corpses in a pond. Their tentacles terrified him, like a nest of worms clutching those colossal crystals. It was all he could do to keep his sanity intact.

"I've got it!" Desmond yelled as he input commands. Final Sky slowed for a moment and then the stars beyond the wide pane began to slow as the mech righted itself.

"I'll work the thrusters, just get us out of here!" Desmond called, mopping his brow with the back of his hand.

"We're going to dive-bomb the bastard!" Rezin announced. "The battery on the cannon is spent, so all we have left is the blade!"

"What about The Chain!?" Liam cried, his teeth clacking together as Final Sky coughed and bucked.

Desmond shot a look over at him, his eyes like fire. "Fuck The Chain! We're dead if we go for it!"

"What are you talking about!?"

"Jesus, Liam, what do you think this moron is going to do!? Can't you piece that together yourself?!"

Liam looked at Rezin's back but wasn't spared a glance from the frantic pilot. The world beyond the window rotated and suddenly all Liam could see was the towering head of the last Old Horn. The spinning vortex in its head absorbed his vision, the massive yellow pit exploding with electricity, dancing off the iron links that disappeared into the anomaly.

"Oh no, no, no!" Rezin screamed suddenly, the alarms still howling all around them. "Desmond, tank us! TANK US NOW!"

Liam looked out the window, and what he saw filled him with absolute terror. The Old Horn's flesh had come apart, releasing a maelstrom of roaring lights headed straight for them. They streaked between the stars at a terrifying speed, millions of them, the cosmic god outlined in their haunting glow.

Desmond responded immediately to the command, and Liam felt his stomach drop as Final Sky ripped through space, jerking them down at a speed that blurred his vision. As the mech plummeted desperately, Rezin brought the hundred-foot blade up and swept it horizontally, using the flat of the weapon in an attempt to block some of the incoming barrage.

The impact followed almost instantly. The cockpit screamed as the lights exploded along the length of Final Sky, each detonation rattling Liam's teeth. The universe flipped and twisted outside, the dark of space mixing with the blaring neon of the attack. Desmond was screaming and smoke poured from the panels along the walls. The lights dimmed, then went completely out, only to reignite a moment later as Final Sky gasped to life once more.

A great eruption from below shook Liam in his seat and then, without warning, he went flying as his strap broke. He tumbled across the room and crashed into the wall, the blow exposing stars behind his eyes. He coughed in the suffocating heat and tasted blood trickling down the back of his throat. He heaved some of it up, gagging, and fought to find his sight.

Rezin was clutching his control panel, the window before him now cracking dangerously. Desmond, still screaming, had released his controls and was clutching his head, fear overwhelming him.

Desmond's fear sparked an anger in Liam's chest, an unexpected thing considering what was happening all around him.

"We're gone below the waist!" Rezin was roaring, fighting to regain some kind of control. "The bastard blew our GODDAMNED LEGS OFF! DESMOND, WAKE THE FUCK UP, I NEED YOU!"

But Desmond was losing it, his mind crumbling beneath the horror between the stars. Sweat poured down his face as he clutched his head, his mouth wide in a scream.

"Desmond, I need you to divert all we got back into the main engine! We only got one shot at this! DESMOND!"

Liam hauled himself to his feet, feeling dizzy and shaken. He fought for balance, clinging to whatever he could find as he made his way over to Desmond. Around them, the great machine fought to stay alive, smoke and light strobing through the cockpit like a burst dam.

Liam grabbed Desmond by the hair and slammed his head back against his metal seat, his voice thick beneath the smoke.

"Do what he says! We're fucking dead if you don't! DESMOND!"

Desmond winced, his eyes dancing wildly in their sockets. He looked up at Liam, and some of the fear was replaced by loathing.

Liam released the man and pointed to the control panel before him. "Do what he says! HURRY!"

But Desmond was shaking his head, his voice a rattling echo from the back of his throat. "I won't. He's going to bury us in that thing! I won't go! I WON'T GO!"

"GODDAMN IT!" Liam howled, sweat stinging his eyes. He grabbed Desmond by the throat. "Can't you do ONE good thing!? Why don't you stop thinking about yourself for ONCE and help the rest of us out? Divert the power you selfish, cowardly FUCK!"

"I've done enough!" Desmond screamed, his voice hoarse. "I won't go in there! Not there!"

"The hell is he talking about!?" Liam yelled, still gripping Desmond by the throat.

Rezin fought to keep them moving, the Old Horn growing closer through the window. "We have to kill this thing, but if we do, it'll release The Chain! If it does that, then Tectonic is gone! We can't let that happen!"

Liam braced himself against Desmond's chair as the cabin shook once more, the metal sheeting rattling around their bolts.

"So what do we do!?"

Rezin looked over his shoulder at Liam, his face blackened by smoke and grime. "We have to kill it and keep The Chain from slithering out of that vortex! We have to go inside Liam!"

Liam felt a sudden sickness grip him, and his eyes went to the window, toward the vortex growing out of the face of the nightmare monster. The Chain buzzed with electricity as the storm continued, snaking white-hot bolts down its links.

"Forget him, I'll do this myself!" Rezin said, returning to the controls. His fingers blurred as he worked, the air in the cabin growing thicker. The lights continued to flicker as Final Sky hung onto consciousness by a hair. If what Rezin said was true, then they had been torn in half at the waist by the storm of lights, severely limiting their movement.

"We only have four batteries left!" Rezin yelled. "I don't know if that'll be enough to get us into the vortex, but we have to try!"

"What happens if we're not fast enough?!" Liam yelled up to him.

"Then that monster swats us aside and we're dead before we can even register what happened!"

Suddenly Desmond surged from his seat, hands going for Liam's collar. His eyes were wide and his voice was a terrifying plea.

"Don't let him do this! Please! You have no idea what's in there!"

"And neither do you!" Rezin yelled angrily.

Liam ripped Desmond away and threw the man to the floor. He slammed his knee down into the man's chest, keeping him in place. He leaned down, sweat dripping from the tip of his nose.

"Touch me again and I'll rip your eyes out. At least then you won't have to see what's coming."

"We heard the voices!" Desmond wheezed. "There's something terrible in there! THINK ABOUT WHAT YOU'RE DOING!"

"I am!" Rezin yelled back. He slammed his hand down. "All the juice we got left is in the main engine now! Liam, hold onto something! This is going to get bumpy!"

Reaching for Desmond's seat, Liam pulled himself up and strapped himself in. He grabbed Desmond from the floor and pulled him up into a sitting position.

"Don't you dare die yet," Liam snarled, holding the petrified man against his side.

"Activating all power! Here we go!" Rezin roared, igniting the main engine, the great machine exploding in a wave of heat as it rushed toward the Old Horn at a terrifying speed.

Liam felt himself pushed back into his seat as the forces around him blurred past. The cockpit filled with a blazing whine as the engine rocketed the fragmented craft forward, the Old Horn filling the windshield as they raced toward it.

As they neared the monster in a wave of magnificent heat, Liam felt his teeth clink together hard as Rezin slammed his hands down over the control panel, jerking their trajectory into a sharp roll. From outside the window, Final Sky's massive blade came into view, arched back in preparation for a strike.

The control room was a screeching sauna as the Old Horn swung at them first, its arm flashing into view like a mountain falling across space. Liam's eyes watered as smoke clogged them, and he felt himself thrown against his restraints as the great craft bucked wildly, still rolling and barely avoiding the massive blow that had been aimed at them.

As Rezin corrected their positioning, Final Sky swung its blade.

The strike connected with the Old Horn, a biting slash across its throat that brought a geyser of color exploding throughout space and into the cabin. Rezin was howling amid the smoke, the shuddering machine plunging for the vortex as the monster outside gurgled on its neon plumes.

"We got it!" Rezin screamed as a wave of electricity cascaded across the mech. "They're dead! They're all fucking *dead*!" He let out a cackle of disbelief as the cockpit vibrated and smoked, the vortex consuming the forward window. Liam barely heard him, clinging for his dear life as another spider web of power fell over Final Sky, causing half the machinery in the cabin to short out.

"We're going through!" Rezin yelled back as sparks sprayed them from all sides. "Dear god, brace yourself! We're passing into the vortex!"

Desmond had his eyes closed, his face coated in slick terror. He clutched Liam's seat as the broken craft swayed madly, the engine sputtering as it was stroked by the storm of electricity between the colors.

Liam slammed his mouth shut and clenched his jaw, The Chain dipping into vision, emerging from the vortex like a tongue out of a throat. When Liam spotted it, he squinted and then his heart skipped a beat.

The Chain was slowly, terribly, sliding out of the dead titan, its grip surrendered as death took its master.

And then the world vanished in a rupture of flashing light.

In his mind, Liam knew that they had just passed into the depths of the vortex, but the sudden immersion obliterated all rational thought. He panicked, hands reaching to find something in the blinking, stuttering darkness. The cockpit gasped in the flaring emergency lights, tides of red splashing across the smoking metal. Desmond was screaming and coughing, begging Rezin to pull out. The window outside flashed with what looked like lightning, but all sound was drowned out. Final Sky jolted viciously, the bolts of its frame cracking and rattling in their seams.

Liam felt his stomach drop away in a free fall and he gasped for breath as he became weightless. As they fell into the void, the lights in the cabin went dark and all that could be seen was filtered through the quick, biting flashes of light from beyond the forward window.

I'm about to die.

The thought came a second before a crunching eruption shook Liam in his seat, rattling his skull and causing him to wince painfully. He grabbed onto Desmond so the man wouldn't split his head open, and he could hear Rezin yelling something, but his voice and form were lost in the smoking cockpit.

Final Sky bounced hard over some kind of surface, and Liam could hear metal tearing away from somewhere below. The heat was sucked out of the cockpit and replaced by a biting cold that rose up on the heels of the screeching grind below. Sparks lit the windshield and sprayed past like electric rain, and from outside the flashing lights continued on a slow rotation.

Pain thudded through Liam's body as the great craft skidded across whatever they had fallen onto, but through the trembling collision, he could feel them slowing. He released Desmond as more sparks flooded past the windshield, the whining grate of metal winding down to a dull groan.

The smoke seemed to clear some and Liam coughed, waving his hand in front of his face. He squinted in the dim light, amazed that he was still alive and that the machine hadn't shattered into pieces on impact.

He was about to call out to Rezin when he felt the cabin shift, a dull crunch echoing from outside, followed by a shrieking squeal.

Rezin's voice came from the clearing smoke. "I...I got it. Pegged the bastard." Panting, then a heavy, desperate noise. "Holy shit...actually got it..." a chuckle followed, but it sounded worn-out.

Slowly, Liam let his eyes adjust to the dark. He wiped his face, his voice thick. "We all still alive?"

"I think so," Rezin answered, sounding absolutely exhausted. "I still got all my parts, it seems."

Liam unclipped his restraint, eyes going to the windshield. "Where... where are we?"

"In the belly of the beast," Desmond answered miserably from the floor. The man picked himself up, the whites of his eyes bulging in the dim light.

"We made it through?" Liam asked quietly.

"Barely," Rezin responded, unfastening his harness. "And look. Outside. I pinned the bastard as we landed."

Confused, Liam walked toward the window and peered outside. He wasn't sure what he was looking at. He wiped soot from his face and looked again.

"My god," he whispered.

"It'll hold," Rezin said, allowing himself a small smile. "It has to."

The Chain was pinned to the ground, to *a* ground, the massive coil of iron hanging from an alien sky to drape across the eerie landscape. Rezin had driven Final Sky's blade through one of the links, nailing it in place.

"It was sliding away..." Liam said, eyes wide.

"It's not going anywhere," Rezin said, swallowing hard. "Though it looks like we were running out of runway. There were only a dozen or so links left before it would have slipped out. You see them?"

"Yeah, I see them," Liam said, staring at the end of The Chain, now only a couple hundred yards away. He traced the iron loops across the strange ground and up into the sky where it seemed to disappear inside a phasing yellow tear.

"What the hell is this place?" Liam whispered as he stared up at the blinking anomaly.

"I don't know," Rezin said quietly, "but I feel...different somehow."

Liam mentally inspected himself and realized that Rezin was right. He did feel different. It took him a moment to understand what the exact sensation was.

Complete numbness. He wished he had a more exact way to describe what he was feeling, but that was the closest he could come up with. He wasn't hungry or thirsty, his body oddly didn't ache, his head was clearing, and he almost felt weightless. He looked down at his hands and then up at Rezin.

"This is strange," he mumbled clumsily. "It's almost as if..."

"Almost as if we're dead?" Desmond cut in, stepping toward them. "As if we've entered some kind of plane of existence that's in between any sense of sanity? Are either of you *seeing this*!?" His voice was cracking and Liam could tell he was growing hysterical. "Do you SEE where you've taken us!?" he jabbed a finger at the window, his voice rising into an accusatory roar. "Everything you've been looking for is right out there along with those... those...!" he trailed off in a shrill screech and turned away, hiding his eyes from the window, his whole body shaking.

Liam turned back to the window and looked. This time, his eyes took him past The Chain toward what lie beyond.

And his breath was taken away, his stomach plummeting.

The place they had entered was unlike anything he had ever seen before. They had landed on some kind of expanse of smooth rock or marble, the world a flat sheen of shining stone. Hills and mountains jutted out from the landscape, but they were all sharp angles and odd, tilting rectangles.

A smattering of gravel littered the ground, covering the odd world in thin patches where the shining surface wasn't visible. Everything was gray, like the color of a storm. In the distance, amid the rising angles, were strange, broken pieces of machinery. It looked like a junkyard, a tangle of crumpled metal and exposed wire. As he stared at it, he realized that he was looking at ruined, toppled buildings and massive, eerie machines that were overwhelming in size. From one of them, a colossal half-halo that held countless bay windows, Liam could see light flickering from inside, almost as if whatever the craft was still functioned.

"Shit…" Rezin whispered at his side as he stared out at the great mountain of tech. "Oh shit…"

"What is it? What is that?" Liam asked.

"Upper Heaven," Rezin said grimly, "Or at least, what's left of it. Seems like it got sucked into the vortex. Must have been why we were still picking up those transmissions…"

"You mean there might still be people alive in there!?" Liam gasped.

"I don't know," Rezin muttered, looking distraught. "I doubt it. Not now. But I have no idea how this place works or what it is."

"This is hell," Desmond said darkly from the shadows. "You've driven us straight into the mouth of it. This is where everything goes to die. Every life and machine that has ever stood in the way of the Old Horns goes *here*. Look at it. Look out there at that wreckage. Look at the *sky!*"

Liam craned his head back and for a second time, he felt his breath stolen from him.

The sky above was filled with dead, broken machines, too strange or unfamiliar for Liam to even process. Great towers floated lazily across the empty night, broken relics from worlds unknown. Crafts of incredible size joined the expanse, long-dead wonders of alien engineering, all of them broken and lifeless and dark.

Behind the clusters of metal were chunks of rock, far greater in mass. They were hundreds of miles away, a testament to their size, but visible from where Liam stood. He could make out mountain ranges and darkened cities, massive open plains and jungles long rotten. It was as if a massive fist had shattered a galaxy of planets and left them to float like gravestones where they had died.

"This is..." Rezin said quietly, his voice not quite his own, his eyes glued to the sky. "Is this what happens to everything the Old Horns encounter? Ripped away and thrown into this horrible place? Why? What's the *point*?"

"I think they just want to stare at their trophies," Desmond growled from the back. "I think they want to gawk and gloat about what they've done to us. To everyone and everything that's ever gotten in their way. It's like killing an animal and mounting its head on your wall. Except everything is an animal to them."

"But they're dead," Liam said, turning. "We killed them! Didn't we, Rezin? Tell him! Tell him they're dead!"

Desmond pointed back out the window. "I don't think we did."

The lights flashed again, a quick succession of blinking white from beyond the strange, squared mountains.

And that's when Liam saw them.

They were masked by a thick wall of fog, their towering figures illuminated by the light. As Liam's eyes rose, he felt his throat tighten with fear.

In the far distance, hundreds of miles beyond the flat expanse, rising from the eerie mountain range, were five figures. Their size scraped the heavens, a cluster of frozen silhouettes that flashed and pulsed as the lights around them buzzed with life. They were humanoid in shape, legs and arms hanging motionless where they stood like statues. But jutting from their heads were long, rising horns, twin blades of sharpened darkness.

They stood, frozen behind the mountains as dark shadows, gods behind the fog, visible only as inky silhouettes as the silent lights continued to flash all around them. They did not move. They did not breathe. They simply towered over the glassy, broken world and watched from the mists.

Liam backed away from the window, feeling his heart begin to race. Despite his fear, he couldn't seem to take his eyes off the five shadows. Their enormous size and presence seemed to consume his mind, draining it of all thought only to be replaced by cold, freezing terror.

"We...we killed them," Liam whispered, his words as broken as the sky above him.

"Of course we didn't!" Desmond cackled loudly from their backs. "How the hell could we kill something as powerful as THAT!?"

Liam licked his dry lips. "No, wait...no...those things...the monsters and the vortexes...we killed them..."

"Oh, yeah!?" Desmond yelled, his voice cracking. "And what were those things REALLY!? Maybe they were just puppets! Maybe those...those SHADOWS out there are *really* the ones in charge! Maybe the monsters we killed were just TOOLS or VESSELS of the real threat! You ever think about that!? Did you really think we could kill something like the Old Horns with mere machinery?! DID YOU!?"

"Shut up," Rezin said quietly, turning away from the window. Liam could see that he was frightened. He turned to Desmond and waved a hand. "Just... shut up. It doesn't matter."

"Doesn't matter what he says!" Desmond howled, throwing his arms up.

"The Chain is secure. Tectonic is safe." Rezin shot a nervous look out the window and then back to Liam. "I don't know what it was we actually killed, but they're dead and Final Sky is keeping The Chain in place."

"And what about us!?" Desmond yelled, storming forward. "Congratulations! You saved everyone from immediate destruction, but what about US!?"

Rezin turned away. "I don't know. It doesn't matter. Our mission is complete. I did what I set out to do. I'm not sure what those things are out there, what it was we killed, but knowing that won't change where we are now. My purpose, my mission, was to keep The Chain safe from danger. To keep Tectonic safe. And that's what I've done. That's what I will continue to do."

Desmond stepped toward him, his eyes slits. "So what, you're just going to...to sit here and WAIT!? You're just going to put your feet up and see what happens!?"

Rezin shot him a frustrated look. "You got a better idea!? Do you know something I don't? Have you been here before!? Is there a way back that you want to tell me about!? No? Then yes, Desmond, yes, that's exactly what I'm going to do. And do you know why? It's because I have a DUTY to those people down there—the ones still alive! I swore to protect them with my life, and that's exactly what I plan on doing!"

Desmond blinked, his face going slack. Then he threw his head back and laughed. The sound made Liam feel sick, the man's sanity cracking along the edges of his humor.

"And what about that?!" Desmond laughed, pointing to the yellow tear in the sky. "Why don't we just go back out!?"

Rezin slumped down in his chair again, suddenly looking exhausted. He rubbed his eyes as he answered. "Did you hear anything I just said? Final Sky is pinning The Chain in place. Even if we COULD move, I wouldn't. We would send Tectonic plummeting into the Void."

"So we're just going to sit on our asses and die, is that it!?"

Rezin waved a hand. "You can leave if you want. I don't know what it's like outside, but you're free to find out."

"I am NOT dying here," Desmond snarled, his eyes bulging, spittle flying from his lips. "And I am DONE doing what you tell me. You've gotten us into this mess, and I'm going to get us out of it."

While Desmond was ranting, Liam had slowly positioned himself behind the man, feeling the tension reach a breaking point. When Desmond lunged for Rezin, Liam was ready. He shot forward and grabbed him by the armpits, hauling him backwards.

Snarling, Desmond went into a frenzy. He whipped his head back and Liam felt his nose explode in pain. His grip faltered some, and that was enough for Desmond to wriggle free.

"I'm not dying in this place!" Desmond roared, launching himself at Liam.

Desmond collided with him, knocking the air from Liam's lungs and sending him soaring backwards against the wall. Liam's head smashed against the metal wall and stars danced before his eyes. He swung wildly, but Desmond was like a wild animal. He shoved himself off Liam and then kicked him in the ribs hard before spinning around as Rezin advanced, his guard up.

"Stop this!" Rezin yelled, ducking as Desmond took a swing at his head. "This isn't solving anything! Final Sky is dead!"

"That's for me to decide!" Desmond snarled, throwing himself at Rezin. The two went to the floor, pieces of metal flying as they collapsed heavily against the control panels, breaking them into shards.

Rezin grunted and squirmed as Desmond positioned himself on top of him. He brought his fists together and smashed them down into Rezin's face, once, twice, each blow bringing blood.

Liam pulled himself up and wiped his face. His blood was boiling.

He threw himself across the room and plowed into Desmond, bringing him off Rezin. They bounced and skidded across the dim cockpit, fists wailing, teeth gnashing, legs kicking. Liam felt himself take a multitude of blows across his beaten body, but he didn't let up. As he bucked and wrestled with the murderous man, he felt his anger bubble over into hatred. Hatred for everything Desmond had done to them over the course of their journey. For all the violence and senseless death, the heartbreak and pain he had caused.

For taking away the one person who made the world a little brighter.

Liam found himself on top, his knuckles thudding into Desmond's side, his face contorted into a snarl. He could feel the man's body tense with every blow he delivered, and it fueled his rage. It felt good. It felt wonderful—like a poison being bled out with every punch.

"You're an animal!" Liam spat, his face coated in sweat as he pummeled Desmond. "A goddamn animal that needs to be put down once and for all."

Desmond didn't have the breath to answer, his teeth exposed as his lips pulled back. He grunted beneath the beating, his hands flailing at his sides, searching for something, anything to stop the pain.

Liam wrapped his hands around Desmond's throat and began to squeeze, feeling the man's esophagus bow beneath his grip.

"This is for what you did to Avalice, you fucking monster," Liam hissed. "I hope you—"

His breath was cut short as his stomach exploded in pain. It was as if a white-hot coal had been shoved deep inside him. He hitched a breath, his grip falling away, and felt his eyes go wide.

Something's wrong.

He tried to breathe and found it difficult. That worm of burning heat wriggled deeper into his guts, eating away at him. Something warm was dribbling from his lips, down onto Desmond's delighted face.

Liam looked down and saw a sharp piece of metal jutting from his stomach. Desmond held the other end, his hand covered in blood.

I've been stabbed. Oh, god, I've been—

Desmond shoved the sharp metal in further, and Liam felt blood spray from his lips in a rush of agony.

"I'm—not—dying—here," Desmond panted, each word coming between breaths. The bastard was smiling and Liam felt disbelief consume him. He had been stabbed. He was bleeding. His strength was fading. The world was swimming.

No. Not like this. Not yet.

Something else joined the pain in his guts, a furious volcano of outrage and insanity. Liam threw his head back, his muscles ignited with adrenaline, and let out a bellowing cry of anger. He grabbed the metal sticking out of his stomach and jerked it out. He screamed as he did, blood dribbling over Desmond as the weapon was wrenched from his grip.

Eyes wild, Liam raised the bloodied weapon over his head and plunged it down into Desmond's left eye. The sharp edge passed through effortlessly, popping the eye with ease, sinking deep into the man's socket.

Desmond screamed, his whole body convulsing as Liam leaned down and placed both his palms on the end of the weapon. His voice came out wet and furious.

"You don't get to watch me die."

And then Liam pressed the metal into Desmond's brain, killing him in an eruption of blood. Desmond's body convulsed as his nerve endings danced, shrieking as the life was forced out of him.

It was only a matter of seconds before Liam was sitting on top of a corpse. Panting, he stared down at the dead man, at the carnage he had delivered. He then spat on the lifeless body, wishing he would come alive so he could do it all over again.

"Fuck. Hell. Oh hell, Liam your stomach…"

Rezin's voice floated over to him from somewhere in the growing haze. He blinked lazily, his hands going to his drooling guts. He could feel the parted flesh around his fingers but felt no need to inspect the wound. It was bad. He could tell by how dizzy he felt. He was losing blood at an alarming rate, and the pain seemed to be slowly ebbing away.

Rezin's beaten face filled his vision, his eyes wide and frantic.

"Oh, shit, he got you good. Oh, god, that son of a bitch…Liam? Liam, you with me?"

Liam nodded and felt blood running down his throat. "I'm…still here."

Rezin helped him off Desmond's corpse and into one of the chairs where Liam slumped down miserably. He could feel warmth running down his legs. He wiped his face and spat a wad of red onto the floor. Rezin was on his knees in front of him, tearing away pieces of his shirt.

"We have to stop the bleeding, if we don't then—"

Liam caught his hand and pushed it away. Rezin looked up at him, shocked and confused, his face an open canvas.

"What are you doing?"

Liam grunted, the pain continuing to drift...drift...drift away.

"Don't bother, Rezin. Look at me. Look at where we are."

Rezin bunched his hands around the strips of cloth in his fists. "I can help you. I can fix this."

Liam swallowed. It took a long time.

"No," he said thickly. "It's done. I'm done...fighting. So tired of..." he took a long, shuddering breath. "Tired of fighting..."

"Shit," Rezin gasped, slumping on his knees, staring up at Liam. "Oh *shit*. Liam, I'm...I don't even know what to say. Please...don't do this."

Liam pushed himself up in his chair and stared out the window, out toward the towering horned shadows beyond the fog, across the horizon. The lights flashed soundlessly around them, dancing off the eerie geometric mountain scape before the hidden creatures.

"How the fuck did we get here?" Liam whispered, blood and drool leaking from his chin.

Rezin shook his head and let out a surprised gasp. "I don't know. I don't know, Liam." He looked out the window, out at the strange, alien world. His eyes traveled over The Chain, held in place by Final Sky, and then out past the rectangular mountains and up the fog wall at the colossal shadows.

"I think those are the real enemy," he said quietly. "I think those shadows, those things in the mists—I think they're the ones controlling the monsters we fought. They're kind of scary-looking, aren't they?" He barked a laugh and seemed surprised by it, his eyes wide. "Statues in the fog. Do you think they can see us?"

Liam's mouth tasted like copper and he spit some of it out before answering. "I don't know. Probably. But I don't think they're going to do anything. At least not for a long time."

Rezin nodded. "Not until they find more puppets to control. Or create. Jesus. Listen to what I'm saying." He shook his head and seemed to be slipping into a state of shock. "You know, all these years I thought those monsters with the vortexes were the real enemy. That they were hunting us and infecting us with Rockflesh. But now that we've seen them? Now that we've seen those giant crystals they were holding with those...those goddamn *tentacles*? I think that the disease was just a coincidence. I think Rockflesh was just...I don't know...the fumes coming off of those crystals. Like an engine's exhaust. Maybe they were just using those crystals to travel. Does that make sense?" He looked up at Liam and snorted. "Of course it doesn't. We're talking about madness here. I'm sorry. I'm rambling. You're dying and I'm fucking scared. I'm *scared*." He looked at his hands and saw that they were shaking. "I'm going to be alone soon."

Liam could feel himself beginning to fade, the world beyond the window swaying left to right in a blink of darkness. He cleared his throat and looked down at Rezin.

"You're a good man. You shouldn't be afraid."

Rezin looked up at him, his eyes helpless.

Liam smiled and felt his stomach flare with pain, but it was a distant thing now. "I had no idea what I was signing up for when I took this job way back in Maltor," he grunted. "That seems like a lifetime ago, doesn't it?"

Rezin reached out and took Liam's hands and squeezed them. "You helped save Tectonic. Remember that. I couldn't have done it without you. You're a hell of a fighter, Liam. I'm so sorry this journey cost you so much."

Liam smiled weakly and felt blood dribble from the corner of his mouth. "Least I get to see her again. Real soon now. Me dying is my ticket back to her. Don't feel too bad for me. We did a good thing, you and me. All of us."

Rezin smiled and his face filled with pain. "You think Isaac and Dekker are OK down there?"

Liam felt his mind relax a little as the faces of his friend's filled it. "Nothing could kill those two. Not while the other is alive." Liam felt his chest hitch a little and he gritted his teeth. "Ah, damn. I'm going to miss them."

Rezin took a long breath and looked out the cracked window, out at The Chain and the strange, mechanical sky.

"I never thought my coffin would be so big," Rezin said quietly.

Liam squeezed his hand with the last of his life. "I'll wait for you."

204 • ELIAS WITHEROW

Chapter 18

Isaac watched the sky. A cool wind cut through the cold air, but he hardly felt it at this point. He wasn't sure how long he and Dekker had been sitting there beneath the carcasses of the cosmic monsters. They continued to float hundreds of miles overhead, their tentacles still, the vortexes silent. The Chain hung as it always had, unmoving, its massive links disappearing into the middle creature's maw.

"I don't think they're getting back up," Dekker said.

Isaac looked at the old man next to him, his eyes softening. "Nothing we could do even if they did."

"It is an eerie sight, isn't it?" Dekker continued. "How long do you think they'll lay up there like that? Weeks? Years? I'd rather not have something like that hovering over us for that long."

Isaac said nothing and watched the clouds. They seemed to be thinning. It was something he had noticed some time ago. Now he was sure of it. The thick blankets of gloom seemed to be dispersing. His eyes rose toward the giant, lightless crystals that were entangled around the dead creature's tentacles. Had they brought the gloom? What else had they brought?

"Staring at them isn't going to solve anything," Dekker said, chuckling and then wincing. "I just hope they're actually dead and that The Chain holds. Seems it's stuck in one of those dead thing's mouths. Creator above, I never thought I'd see something like this." The old man rubbed his chest and coughed before continuing. "Sure would like to see the sun one more time before I go."

Isaac looked sharply at him. "You're not dying."

"I mean, one day I will."

"That day will have to wait."

"If you insist," Dekker said, rolling his head back to stare up at the bizarre spectacle above. "You see any sign of Liam or Rezin?"

Isaac shook his head.

"Me, either. That machine they were piloting looked like it took a beating before it vanished."

"They'll be back," Isaac said quietly, watching as the clouds continue to part, the gray lifting like a veil.

Dekker looked around at the barren wasteland. "Boy it's going to be a long walk back."

"What are those things, Dek?" Isaac asked softly as he continued to stare up at the dead titans.

Dekker shrugged. "I don't know, son. But the sky seems a little brighter now that they're dead, doesn't it?"

"What did we *do here*, Dek?" Isaac asked. "What was all this for?"

Dekker reached out and patted the young man's leg. "I think we stopped something very bad from happening. I think we saved a lot of people from a very nasty death." Dekker trailed off for a moment. "I believe we did some good here, Isaac. That's what I'm walking away with."

"But we lost Liam up there," Isaac said. "And Avalice…"

Dekker smiled sadly. "Hey. Didn't you just say Liam would be back?"

Isaac nodded.

"Well, then, he'll be back. And he can tell us all about what it was like to fly. I'm sure he was scared out of his mind," Dekker chuckled. "I know I would be."

"Dek, look. The sun," Isaac said, pointing.

Dekker looked up toward the sky, and was washed with warmth. Golden orange ripples fluttered across the horizon and bathed the two men in light. It was a gentle, calming light, a last gasp before sunset, lingering just long enough to take their breath away.

"Well how about that?" Dekker whispered, his body engulfed in the sun's brilliance. "Makes a man never want to leave this spot."

Isaac closed his eyes and exhaled, feeling his whole body relax. His voice was gentle and filled with peace.

"Let's sit a little while longer." Then, almost a whisper now: "I want to be here when Liam comes back."

The End

ELIAS WITHEROW lives in New England and can usually be found muttering to himself and staring blankly out a window. Having written over sixty short stories and six novels, Elias hopes to continue to provide horrific entertainment to his readers.

Twitter: @EliasWitherow
facebook.com/FeedThePig
www.reddit.com/r/feedthepig

The Last Tower
—Elias Witherow

The Black Farm
—Elias Witherow

The Worst In Us
—Elias Witherow

The Third Parent
—Elias Witherow

Before The Farmhouse Burned Down
—Holly Riordan

**THOUGHT
CATALOG
Books**

THOUGHTCATALOG.COM
NEW YORK·LOS ANGELES

Made in United States
Orlando, FL
01 May 2024

46389390R00129